The Don's Doorstep Baby

ASHLIE SILAS

In no way is it legal to reproduce, duplicate, or transmit any part of this document in either electronic means or in printed format. Recording of this publication is strictly prohibited and any storage of this document is not allowed unless with written permission from the publisher.

All rights reserved.

Respective authors own all copyrights not held by the publisher.

CHAPTER 1

Katerina

10 YEARS BEFORE

Three things I hate about myself. My inability to connect with people my age. My inability to turn off my brain. And my inability to arrive to places on time. Basically, I'm an antisocial over thinker who also has trouble with time management. Although my sister does like to say I'm not antisocial, just a girl with a resting bitch face that tends to drive people away before they can even get to know me. I've never understood that, I think I'm a perfectly nice, approachable person.

Anyway, my issue with time management is the reason I'm practically running as I head for the library in the middle of campus where a meeting is currently taking place. A meeting I should have arrived for, five minutes ago.

I'm crossing the lawn in the Yard when someone bumps into my shoulder effectively knocking away all the books in my hands.

"Watch where you're going!" I snap, glaring at the girl.

Her eyes widen and she stammers out an apology before rushing off, without bothering to help me pick up the books. Maybe I do have a resting bitch face. I run my hand through my hair in frustration, before getting on my knees to pick up the books. There are four of them and the only reason I'm carrying so many is because I'm meant to return them to the library.

"Damn," someone chuckles, bending to help to pack my books. "You looked like you were about to kill her."

I look up and staring at me are the most piercing green eyes I've ever seen. Eyes that draw you in with their intensity. My mouth dries for a second as I stare dumbfounded. Thankfully, it only takes a second for me to recover. I grab the last of my book off the ground, getting back to my feet. He stands as well, holding onto the textbook in his hand.

"I wouldn't have killed her. Committing murder in the middle of campus wouldn't be tasteful."

He grins. "A pretty girl that can make jokes about murder. You don't see that every day."

It's cute that he thought I was joking. I can't help but consider his good looks again. His dark hair falls in messy waves, giving him that sexy just rolled out of bed look. He's also tall with an athletic figure and lean muscles. In the back of my mind, I'm thinking that he's exactly my type but I don't have time for this. I'm already ten minutes late for the group meeting I was meant to be at.

"Okay, well I have to go, so you won't be seeing me again. Can I have my book back?" I ask stretching my hand.

He holds it out of reach. "Relax, princess. Where are you off to in such a hurry?"

"I have a meeting in Widener," I say glaring at him. "And I'm late."

"Exactly. You're already late, might as well chill."

I take in a deep soothing breath, searching for inner patience.

"What do you want?" I question.

He pretends to ponder it for a second. "You're in my Computer class. I saw you a couple of days ago."

"And?"

"And I'm wondering why a freshman is taking that course. And also apparently, already studying criminal law," he says waving my textbook in my face.

"I like to stay ahead and it's none of your business," I snap, trying to grab my book from his hand.

He relinquishes it with a small smile.

"Alright fine. My approach could use some work. Since you're in a hurry, I'll just rip the band aid off. I'm here because I want to ask you out," he says bluntly.

I'm slightly taken aback. Where was the preamble? The build up? Who just asks a stranger out?

"Ask me out," I repeat blandly.

"Yeah," he says on a shrug. "For some reason, I'm feeling some chemistry between us princess. I want to see where it goes. So, what do you say?" he asks with a smile.

His smiles are a little unnerving. Plus there's a hint of mystery in his gaze and a mischievous spark that guarantees trouble.

I decide it would do me well to stay away.

"Is this some kind of dare?" I ask still a little confused.

He shakes his head. "Nope. I'm here of my own free will."

"Okay… I'm not interested and you look like every typical frat boy, not my type," I'm totally lying but he doesn't need to know that. "No offense," I add.

His eyes narrow. "Saying no offense doesn't mean I'm not going to take offense, beautiful. Come on, you don't even know me. Take a chance, think about it. You and me, a date. Anywhere you want. Do you like sushi?"

I groan softly, looking up at the sky and cursing my luck. Then I'm looking back at him.

"Alright fine, I've thought about it," I say. He perks up, looking expectant. "After much consideration, I'm going to have to decline. Sorry."

His face falls. I get the feeling he's not used to being rejected. And I get it. I'm sure he doesn't get rejected often with a face like that. But sometimes you need to do God's work and keep guys like him humble. I push past him, going on my way. Of course he follows me.

"You're like a lost puppy," I mutter. "You realize that."

"Oh chill out, princess. I'm not following you, our destinations just align."

"Yeah, right," I say sarcastically.

We continue walking. Him a couple paces behind me. A minute or two later and I suddenly can't hear his footsteps anymore. I turn around and realize he's turned a corner. I watch his back as he walks away, surprised he actually gave up that easily.

Just when I'm about to move along, he suddenly turns, walking back towards me with a grin. I arch an eyebrow as he stops in front of me.

"So, how did that feel?"

I shake my head in confusion, "What?"

"Me leaving. Let me guess, you got this sinking feeling in your gut. You were probably thinking it was a mistake to turn me down. Listen to those thoughts, beautiful and just go on one date with me."

Despite myself, I laugh. "Yeah, I definitely wasn't thinking any of those. If I'm being honest, I was just glad you were leaving."

"Then why were you staring at me for so long as I walked away?"

My mouth falls open. "I wasn't staring."

"You were. For about twenty seconds. I counted. If you turned around and left after ten seconds, I would have given up and accepted you weren't interested. But you didn't. You waited, meaning you are interested," he says, green eyes gleaming.

My head tilts to the sight as I look up at him.

"You're not very good at taking no for an answer, are you?"

He shakes his head. "Nope. Unfortunately it's a product of my upbringing. I can tell you all about it if you go out with me."

I sigh softly. "Fine. I'll go on one date, just to get you to back off."

"How enthusiastic," he says, with a small wink.

I roll my eyes. *Why do I have a feeling I'm going to regret this?*

He brings out his phone and hands it to me. "I'm going to need your number so I can text you."

I grudgingly input my number and he places his phone back in his pocket.

"Just one slight thing and I feel the need to apologize about it," he tells me.

"What?" I question curiously.

"I'm notoriously famous on campus. Girls who go out with me tend to become crazy obsessed with me. It's an unfortunate consequence of my charms. I'd hate for you to turn out like them, but it might be inevitable."

"Don't worry, I'm sure I'll be fine," I say drily.

He chuckles, "Alright. I'll see you later…" he trails off, leaving me to fill in the blank.

"Katerina," I supply.

"Katerina," he repeats with a smile. "I'm Xander."

"I would say nice to meet you Xander but it's really not, considering your pestering has made me late for a meeting."

"Eh, you were already late anyway. I'll see you later for our date."

He starts to walk away after one last bright smile.

"I hate sushi by the way," I yell at his back.

He waves at me over his shoulder, "Noted, princess."

As soon as he's gone, I'm rushing for the library where the meeting is already underway. Thankfully, no one pays me any attention as I slide into a seat at the edge of the table. I always hated group assignments in high school. Mostly because owing to the fact that I had no friends, I was always paired up with idiots and then I always ended up having to do most of the work on my own.

Harvard's different though. Everyone here seems driven, intent on finishing their tasks and moving on to the next. By the end of the meeting, our work has been evenly shared. No one stops to make small talk, there are no pleasantries. They're all intent on minding their own business, which suits me perfectly.

I head for the front desk once the meeting disperses, placing the books I borrowed. The librarian arches an eyebrow when I hand her a list of books I'd like to borrow next. Which if I'm being honest, might be weird. Not a lot of freshmen are reading about criminal litigation.

But I like to read. It's literally the only thing I've got going on in my life.

My sister calls a few hours later while I'm in my dorm room. I'm surprised it took her so long. I've only been at college for a month but I swear Sophia has called me every day since. She's definitely having separation anxiety and I can't exactly blame her since I'm feeling it too. This is the most time we've been apart since we were kids.

"Hey, *sorella*," she greets, calling me sister in Italian.

We're mixed race. Born and raised in America. But our dad's a second generation Italian. His family moved to the U.S when he was just a boy. By the time he became a teenager, he left, trying to crawl his way up to the top, doing anything to survive. He always likes to remind myself and my sister that he built a name for himself out of ashes.

Our mother was Russian. Born and raised in Moscow. She was her family's second daughter. A complete Russian woman but one that like to defy traditions and propriety on occasion. It's how she was able to marry my father and live her home country, which was extremely brave of her. She passed away a long time ago.

"Hey, how was school?" I ask, lying on my bed.

"It was alright. Nothing interesting. I'm heading out to a party in a couple of minutes," she informs me. My little sister's a social butterfly. Where I'm woefully inadept with social interactions, she thrives. I hate crowds, she likes being the center of attention. She's always trying to get me to live a little.

The room is blessedly quiet. My roommate is almost never around which is one of the things that makes living in a dorm bearable. Papa offered to get me somewhere off campus so I'd be more comfortable but I wanted to at least try. The one thing I promised myself when coming here was that I'd do my best to have a semi-normal college experience. Although I seem to be failing woefully, something that Sophia will undoubtedly be pointing out soon.

"That's nice, Soph," I tell her.

"Please tell me you're not in your room alone, on a Friday night."

"Alright I won't."

She groans softly. "Kat, we talked about it. You're supposed to branch out in college. Meet new people, make some friends."

"But why is that necessary?" I retort. "Most people would run for the hills if they knew I keep a revolver under my pillow to sleep. It just seems futile starting relationships that will inevitably end once they get to know the real me."

My sister and I haven't had the most conventional upbringings. Quite the opposite, considering our father's one of the top mafia Don's in the New York, Cosa Nostra. Still, we've gone through great pains to hide who we really are. Our identities are secret. Which means whoever we meet, any relationships we begin are always tainted with a cloud of untruth, and we can never be a hundred percent ourselves with anyone.

Sophia seems okay with it. She's managed to find a balance and some kind of peace with entering meaningless relationships that will eventually end. She's great at putting herself out there. I'm not.

It's kind of embarrassing. Because I'm meant to be the big sister. I can be brave when it comes to anything else. Shooting people, fighting, I'm good at those. Anything I'm not good at, I work hard to be. But when it comes to people, there will always be this gap that I can't seem to cross.

"At least tell me you've done something interesting since arriving at Harvard?" Sophia questions, exasperation in her tone.

"I joined a robotics club."

"What do you even know about robotics?"

"Nothing, which is exactly why I joined. I want to learn."

"You know you don't have to know everything right?"

"Sure, but I do have to be the best."

Sophia sighs softly. "So you haven't made any friends, you've been attending a shit ton of classes and you've joined one club. That's it?"

"Well…" I trail off, wondering if I should share this tidbit of information.

"What? What is it?"

"There's this one guy that did ask for my number?"

"Let me guess, you shut him down hard, glared at him. Or maybe you made him cry?" she laughs.

I smile. "I did that one time. And no, none of the above. I actually did give him my number."

"Are you serious? Oh my God, how did he achieve that?"

"He was annoyingly persistent," I mutter. "And really good looking."

Sophia giggles. "Oh my God, yes! This is what I needed to hear. You need to go out with him. Please tell me you're going out with him."

I roll my eyes at her excitement.

"He technically did ask me out on a date. But he hasn't texted so maybe he's no longer interested," I shrug.

"If he doesn't get back to you, you have my permission to shoot him," she says.

"I'm not going to shoot anyone on campus. Papa made me promise that I wouldn't make him clean up any murders in college."

I'm only half joking. Obviously I'm not some psychopathic bitch who goes around shooting people. But my father really did make me promise not to be involved in any murders. My move to Boston was allowed only on the condition that I remained low key throughout my entire stay. When I'm here, I'm not a mafia princess. I'm just Katerina.

The problem is, Katerina doesn't know how to be herself outside of the mafia world. It's been hitting me that I have no identity apart from my family.

"Fine, don't murder him. But a swift kick in the balls the next time you see him?"

"I'll put it under advisement," I tell her.

She's telling me about a fight that broke out at her school when my phone pings with a text. I lift it from my ear and it's an unknown number. But the contents make it pretty clear who it is.

> Hey beautiful. You like bowling? You, me, tomorrow afternoon?

"Sophia, it turns out might not need to murder him after all," I inform my sister.

After replying Xander's text and agreeing to the date, I spend the rest of the night wondering at my choices and plans for my future. I might not know who I am but I've always known who I wanted to be.

THE PROBLEM WITH PLANS THOUGH, is that they have a way of getting derailed. In painful, unexpected ways. But before the derailment of my plans, I get the chance to fall in love. And I also the get the chance to lose that love, leaving me more broken than I was before.

CHAPTER 2
Xander

People make a lot of mistakes when they're young and dumb. My mistake, was falling in love.

10 YEARS BEFORE

"Come on, baby. It's my senior year. And it's literally the last time I get to attend this rally. Let's go together," I implore.

Katerina's lying face up on my bed. Long sexy legs crossed, blonde hair fanning out behind her. She has a tablet out, staring up at it and seemingly not listening to me.

It's only been three months since this amazing, gorgeous woman agreed to date me. And sometimes it's still crazy that she did.

"No," she says without even looking at me.

I take a seat on the beanbag and stare at her for a couple of seconds. With Katerina, it takes incentives to get her to do things she doesn't want to. I just have to think about something she wants more. Dating her has taught me diplomatic negotiating. I love every second of it.

She finally turns her head to look at my face, big brown eyes narrowing.

"I can practically smell the smoke, Xan. You're not convincing me to go to that rally. No way. Rallies are loud and messy and uncomfortable. There'll be too many people."

"Yeah, but I'll be right beside you."

She rolls her eyes, "You're exaggerating your importance in this scenario."

"Oh come on, beautiful. I'll take you to see that play you wanted to see."

"I can take myself," she says dryly, eyes going back to her tablet.

I chuckle. Katerina's a woman that doesn't take any bullshit. Dating her could pose some challenges to most people. But I've always liked a good challenge. Enjoyed it even. Seeing her fires up something in me. Makes me strive to be even better.

But if there's one thing I've learned dating her, it's that no one's better than her. I come from a home where everything was turned into a competition and I had to work hard every day to be better. With Katerina, that element is still there, but there's less pressure. There's no beating the insanely beautiful, intelligent woman that's my girlfriend. And I've made peace with it. I enjoy it even.

"Alright fine," I say, clapping my hands together. "What's it going to take for you to go to this rally with me, Katerina Petrov?"

She perks up at that, seemingly interested. I fight back a grin as she sits up, her legs swinging down to the floor. She looks at me, brown eyes fierce.

"I want a weekend gateway," she states.

"What?"

"I want one weekend, with just us. None of your friends,

no parties. I want you to myself for three nights. Friday, Saturday and Sunday. We can go anywhere, hiking, camping, any of those shit you like. But I want it to be just us."

Something warm slides through my chest. I stare at her for a couple of moments, completely dumbfounded.

"You hate hiking and camping and all that outdoor stuff," I manage to say.

She shrugs, the shirt she's wearing, sliding off her shoulder. "Yeah, but they're slightly manageable when I'm doing it with you."

My mouth widens into a grin. "So you do love me."

"When did I say that, Xan?" she sighs.

In the time we've been dating, I've said the words a total of twenty four times, she's said it a total of zero times. But I know she loves me. For some reason, Katerina has a hard time saying the words. It's okay though, because I understand her. Better than most people.

I get to my feet, sit on the bed and, pull her into my arms. We both fall onto the mattress, lying down.

"It's okay, baby. I get it. What was that about me over exaggerating my importance again?" I question teasingly.

"Shut up, Xan," she mumbles, punching my shoulder.

I chuckle. "We can go on as many weekend gateways you want, baby. Just say the word and I'll do it."

"Yeah, I know. I'm just worried," she says softly.

I lean slightly away to look at her face. "Worried about what?"

"Well, you're in your senior year. Which means we've only got a couple of months before you graduate. I want us to make the most of the time we've got left."

Something about that statement doesn't sit right with me.

"Woah, princess. Don't tell me you think we're going to break up after I graduate or something. My family quite literally has a private jet. I'll be flying over here every weekend to see you."

She laughs. "Sometimes I forget you're a total rich boy."

"Says the girls who owns every luxury item to exist. Your family's rich too."

Or at least I think they are. I don't really know much about Katerina's family. I know she has a little sister and her mom passed away a couple of years ago. But she doesn't talk much about them. It's odd but I've been trying to respect her privacy. I don't want to be too pushy. She'll tell me when she's ready.

She's still smiling when I tilt her head up. Our eyes meet and a shiver rolls through me. I'm still not sure what I did to deserve her. My heartbeat pulses in a way that makes me feel alive. Promises and assurances swirl around us. Her eyes darken before flaring to life. She meets me halfway as I bring my lips to hers. Her lips part immediately. One second she's lying by my side and then the next my body is over hers, her arms wrapped around my neck.

It's all a rush from there. Clothes, underwear. Everything comes up as I kiss my way down her neck and chest. Every single time I'm with her I feel alive in a way I've never felt before.

My fingers find their way to the heat between her legs.

"Always so wet for me, Katerina," I say her name in a purr.

She's breathing heavily as she says, "You know you only ever say my full name when we're having sex?"

"Really?" I ask, before closing my mouth over one puckered pink nipple.

She lets out a small whimper as I lick and suck, pulling my hair hard enough to hurt.

"Xander," she gasps, bucking against my fingers which are in between her leg in a search for more friction.

I continue thrusting inside her, while my thumb teases her clit. My teeth grazes over her nipples before I soothe them with soft, leisurely licks. My thumb continues to play with her clit, lingering over the spots that I know drive her wild.

"Tell me what you want, baby," I prompt.

"I want..." Her hands fists the sheets as I add another fingers inside her, hitting a spot deep within.

My mouth trails down her stomach. Her skin is hot to the touch, tiny trembles wracking her body the closer I get to her clit. I pause at the juncture to her thighs and look up, soaking in the sight of her flushed face and hazy expression.

"Answer me, Katerina."

"I want you inside of me," she pants, squirming and clenching around my fingers with obvious need.

I pump inside her slowly. My body practically vibrating with the need to thrust inside of her and taste her as she comes. But I want to draw this out as long as possible. To savor every second, every sound that comes out of those gorgeous lips. "Be more specific. What exactly do you want inside of you?"

"Your cock. I want you to fuck me," she says, the words escaping in a plea.

She once confessed to me that for the longest time she didn't like having sex because it was the only time she has ever felt helpless and out of control. I worked hard to become someone she felt comfortable with relinquishing control with. And I'm damn proud of the fact that she chose me to be that person for her.

I groan softly before pulling my fingers out of her and burying my face between her legs. I lightly circle her clit with my tongue, letting the taste and scent of her distract me from the ache in my cock.

"I'll fuck you, Katerina, I promise. But first I want you to be a good girl and come on my face."

Her moans grow louder as I feast on every inch of her. My blood surges with every cry, the way she arches into me, greedy and searching. I grip her thighs, resting her legs on my shoulders so I can continue to thrust inside of her. I lock her in place as my tongue fucks her, thrusting inside and licking her until she finally comes with a loud cry. Her entire body shudder and her arousal coating my tongue.

"Holy shit," Katerina pants.

"We're not done yet, baby," I tell her. One upward movement and I'm inside of her, sinking in slowly, to draw out the pleasure.

"Oh God, Oh God," Katerina says continuously.

I grit my teeth, trying to imagine something that'll stave off my impending orgasm. Naked grandmas are always the best bet. I exhale deep, ragged breaths each time I pull out and push in, making sure to hit her most sensitive spots.

Katerina clings to me as I drive in deep, harder and faster until we're both gasping for hair. The headboard slams against the wall with each thrust. Pleasure starts to burn bright inside of me. I grunt softly as I fuck her, feeling myself about to be taken over the edge. I reach for Katerina's clit, massaging lightly.

"Come for me, baby," I whisper against her ear.

My words are a detonator. She explodes around me, her pussy gripping my cock like a vice as she comes with my name on her lips. I have to slow down a little, my hands gripping her hips as I thrust into her. Katerina offers me a dopey sex hazed grin.

Her hand moving up to my forehead that's slick with sweat. She pushes a few strands away.

"Let go, Xander," she says softly.

And that's all I takes. I come with a hoarse cry, my legs giving out from under me. Every bone in my body liquefies. I fall down onto the bed beside her. Katerina holds me as I recover, placing soft kisses against my chest.

My heart continues to pound in my chest. I love her. It's not really a realization. More a promise to myself, to her. I've only known her for a couple of months and I can't even begin to imagine a future without her.

"You're stuck with me, princess. Okay?" I ask, kissing her cheek.

She lets out a soft, satisfied sigh, "Okay."

My mother always used to tell me that the people you fight the hardest to keep are the ones you end up losing in the end.

I just never thought Katerina would be one of those people.

CHAPTER 3

Katerina

9 YEARS BEFORE

I've always had a clear path to my future. First born child of Eduardo Mincetti, heir to his empire. That was always the plan. I've never strayed from that plan, not once. I tried my hardest to be the best. I conformed to my father's ideas. I let him mold me in his own image. I wasn't just a princess. I worked hard so that I would be known as an ice queen when I eventually take over.

And now every plan I've ever had, everything I've ever wanted for myself is practically evaporating before my eyes. And all because I made a mistake.

Tears well up in my eyes as I stare at the mistake. And I immediately feel guilty. His big green eyes blink up at me innocently. So much like his fathers.

"You're not a mistake, my baby," I say softly, holding him to my chest. "You're perfect. So, so perfect."

Someone walks into the room, and I hear his footsteps but he doesn't speak for the longest moment. Giving me time to recollect myself. Eventually, I lift my head to look at him.

"Yes?" I ask, my voice as cool as I can muster.

"I'm sorry to disturb you, Miss Mincetti but the pilot is ready to fly you back to the U.S," Cole informs me.

I nod, getting to my feet unsteadily. I only just gave birth two days ago. I haven't left this room since then. Cole helps me in packing up all my stuff. My baby is still wrapped in my hand. When he offers a carrier for me to hold him, I shake my head. We head outside the building where a car is already in wait. Cole gets behind the wheel driving us to the hanger.

"And you're sure my father isn't aware of any of it?" I ask him during the ride.

"The Don believes you'll be arriving home tomorrow and not today, ma'am. He was worried about you but I assured him you were fine and safe."

"Good," I say softly.

My baby stirs in my hands, his eyes blinking up at me once before he goes back to sleep. I need him to be calm for this.

"And Sokolov?" I question.

"He's chasing after a fake lead in Arbat. He has no clue you're leaving Moscow."

"Alright," I say letting out a soft breath. "Thank you, Cole."

Cole's a brown haired man in his thirties who has been my bodyguard and driver for as long as I can remember. Even in college he was never too far away. Always a call away if I was in any trouble. He came to Moscow with me when I arrived a couple of months back. And has been at my side, helping me to stay alive. Helping to keep my secrets.

He's already done so much for me here. I just wish I could trust him to continue to do so when I return. My pulse races as I consider the inevitability of my actions.

We arrive at the hanger and he leads me towards the plane that'll fly me back. At the boarding stairs, I face Cole, my baby still in my arms. His brown eyes are dull, his expression set.

"You already know what I'm going to do," I say softly.

"I've known you since you were little, Miss Mincetti. Of course I know what you're going to do."

"I'm so sorry."

"I understand. You can't afford for there to be any loose ends. Not if you want them coming after your baby."

My hands shake as I reach for the gun in my purse. I've killed people before. And sometimes I like to tell myself that it gets easier. But this might be the hardest one of all. Because he doesn't deserve this. I know he doesn't deserve this.

"Keep him hidden, Katerina. Make sure he's not exposed to this world," Cole says grimly.

I nod once, as tears well up in my eyes. One shot and it's over. My finger rests on the trigger. There's a silencer attached to the gun so it doesn't make too much noise.

"You're a good man, Cole."

He offers me a small, sad smile. "There are no good men."

I finally pull the trigger and the bullet hits him in the chest. He falls to the ground. My hands are shaking so badly but I manage to hold on to my baby and the gun. Cole's eyes are closed and I feel so sick. I think I might throw up. But I also have to be strong.

I take in a deep breath to steel my nerves. Then I send a text asking someone to take care of the body. My eyes fall shut briefly before I walk up the stairs and enter the plane. It doesn't take long for the pilot to start and then we're up in the air. I spend the entire plane ride hating myself and the things that led me to this point.

Cole was right. There are no good men in our world. And I'll do whatever it takes to protect my baby from everything.

THE DON'S DOORSTEP BABY

I NEVER WOULD HAVE THOUGHT I'd have a baby at 19 years old. I also never thought I'd be a mother that would place my baby in front of a doorstep to be found. And yet I find myself doing it. The first thing I did after arriving in the U.S was to find my way to D.C. To the home of a person I'm sure probably hates me by now.

And if he doesn't, he's about to. My baby smiles up at me as I drop his carrier at the foot of the steps leading into the house. My heart swells and drops in the same moment.

"I'm so sorry, baby," I whisper, trying my best not to cry.

After making sure he's comfortable, I step back and then I continue taking another few steps, until I can't see the carrier anymore. Until I'm completely hidden from view. After, I pull my phone out and send him a text.

> Hi, Xander.

The house is dark and the shutters are closed but I know he's home. Probably asleep. I'm proven right when one of the rooms light up. But it takes a couple of minutes for him to reply my text.

> What the actual fuck, Katerina? Where the hell are you? How could you disappear for months?

> I'm sorry I disappeared. But everything I did, I did because I had no choice. And I need you to understand that what I'm about to do now is also because I don't have a choice.

> What are you talking about? Is this because my family found out who you are? I don't care that your last name is Mincetti or that your father is some kind of crime boss. I just want to talk to you.

A sob wells up in my throat, but I don't let it escape.

> You can't talk to me, Xander. I have to stay away from you. It's what is best.

> Like hell it is.

> Xander, I need you to go outside.

> What?

> Go outside.

It takes a minute but suddenly all the lights in the house are coming on. My heart practically climbs in my throat when the door opens. Xander stares at the baby in front of him in shock for a couple of seconds. Then his expression morphs into disbelief. He looks around like someone is playing a practical joke on him or something.

Then he seems to remember the phone in his hand.

> What the hell is this, Katerina?

> He's your baby. I know you're probably confused and none of this makes any sense. But I got pregnant before I left. I had your baby two days ago on the 25th. I haven't named him yet. I thought you might like to do that. And I know you'll take care of him, Alexander. Because I can't do it. I have to go. I have to disappear from both your lives. Please, don't come looking for me.

He looks so distraught. I watch as understanding starts to dawn in his expression.

> If you do this, I will never forgive you.

> I know you won't. Take care of him, Xander. I love you.

I watch as he starts to text again but he won't be able to reach me. I switch off the phone and as I walk away, I toss it into the bushes. I keep on walking, trying hard not to run away. Not to turn back. Every part of my heart wants nothing more than to go back to both of them.

They're my whole entire heart. And they'll never know. Not if I want to protect my family's legacy. Not if I want them to be safe.

PRESENT DAY

I hear my little sister before I see her.

"Kat," Sophia sings from the other side of the door before bursting inside.

I arch an eyebrow as I lift my head from the giant screen in front of me, surveilling Sophia and the toddler strapped to her chest. My little niece, Nova Annalise Legan is the most adorably, sweet thing on the planet. She's almost two years old, with bright blue eyes like her mommy, and her curly dark hair like her dad. She beams when she sees me, lifting her hand to wave. Her mom puts her down and she's waddling towards the table as fast as her little legs can carry her.

"*Zia* Kat, *Zia* Kat," she exclaims reaching her arms out for a hug.

I smile, hurriedly switching off the computer so she doesn't see the footage of the man being tortured on the screen. She climbs into my lap and I pull her closer, relishing in her warmth. She's so small and fragile. So bubbly.

"I missed you so much, Nova. How are you *angioletta*?"

She babbles excitedly, trying her best to form words. "Doggie, Zia. Doggie," she says looking around for Rocky. A dog I recently got a few months ago. It was an impulsive decision and one Papa absolutely hates.

But like Nova, Rocky's adorable and I love having him around.

"I'll have one of the men bring Rocky to you," I tell my niece, reaching for my phone to send a text asking for the dog to be brought in. "For now, why don't you go to the couch and play with one of your toys so I can talk to your mama?"

She nods, understanding my words fairly easily. She slides off my lap and walks past her mother to sit on the couch obediently. My sister steps forward, sitting on the chair in front of my table. Her blonde hair is in a messy bun on top of her head. She's practically glowing. Having a daughter and her family really agrees with her.

"You know for a kid being raised by Anthony, she's surprisingly well behaved," I say, pointing at Nova who's currently playing with a toy car.

Sophia laughs, "Don't be mean to my husband."

"I'm never mean," I say smiling. "Anyway, what's up? I

love seeing you and Nova but I was in the middle of something."

"You're always in the middle of something, *sorella*. I just dropped by to check up on you. Tony's on some business trip with Roman. And I had a day off from work so Nova and I thought we'd surprise you. How's Papa?"

"He's fine," I reply. "He's currently not home though. I have no idea where he is. Now that he's not the boss anymore, he seems to have found other things to keep himself busy."

"I'm not the only one worried about what those other things could entail, am I?"

"Nope. Knowing Papa, it's undoubtedly dangerous. But I'm sure he'll be fine. Plus, I'm sure Zio Frederico will keep him out of trouble."

At the moment, Rico, our cousin walks in, holding the puppy. Rocky's a golden retriever with fluffy, golden fur and floppy ears. His tail waggles and he lets out a loud bark. Nova lets out a giggle as Rico walks over to the couches in the office and places the dog on the floor.

"Doggie," she yells in excitement, getting on her knees in front of the dog.

Sophia clears her throat, "Aren't you going to greet *Zio* Rico, Nova?"

The toddler looks up at her uncle bashfully. "Hi, *Zio* Rico."

Rico smiles, placing his hand on her head. "How are you, *mi amore*?"

She starts babbling something and Rico listens to her attentively, while my sister turns back to me.

"Anyway, how are you?" Sophia questions.

I shrug. "As well as I can be."

Her eyes narrow. "I could ask you the same question on a

day you have a bullet wound and you'd still give me the same answer."

"My problems do not concern you, *sorella*. Not anymore."

Sophia frowns. I don't meant to guilt trip her or anything, but she left the mafia willingly when she found out she was pregnant. I know without a doubt that she made the right choice. But sometimes I really miss my sister.

"Sure, they don't," Sophia says, recovering quickly. "But I happened to be married to a man I can get to help you if you need it."

I offer her a smile. "I'm fine. It's honestly nothing I can't handle. Just a drug deal gone wrong."

"Okay."

She starts telling me about work and I hear some fun stories of the adventures of Tony and Nova. She's living a happy life and I'm so glad. By the time we're done speaking, Rico has left with the dog and Nova's asleep on the couch.

My sister and I get to our feet, heading over to look at her.

"She is so adorable," I say. "Despite the fact that she looks so much like Tony."

Sophia laughs, shaking her head. "The both of you are weird. I know you like each other but you keep insisting otherwise."

"As if," I scoff before looking sideways at my sister. "So, have you ever thought about having one more?"

"Well... Tony and I had a conversation a couple of days ago. And we both decided to wait for a little while longer. We're still content and Nova's an energetic little monster right now. Adding a baby into the mix might be a bad idea."

"Whatever you choose will be great."

"How about you?" Sophia says, shifting closer and

nudging at my shoulder. "Have you ever thought about having kids of your own?"

"You mean will I be having kids with the imaginary boyfriend I currently have?"

She laughs. "Do you want me to set you up? I hear dating apps are all the rage these days. Maybe you could meet someone?"

"Who on earth would actually be comfortable dating a woman that's the head of a mafia crime syndicate, Sophia?"

My sister sighs. "Maybe they don't have to know?"

"You especially should know that's a terrible idea, Soph," I mutter.

We both know that.

"Fine. But you can't be alone forever. I want you to be happy. With a man and kids of your own."

"What if I don't want kids?" I ask, feeling my heart clench.

The weight of those words are heavy on my chest. A reminder, a searing hurt.

"Then that's okay," Sophia says easily. "As long you're happy."

"I am happy. I have you and Nova and Rico and Papa."

"That's not enough. You deserve so much more, Kat. You deserve love."

She wouldn't be saying that if she knew the truth. I'm the least person that deserves love.

CHAPTER 4
Xander
PRESENT DAY

I line up for my next swing, trying to get the perfect balance of speed and accuracy to sink a putt. A breath leaves me as I take the swing. Someone lets out a chuckle before clapping.

"Excellent form, Xander. Have you been practicing?"

I turn to look at the middle aged man in his fifties. Graying brown hair, light brown eyes. He's wearing a white polo shirt, paired with blue gold pants. I shift the visor on my head slightly before shaking it.

"Not really," I inform Mr. Rojas.

I hate golfing. But when you're in a business that involves having meetings on a golf course with old billionaires who enjoy the sport, you tend not to have a choice.

"Could have fooled me," he says.

Mr. Rojas is one of my father's oldest friends and business partner. He's partnered with us our company on a variety of projects over the years. And I'm here today to try and cut a deal with him for our next partnership.

"So have you heard about our latest project, sir? The one

with holographic interface?" I ask, as he gets ready to take his own swing.

Rojas chuckles. "You Steeles are all the same. Haven't you learned not to mix business with pleasure?"

"Considering right now was the only appropriate time I could have met you that fit into both our schedules, sir, I think it's the perfect situation to mix business with pleasure."

He smiles before taking the swing and absolutely missing. He doesn't seem too bothered by it though. He turns to me with a sigh.

"I already saw the proposal. Cutting-edge technology like that could revolutionize the market. But the financials are a tad bit worrying."

"Which is why I'm here. We'd like to ask for your help with financing the project. We'd offer you a competitive licensing deal for it."

His gaze is thoughtful as he says. "I see the potential but I also need to ensure that our interests align. It's a big project. And I'm not feeling that pull yet."

My jaw clenches. *What more could he possibly want?*

"What do I need to do in order to get you to feel that pull?" I ask.

He places his hand on his jaw thoughtfully before offering me a small smile.

"Remember my daughter who's around your age?"

"Vividly," I say dryly, already aware of where this is going.

It wouldn't be the first time he's mentioned his amazing daughter who would make the perfect wife for me.

"She recently returned from Chile a couple of weeks ago. Went there for volunteer work. But she's back now. Would you like to go on a date with her?"

"If I go on a date with her, will you invest in the tech?" I question bluntly.

He laughs. He really laughs way too much. It's unnerving. No one should be so jovial. Especially not a man who's built a multi-million dollar corporation. There's no way he got so far without occasionally getting his hands dirty.

"Careful, Xander. You're making it out to be like I'm blackmailing you."

Because you are.

"Of course not, Mr. Rojas," I say with a disarming smile. "I'll go on a date with your daughter. It wouldn't be the first time. But it doesn't seem to matter how many countries she visits for volunteer work or how many dates we go on, our interests don't seem to align."

"That's true. I have another daughter though," he says grinning.

"Sir," I say on a sigh.

"Alright, alright. You can't blame me for trying. You'd make a great son in law, Xander. I'm surprised no women have snatched you up by now. Try not to remain a bachelor for much longer."

"Of course."

"I'll get back to you on that investment," he assures me. Then his eyes brighten. "Which reminds me, I hear your father's opening a branch in New York."

"Yes. It's in the last stages of development before the grand opening in a month or so. It's a move to tap into the bustling tech scene over there in New York."

"Who's he sending to oversee things there?"

"He hasn't told me. I'm sure it'll be one of the managers."

"New York's a big city. He'll have to send someone he really trusts to take care of things."

I shrug. "That's his decision."

Truthfully, I haven't thought much about the New York

branch being opened. It was always inevitable considering New York's large market. I'm glad father's finally pushing on with it, but with everything I have to take care of here, it's barely in my headspace.

The meeting or should I say the game with Mr. Rojas ends and I'm about to head home when I get a call. As soon as the caller id flashes on the screen of my phone I pick up. Like I always do. No matter where I am or who I'm meeting.

I hear my son's voice as soon as I pick up.

"Hey, dad."

"Hi, sport. What's up?"

"Nothing much. There was a spelling bee in class today."

"And?" I prompt.

"I got twenty five words right out of thirty. Disappointing right?" he asks.

I chuckle. "Actually, sport, I'd say that's pretty great actually."

"No, it's not. I could have gotten all the words right."

"And I'm sure you will next time, my little over achiever."

"Whatever," he says, a little attitude in his voice. The more he grows, the less he acts like my adorable baby. We've come a long way. "Are you coming home tonight?"

"Uh.. I don't know, sport. I've got a pile of documents to get back to in the office."

"But you haven't been home in three days. And you promised to have dinner with me twice a week. We've only had dinner once this week and the week's almost over."

"Excellent deduction," I say dryly.

"Will you come home or not?"

"A little demanding, are we?"

"I miss you, dad," he says in a low voice and just like that my heart warms.

"I miss you too, Nate," I say, inhaling softly. I hate this. How much I have to work, the way it feels like I'm failing him, every single time. "I'll be home by 8pm."

"Yay! I'll let grandma know so we can have dinner by 8."

"Is your aunt around?"

"She said she was tired and went up to her room a couple hours ago," his voice drops to a whisper on the next sentence. "I think she's just getting drunk because she's sad she got dumped by her boyfriend."

A smile involuntarily creeps across my face. "And you know this how?"

"I heard it. And then I pieced the pieces together," he informs me. "She had that look on her face that she gets when she's heartbroken. I called it a poopy face and grandma laughed at me. She was also wearing the perfume she wears when she goes on a date but she looked sad when she came in so it wasn't hard to know why."

Nathaniel's a nine year old with an affinity for eavesdropping, add that with an uncanny desire to know and understand everything and anything and I've got a little detective on my hands. He's a kid who spends his free time solving puzzles and taking apart computers. When he's not doing that, he's either reading some book or doing school work. He never causes any trouble, extremely well behaved and polite and also a little antisocial.

Honestly, he's a perfect kid. And I'm grateful every day that I have him in my life. He's the most important thing to me.

"We'll question your aunt about the break up over dinner," I assure him.

"Okay, dad. Drive safe." He hangs up and I debate heading to the office or just calling it a day so I can spend more time with my son.

In the end I choose to head home. Nate will always be my priority. The large gates into my family's home swing open with only one press of a button in my car. I can't see it, but there's a facial recognition security software running as I drive past the gates to confirm my identity. We don't have guards or people to protect us. All we have is technology.

The mansion is huge, with more rooms than I've ever had time to count. It's built on an expansive land that has the house, a cottage and even a horse racing track in the back. I grew up here. All my childhood memories are here.

I drive up to the front of the house where our personal valet is already waiting to drive the car into the garage. He accepts the key from me once I step out. I offer him a short nod before heading up the steps leading into the house. It's quiet, echoey. It's always been like that, which makes sense considering only five people live there. Apart from the help of course. The house is huge, much too large for us. I used to hate it here. It made me feel so small and growing up here was lonely. Then I met Nate and his presence has helped greatly with the hollowness in my chest.

I find him in one of the living rooms with his grandmother. He comes running at me as soon as I appear in the doorway. I'm already in position. Knees bent and body braced for impact. Despite bracing myself, the force of his hug manages to knock me slightly backward. My breath leaves me in a rush as I hold his body to mine. He's so much bigger, already five feet tall. He's a bit lanky but he's growing faster.

"Damn, sport. You're getting way too big for this," I say affectionately ruffling his head full of curly brown hair.

"Hi, dad," he says, leaning backward so he can look me over. "You look tired."

I smile. "Thanks, Nate. That's what every man wants to hear."

"You'll never guess what I did today," he starts telling me, his green eyes gleaming.

He has a line of freckles dotting under his eyes and over his nose.

"Considering I'm never able to guess half the things you do, I'm sure that's correct."

"Grandma showed me how to fertilize the plants. We used manure. Do you want to know what kind of manure?" he says, his voice going lower. "Horse manure. We went our back to the racing track and got it. Manure is horse shit."

I make a face. "First off, you're not allowed to say shit-"

"You say shit all the time."

"That's because I'm old," I counter. "Also, you're telling me you were packing horse shit? That's gross, sport."

He giggles. "You just said shit again, dad."

"Yeah, I'm gonna need you to step back, Nathaniel. Don't want you contaminating me," I say, taking a step away.

He raises his palm towards me. "Its fine, dad. I already washed my hands."

I shake my head vigorously. "Nope. Stay away from me."

I pretend to run away and he's jumping on me in a bid to tackle me. I actually do end up on the floor, his small body above mine.

"Dad, I can't stay away from you. It's you and me, remember?" he asks, sitting on my stomach.

My mood sobers up pretty fast at that. I used to say that to him all the time growing up.

"Of course, sport," I say softly, looking into those green eyes that mirror mine.

I've always been glad he has my eyes. Better mine than his mothers'. It would have killed me having to stare into her eyes all the time when I'm with my son.

He finally gets off me and once I'm on my feet, I notice

his grandmother has moved closer. She's staring at us with a soft smile. Isabella Steele in an elegant woman. Pin straight black glossy hair, caramel brown eyes, and brown skin. She's in her forties but she looks younger. Much too young to already have a nine year old grandchild. She doesn't though. Not really.

She's my step mother, meaning she's technically not related to Nate or I by blood. But she's his grandmother because she stepped up to fill the role.

"Hey, Isa," I greet.

"Hello, Xander. How was work?"

"It was alright. Is dad home?"

She shakes her head. "No, it's just us. He's on a business trip to Virginia. Apparently, he won't be back for a couple of days."

That suits me perfectly. This house is much less stifling when my father isn't here. It's much easier to breathe. There's a shadow in Isabella's eyes that has me arching an eyebrow. There's something she's not telling me.

"Okay. I'll go wash up and then we can have dinner."

Nate pulls at my pants. "But dad, I wanted to show you something cool I made. It's in my room."

"I'm sure you have many amazing things to show your father, my love," Isabella states. "But you'll do all that after dinner, alright? Come on, we can go check on how the meal is coming in the kitchen."

He pouts but nods, obediently moving to his grandmother's side. I smile at him before leaving, heading up to my bedroom. The tie around my neck comes off before I step inside. When I walk through the doors though, I pause in my movements. Lying on the bed is my little sister. She's spread eagled, staring up at the ceiling. She doesn't so much as shift, or acknowledge my presence.

"Mikayla," I start. "Fancy seeing you here."

"Big brother," she says sweetly without looking at me.

I notice the bottle of wine next to the bed. "Isn't it in poor taste to get drunk before 8pm?"

That makes her look at me. "Who says I'm drunk? I might have indulged in a few sips but I'm perfectly sober."

The statement would have much more believable if it didn't end with a small hiccup. I smile.

"What are you even doing in here, trouble?" I ask.

"I like your room," she says with a sleepy smile.

Mikayla's 25 years old, 5 foot 7 with eyes like her mother and a smart mouth. I call her trouble, because I've had to bail her out of so much shit over the years. Even jail on one occasion. She's the epitome of living life on the fast lane. It can get a little worrying, but I think it's her way of coping.

We all grew up in a high stress environment, Kayla just finds a way to release that stress. I just wish it didn't entail stripping at parties, getting drunk or having poor taste in men.

"Nate says you got dumped."

She sits up so fast I'm surprised she doesn't get whiplash. I snicker.

"How does that little imp even know? I haven't said a word!" she exclaims.

"He has a talent. So which guy is it? The biker one? Do you want me to send someone to rough him up a bit? Why did he break up with you?" I question. "Just to be clear though, I'm asking this out of concern for you, but I am glad the relationship ended."

"Your honesty is appreciated," she says sarcastically before reaching for the bottle of wine. I step forward and take it out of her hands.

"That's enough."

"You're no fun," she murmurs, running her hand through her curly dark hair.

"Here's what's going to happen, I'm going to go in there and change. When I come back out, you should be at least semi-sober, okay?"

She gives me a thumbs up before falling back into the bed and shutting her eyes.

"I said semi-sober, Kay, not asleep," I add.

She mumbles out an incoherent reply. I'm stepping towards the closet when I hear her voice.

"He said I was unlovable, Xan." Her voice is low but I'm still able to make out the words.

I still, "You're not," I say assuredly without looking back at her. "I love you."

"Awn, I love you too, big brother."

She and Nate are the only ones who ever hear those words. I haven't said them to anyone apart from them in a long time. My son and little sister are the most important people to me. I'd protect them with my life.

"You okay, Aunt Kayla?" Nate questions as we walk into the dining room where he's already seated with his grandmother.

"Not talking to you, Nancy Drew," Kayla mutters, unable to walk a straight line.

I laugh softly while Isabella sighs as I place her in one of the chairs. I cross over to the other side of the table to sit down beside Nate. We get to sit more informally when dad's not home. Usually, we have assigned seats at the table.

"She's fine," I mouth at Isabella but she only shakes her head.

Dinner commences with Nate talking my ear off between bites. Another thing he wouldn't be able to do if my father was here. Just before we're done eating, Isabella suddenly lifts her head, looking at me.

"Oh yeah. Did you hear Gray's coming back?" she questions.

My eyebrows go up and I look at Isabella accusingly. She looks away guiltily.

"I was going to mention it after dinner," she says, glaring at her daughter. "Your father has allowed him to return home."

"Why?"

I might call Mikayla trouble as a joke, but my brother, Graham has a tendency of actually inciting trouble anywhere he goes. And it's not the kind of trouble that's easily managed.

"He needs someone to manage the New York office," she informs me.

I scoff. "Dad would never send Graham there."

"You're right," Isabella says gently. "Which is why I think he's considering sending you instead, Alexander."

The implication of those words takes a while to hit me. When they do, my hands curl into a fist.

"He wants me to move to New York?"

"He's considering it," Isabella states.

My jaw clenches. "I'm not going."

Her expression turns sad, "Honey, I don't think you'll have much of a choice."

My chest rises and falls with each breath. Beside me, Nate taps my hand but I don't look at him. I haven't set foot in New York in ten years. That's the one city that I've been steadfast about keeping away from. Because she's there.

And I want nothing more than to stay the hell away from her.

CHAPTER 5
Katerina

When I was seven, I asked my dad to take me with him to a shooting range because I wanted to learn how to shoot. He was hesitant because I was so young, but I think he was also proud, because I took the initiative to go after something like that on my own. He did take me though and I continued practicing after that, every chance I got, until I was perfect.

That's how things have been my entire life. Me going after the things I want. Or should I say the things guaranteed to make my father proud of me. My mother was still alive then. And she hated me learning to shoot. We tried to hide it from her but she found out eventually. She tried to make it stop but in the end realized I didn't mind. I was happy shooting, comfortable with a gun or a pistol in my hands. I don't think I was ever normal as a kid. My dad always says that I was born for this life.

I didn't choose it, but it chose me and I've learned to accept that.

The shooting range is a dimly lit space, with the sound of gunshots echoing against the walls. The air is filled with the distinct smell of gunpowder. Rows of booths, line the range, each equipped with targets at various distances. My eyes are fixed on the target in front of me, my feet planted on the ground.

Beside me, Roman De Luca is just as laser focused. He's wearing a tailored black suit with a hint of menace in his dark blue eyes that never seems to leave. Roman and I recently started coming out here, ever since we bonded over our shared responsibilities as the heads of our respective families. Owing to our similar positions, we have a lot in common. He's also pretty cool. I'm pretty sure he's a friend, although I wouldn't say that out loud.

I adjust my grip on the sleek black handgun, my fingers wrapping around the textured grip.

"Ready, Mincetti?" Roman questions.

"Promise to pay up when I win."

"I'm a man of my word, Katerina," I hear the smile in his voice. "But you're not going to win," he says in Italian.

I take in a deep breath and align my sights before squeezing the trigger. With each shot fired, there's a recoil pushing against my hand, but I maintain my stance, eyes fixed on the target. When we both reload the firearms, Roman speaks.

"I heard on the grapevine that you're going after a few politicians for extortion."

"It's for charity," I say dryly as I fire three shots in quick succession.

"Oh yeah?" Roman asks and even though I'm not looking at him, I can see the grin on his face. "What charity?"

"Half the money gotten is going into providing homes for the homeless. The other half is funding for some farms in Moscow."

This time, Roman laughs. "What kind of farms?"

"Medicinal ones," I reply. "You want in?"

"That depends. Who are you going after?"

"A couple dirty senators. They're based in D.C but are always here in New York to do shady stuff. I dug into them and got proof of it. Now, they'll do whatever I ask them to. It'll be fun."

"Careful, Katerina. Don't poke bears that can bite."

"Bears tend to maul people first before resorting to biting," I say on a smirk.

"Just be careful, alright? Extortion's alright but your father built his empire on staying low key. Doing this might bring in some unwanted trouble."

"I have nothing to be scared of," I state before shooting my last round.

Roman does as well. Once we're both done, I tip my head at one of the men behind us who walks towards the targets, bringing them closer so we can get a good look. Most of my bullets were right on target or close to it. More than Roman's. I look up at him with a smile and he rolls his eyes.

"Do you have to be so annoyingly good at everything?" he questions, gesturing for one of his guards to step forward.

"Of course."

He's handed a bag which he pulls some cash out of, giving it to me. I collect it happily, passing it off to one of my men.

"Good game. And one more thing. Have you ever heard about a Russian crime boss called Sokolov?"

At the sound of that name, every muscle in my body shuts down. I'm immediately thankful for all the lessons my dad gave me on having a good poker face and never letting your emotions show. My heart starts to thud but I manage a small smile.

"The name sounds familiar."

"Well he's apparently kicking up a storm over in Moscow, causing some trouble. He was thought to be dead up until a while ago but he's resurfaced. I don't think he should cause us any issues since we're here and he's all the way there but most of your family's businesses are in based in Moscow. It's better to be careful."

"Thanks for the advice, Roman. I will be."

He nods. "If you ever need anything just let me know. You're part of the family."

I'm about to say something else, maybe ask who his source is on Sokolov when Anthony walks into the rink. His eyes narrow onto my face. He's wearing a gray shirt and black pants, with a black baseball cap that's on backwards. Very douchey looking but he makes it work.

He looks like every other chill guy on the street but Tony can get a little unhinged. Not towards his family but to those who cross him. Two years ago, my family was one of those. Then he married my sister and we became family.

"I keep telling you both to stop coming here without me," Tony says, brown eyes twinkling with mischief.

He swings an arm around Roman's neck. The latter unceremoniously pushes it off.

"You're not invited for a reason, *cognato*," I say to my brother in law.

"Why? Because you know I'll kick both your asses?" he winks.

I let out a soft sigh. I love my sister, I do but sometimes I wonder exactly what she saw in him. I mean sure, he's hot but he's also an idiot.

"In your dreams, Tony," I state. "Anyway, I have an important meeting to get to. I'll see you both later."

"Don't forget our monthly game night, *cognata*," Tony calls after me.

I wave over my shoulder in acknowledgement. My men start to clear out of the room. Since I became Don, my security's been greatly upgraded with me being unable to leave the house without at least four men accompanying me. I've tried to fight it, but my dad's insisted and I decided to let it go.

Still it irks me that a male Don like Roman can leave the house at any time without any security. Today he was accompanied by two men but it doesn't happen often. But that's not a battle I can fight. Roman's a man and I'm a woman. Our situations and experiences are vastly different.

Plus, my dad might not be Don anymore. But he still has some influence over our men.

My cousin walks into my office about an hour after I arrive home. There's an expression on his face that immediately has me arching an eyebrow.

"What's wrong?" I ask.

Instead of answering me, my cousin's eyes go to the desk then back to my face.

"You know it'll never not be weird seeing you in Eduardo's chair."

"Tell me about it," I mutter. "It feels uncomfortable. Like it's wrong that I'm here at all."

"It suits you," he says sincerely.

Rico has always been steadfast about supporting my position. There are some people who believe he should be Don instead but he likes working in the shadows and on the sidelines. I'm beyond grateful to have a cousin who is so loyal.

"So, I have bad news, two potential issues, not sure if they're problems or not," he states.

"I'm listening," I prompt.

"First off, intel getting to me from Moscow is that Sokolov might not be dead. It seems he's actually still very much alive and running his empire."

I arch an eyebrow. Hearing that twice in one day is definitely worrying. "And you know this how?"

His brown eyes narrow. "You're not surprised, which means you already know."

I sigh. Rico's one of the only three people on earth who are capable of reading me well.

"Yes, Roman might have mentioned it while we were at the shooting range earlier."

"Well, I got confirmation of a sighting from one of our sources in Moscow. He's still alive. You worried?" Rico asks.

"Should I be?" I counter.

He holds me gaze for a couple of seconds before sighing. "There's always been something you're not telling me in relation to him. I'll find out eventually."

Hopefully not ever.

"What's the second issue?" I ask, feigning disinterest.

"Steele industries."

For the second time today, my muscles tense. This time, there's no hiding the way I freeze or the shifting of my expression.

"What?" I ask quietly.

Rico studies me for a second. "Something else you're keeping secret, *cugina*?" he asks.

"No," I say, trying and failing to keep the bite from my voice. "What's up with Steele industries?"

"Well I remembered you used to date that guy who's a Steele, so I thought you'd be interested in knowing that they're opening a branch of the company here in New York."

The casual way he mentions my only real relationship to date, has my heart clenching.

"When?"

"In a few weeks or so. I don't have all the info. I just know cause one of our business partners is their biggest rival in the country."

"I know," I manage to say. I look up at my cousin. "Thanks for letting me know, Rico. Anything else?"

He shakes his head and after a moment's hesitation, he's walking out of the office. As soon as he's gone, I'm opening my laptop to hack into some servers and figure out anything and everything there is to know about the Steele's opening in New York. Unfortunately, there's nothing to find. They're a tech company that specializes in cyber security. I've never been able to successfully hack in. Which is really pissing me off because I need information on this new development.

It takes a while but I slowly start to convince myself not to worry so much. There's no way in hell Alexander Steele would come here to New York. He has avoided this place like a plague for years.

Still a part of me is worried. Rico just asked me about the secrets I'm keeping and the truth is there are too many to count. With me finding out about both Solokova and the Steeles on the same day is suspicious and doesn't feel much like a coincidence.

It's like there's a noose around my neck and it's closing with each passing day. And while I might be perfect when it comes to most things, my Achilles heel has always been the relationships in my life.

I'm terrified that when the truth does come out, the fallout will be irreparable and I'll have lost everyone I love. The past ten years have been hell. And despite the fact that I act like I'm okay, I do so with the knowledge that I could crumble at any moment.

CHAPTER 6
Alexander

My father had very traditional ideas when it came to raising his children. He had a deep set idea of what he wanted us to be, how he wanted us to act, who he wanted us to be. We were raised with iron fists from a very young age. Even his mistress's son, who he eventually married, I believe in order to legitimize his other son's existence.

That might not be completely fair of me. Perhaps he did love her. I'm sure he did. But back then, I was a child, too young to remember anything. What I do remember is having a family that was just myself and my parents. They were both distant and I was raised by a nanny for a good chunk of the time. Then when I turned five years old, I met my brother.

Graham was only a year younger than me and his existence was a complete scandal at the time. It was also the push my mom needed to get out of her marriage. She didn't hesitate. After milking my father for all the alimony she could, she was just gone. She returned a few times over the years. She returned on my father's wedding day to Isabella just to spite her. But she only ever came out of self-benefit. Not for me. My mother was absent for most of my life. I grew up without one.

The first few years after my father's marriage to Isabella, I stayed away from her. In my adolescent mind, she was the reason my parents broke up. I hated her and I hated her son. I understood better as I grew older though, understood that she was just as trapped in my father's orbit as I was. Most people tend to be unable to leave once Richard Steele has stuck his teeth into you. His talent is in controlling people, poking at their weakness. It's why he's being able to maintain his empire, why Steele Industries has flourished under his reign.

While I eventually came to like Isabella, to accept her, the same couldn't be said for my younger brother. Graham Steele is the epitome of brash, rude and uncaring about the way his actions affect those around him. He and I have been pitted against each other since we were young. Forced to compete for everything we wanted. Our father's love, material things, even Isabella's love. She might have been Graham's birth mother, but she tries her best not to let that influence her relationship with me. Not to let the already glaring divide grow.

I think the one thing that annoys me about Graham though, is how similar he is to our father in some areas. I've said as much to him before. Unfortunately, he had the same thing to say about me.

The door to my office at the company's HQ opens and in walks the devil himself. Graham Steele wears a smile everywhere he goes, green eyes twinkling with mirth and mischief. It's all a façade and I've never let that fool me.

"Hey, big bro."

My eyebrows flick up at the casual way he enters my office, without knocking. He steps towards the couch, sitting on it without invitation and placing his legs on the table in front of him. My jaw grinds but outwardly I show no emotion. I refuse to let him know his actions faze me.

I get to my feet and head for the sofa at the head of the table, taking a seat and prepping myself to engage in a semi-decent conversation with him. When I get closer to him though, I can't resist pushing his legs off before taking a seat myself.

He chuckles. "You're so predictable, Xander."

"Welcome back, Graham. How was your Japan?" I ask as politely as I can muster.

Graham was gone for over a year, meeting with foreign investors in Japan and helping to solidify our relationship with partners over there. It was disguised as a long business trip but what it really was, was a punishment. Him being kicked out because of a huge scandal he caused. Our father has never had any taste for mediocrity and he especially hates it when his children embarrass him.

My brother scowls for a half a second, before smiling again to cover it up. It must be exhausting having to keep up a face like that all the time. Then again, whenever I'm not with my family, I give off the illusion that I'm ice cold, unfeeling. I've carved a reputation in the company owing to that.

"You may have been able to convince father to send me there unfairly but I'm back now, big bro."

And its payback time, is what he really wants to add. The words are left unsaid, probably because they're a little immature, but I hear them anyway.

I shrug, crossing one of my legs over the other as I stare at him. Another annoying thing about Graham is how much we look alike. Same physique, with him being only an inch shorter than me, same green eyes, same dark hair. His skin is slightly darker than mine. We could be twins, but there are some defining characteristics that set us apart. He's an asshole, I'm slightly less of an asshole.

"Actually, you weren't sent away unfairly. You were sent away because there were pictures of you released online with your mouth around a stripper's tit. Not very dignified for a Steele," I say with a grimace.

A shadow crosses his eyes. "You sound just like father."

I ignore that. It's a jab he likes to use often.

"So, now that you're back and you have father's ear, you'll convince him to send me to New York as a form as exile in revenge?" I ask bluntly.

He smiles, shaking his head. "Au contraire, big brother. I don't want you going to New York, I wanted to go. But it seems father is intent on sending you. There's an issue there that requires your particular skillset."

My eyebrows furrow. "Meaning?" I question.

Graham simply smirks, relishing in the fact that he has some knowledge that I do not possess. At least not yet.

This whole New York thing has had me going sleepless over the past few nights. My father has still not called me in to discuss it, leaving me to speculate on his plans. I'd like nothing more than to barge into his office and spell it out that I have no plans to move to New York. But you don't enter Richard Steele's office without being called.

"Oh chin up, Xan," he says the nickname mockingly, not a hint of affection in his tone.

Apart from my sister and her, no one else calls me Xan. When my sister does it, it means something else entirely. I can tolerate it. When Katerina did, I relished in it. But in her absence, the sound of it fills me with a sense of biting pain. Something Graham knows, which I'm sure is why he calls me that in the first place.

"There are worse things than being sent to New York," he

continues. "If you succeed over there, you get in good with the board. Might make your transition into the CEO position smoother. Of course, I'll be there to throw some road blocks along the way. Don't think I won't fight you on that. Especially now that I'm back."

"Did you at least learn anything useful while you were away? Become at least a little more mature?" I ask.

He shrugs. "That's for me to know, big bro."

Graham gets to his feet, buttoning up his suit jacket. He looks as pristine as ever, hair cropped short, with only that gleam in his eyes that never fails to make me uncomfortable.

"I'll see you at home, dad will call you in soon," he informs me, heading for the door. "Oh and I'm picking Nate up from school. He called earlier, asked if I was back. The kid missed me."

I roll my eyes. "I'm sure he missed your bad influence. Do not exert that onto my son," I warn.

I would keep Nate the hell away from his uncle but they're actually close. Nate adores him. Graham's a semi-decent human being with everyone else but me and I guess our father.

"Yeah, yeah. See you, Xan," he says, walking out of my office.

My father calls me into his office an hour later just like Graham said he would. I head up as soon as he does, walking through the halls of the company and into the elevator. Thankfully, it's empty. Once inside I press the button for the first floor, going up.

Once I arrive, I'm asked to wait for a couple of minutes before being shown into his lavish office. My father sits at his desk, a pair of spectacles on his face, his expression hard as he looks down at some documents. He doesn't acknowledge me, not immediately. And I'm left standing, waiting for him to do so.

After what feels like forever, but is only a minute or two, he finally does look at me, green eyes intense, face carved in granite. His dark hair is speckled with gray, as is the beard he wears that's been cut short and clean. He's wearing a tailored navy suit. And when he stands, he stands tall, fit, especially for a man as old as he is.

"Alexander," he says. "Sit."

He gestures for the couches and I steel myself for yet another conversation I hope is semi-descent. Pun intended. When we're seated, he doesn't waste any time before getting down to business.

"I'm sure you've heard that I plan on sending you to New York."

"The subject came up," I say dryly, earning me a glare.

I decide to reign in the sarcasm, at least until he's done explaining. I sit up in my chair.

"Yes, I heard. I'd like to know why before giving my reasons for refusal," I state.

He doesn't look surprised at that, his emotions carefully blank.

"The reason I'm sending you to New York is because we have a particular problem, only you can handle. That problem, is Katerina Mincetti."

I feel a whoosh in my lungs at the sound of her name. My heart speeds up and it takes every ounce of my strength to wipe my expression clean but my father sees my reaction anyway. He frowns disapprovingly.

"What has she done?" I manage to say.

"The question should be, what has she not done? My sources have informed me that since coming into power and taking over her father's organization, she has begun to revolutionize some things."

Katerina became boss? I didn't know that. Then again, I make it a point to stay away from any news in relation to her. Still, I can't help a twinge of pride that she actually succeeded. She got what she wanted. I hope she's happy. I also wish to God that she isn't.

"Anyway, she's being quiet for a year or two but it seems one of her plans of action involves extortion and blackmail. Particularly some very powerful people in D.C in order to gain some control over them."

"Seems like a solid plan," I shrug, unsure what he wants me to say. Her family has a mafia crime syndicate. I'm sure extortion's the least of what they do. And my father is in no place to judge. "What are you worried about, dad? She would never touch our family."

I say that with complete certainty. Katerina could never do anything to us. We're her weakness, just as she is ours in a way.

"Of course not, she's not stupid," my father says a bite to his tone. "But she is going after Senator Davies, who is extremely close to our family. We have an alliance. Come after one, come after all, sort of thing. Which is why we need to put a stop to her plans. New York is a crime hub and there's no stopping mafia activities over there. But this Mincetti girl seems intent on leaving her territory and encroaching on ours. I won't allow it."

My breath leaves me in a rush. "What do you want me to do, father? I hear the problem but if you think I'm in any way capable of proffering a solution, you're delusional."

His jaw clenches. "You're in a much better position than any other person," he states. "But that's not the main reason I would have you move to New York. The expansion that's happening, the branch we're about to open, there might be a wrench in our plans."

"Let me guess, Katerina?"

For someone who can't attack us outright, she sure is involved in a lot of our problems. Makes me wonder if it's intentional, although that doesn't seem much of her style. My father shakes his head however.

"This has to do with Colton Industries actually."

I arch an eyebrow at that. Colton industries is our company's biggest rival and the bane of my father's existence. Legend has it that the CEO of Colton and he used to be best friends, until he stole some of the tech he worked on with my father and used it to launch his own company. Legend is probably true. And seeing as they've made a big name owing to their actions, I hate them on principle. Colton is also based in New York.

I wonder if my dad opening a branch there is to spite them. They've never crossed into each other's territories before now.

"There are rumors reaching me that they plan to launch a similar product that we do a week before us."

My eyes narrow. "You mean the product I've been busting my ass on the past couple of months?"

"Exactly. As is their usual behavior, they must have managed to find a way to steal a data and pass it off as their own. I want it stopped, through any means possible."

"And how would you have me do that?" I question.

"Eduardo Mincetti has a twenty percent shareholding in the company. Not surprising that Colton would consort with criminals. Anyway, the Mincetti's are close to the family, which means Katerina Mincetti would be your best chance of getting in. You're skilled, Xander. I'm sure you would be able to put a wrench in their plans to launch the product. You just need to get close enough to do it."

"What are you suggesting I do, father?" I ask through gritted teeth.

"I don't care what you have to do. Use her, manipulate her."

That makes me chuckle. "You think she's someone that can be manipulated? She's fucking brilliant, she'll see this coming a mile away."

"Like I said, Alexander, I don't care what you have to do, as long as you do it."

My jaw clenches so hard, I'm surprised it doesn't crack.

"No."

My father blinks. "Excuse me?"

"I said no. No to moving to New York, no to reentering Katerina's life. No to all of it."

His gaze hardens. "Do you understand the implication of those words? You think because you're the vice president you can do whatever it is you want. I could always send Graham to New York to do your job for you."

That makes me smile. "This is the one thing Graham would be unable to do. I'm the only one capable and I refuse," I say, getting to my feet.

He looks so angry I'm surprised he doesn't combust.

"This is for your family," he says. "Our company!"

"I don't care."

I've cared for way too long, not anymore. I start to walk away when I hear my father get to his feet.

"Alexander," he says roughly. "Sit down. You're a businessman, not a petulant child. Tell me what you want in exchange."

That makes me pause. I turn around and head back to my

seat obediently. I don't waste a second before launching into it.

"I'm only going to New York for a year. And after that year is up, after I've taken care of all the problems and made sure the branch is up and running, I return. And when I do, I want you to step down from your position."

My father is never really fazed. He just nods like he's in agreement. I arch an eyebrow.

"What? That's it?" I question.

"I raised you to go after the things you want, Alexander. Plus, my time as CEO is coming to an end, there's space for new leadership. Is that all you want?"

I would ask for him to stop trying to control my life but that's the one thing I'm never going to get. So I nod once.

"Alright, then we're in agreement. You leave for New York in two weeks," he orders. Then his expression clears a little. "Will you be taking Nathaniel with you?"

The only person my father has a soft spot for is his grandson.

"Of course," I state. "I'll be there for a year. He's coming with me."

His forehead crinkles. "Are you sure that's a good idea? Just let him stay at home. That would be better. I'm sure Isabella would take good care of him."

Considering my son can't go two days without seeing me, I doubt it's in anyway a good idea.

"I'm not leaving him."

"Xander, our family has two private jets you can take at will if you want to see your son. Taking him to New York, where that woman is, is a bad idea."

My pulse starts to race but my expression doesn't change. The decision is made. And he seems to understand it. Surprisingly, the one area he never really fights me on is what's best for Nate. He always has his best interests at heart and he trusts that I do too.

"You keep that woman the hell away from my grandchild, do you understand, Alexander? I want her far from him."

"But you'd willingly throw your son into the belly of the beast?" I question.

"If I didn't think you could handle her, then I haven't raised you right. After so many years, you're older, wiser, you won't fall for the same tricks twice. You can handle her now."

She's not someone I can just handle, I think, frustrated. But I don't say the words. Instead I offer my father a nod and get to my feet, exiting his office.

Trepidation accompanies my every step as I consider what I'm about to do. Entering the belly of the beast is a far too accurate depiction of my move to New York. Katerina Mincetti might not be a beast but she is a siren.

One capable of luring a man in and drowning him.

CHAPTER 7
Katerina

I'm on edge. I'm on edge and I have no idea why. I feel like there's something lurking beneath the surface, just waiting to consume me. I have this feeling in my gut that something terrible is about to happen.

When I was younger, for a while after my mom died, I had really bad anxiety. I was terrified everyone around me was going to die. I was terrified that Sophia was next. I wouldn't leave her side. She probably doesn't remember how bad it got. Bad enough that I had to go to therapy because I couldn't sleep.

The therapist referred to it as hyper vigilance. A constant, overwhelming fear that something terrible is going to happen. Brought on by a traumatic incident. She told me I couldn't go through life like that, waiting for the other shoe to drop. Especially not when there's no basis for it.

Eventually, I got better. I've always hated that period of my life. I felt completely and utterly weak, especially in the eyes of my father. He expected me to always be strong and I crumbled. But I picked myself back up. One thing I never really confessed though, is that the hypervigilance never really went away. I became less protective of Sophia but I was always watchful of her, ensuring that she was safe, scared that she wouldn't be.

But I also learned to always trust my gut and something is definitely about to happen. Something I won't like. Rico notices my mood as we exit the gambling den my family owns. It's not our main business, mostly because it's harder to manage, a lot more public with many people involved, which doesn't go well with my family's desire to be conspicuous. But in the past few years, we've been more open than ever and I'm thinking it's time to come out of the shadows fully.

"You okay, Kat?" Rico asks as one of the men opens the door of the car for me.

I nod once before entering, but my cousin can be annoyingly persistent. Instead of entering the other car which he always rides in when we go out, he crosses to the other side and enters beside me. I raise an eyebrow and he offers me an innocent smile.

"Something's wrong," he insists.

"Yes. But I don't know what," I mutter, looking out the window as the car starts to drive.

"Everything's in order," Rico starts to say. "There's a plan in place to send out messages to the politicians in D.C, giving them a time frame for them to meet our list of demands. Have I already told you how brilliantly bold and dangerous that plan is?"

"Yes, several times," I say dryly.

"Just making sure," he continues. "Anyway, we're making good time on our deals. New York has been relatively peaceful these past few years, with all the major mafia families having an alliance and all. We haven't had any news from Moscow. There's nothing to be worried about."

My eyes meet his brown ones and I suddenly feel

immensely blessed to have him. Rico's my rock. I don't know how I would have handled things without him.

"I know."

He tilts his head to the side, studying me. "Do you want to shoot someone?"

That makes me laugh. "Why? Are you offering?"

"Nah, I'd like to keep my head and you never miss."

"I'd miss if it was you on the other side," I tell him.

"How sweet, *cugina*," he says, brown eyes gleaming. "Anyway, what do you need?'

"Some rest, I guess. It'll be okay. I'm sure it's nothing."

The nothing proves to absolutely be something once we drive into my family's compound and a call enters my phone. It's a private id number and my eyebrows immediately arch. One look at Rico and he's handing me my laptop. I simultaneously start to decode who the caller is and his location while picking up the call.

The person on the other end doesn't speak. My eyebrow rises even further.

"Hello?" I ask, but there's no reply.

Rico taps the shoulders of both men in front of the car, telling them without words to step outside. I focus on finding the location of the caller. Whoever it is, the fact that they have my private number already raises red flags. My cousin waits patiently beside me as my hands fly over the keyboard.

"Who is this?" I ask to keep the person on the line.

There's still nothing. But he or she doesn't hang up. I don't even hear any breathing. Rico gives me a look and points at the phone asking me to put it on speaker. I refuse, shaking my head. His eyes grow hard but he doesn't fight, watching me as I continue tapping away on my keyboard.

The IP address for the number is pinging everywhere

from Croatia to France to Chile. Whoever this person is, he's good. I feel a flush of frustration.

"I'm going to hang up now if you're unwilling to speak," I state.

Finally, there's a throat clearing on the other side. "I was giving you time, Katerina. To try and fail to figure out my location."

My eyes widen and I almost drop my phone out of shock. I haven't heard that voice in nearly ten years. Silky and masculine. The kind of voice that makes women swoon. I'd recognize it anywhere. It's engraved in my mind. I've had dreams about it. But it seems impossible that the owner of the voice is calling me.

"Seeing as you haven't said anything, I'm guessing you know who this is," the man on the other hand prompts.

My hand tightens around the phone. I feel a tremble on my other hand.

"Alexander," I breathe, the name coming out of me in a rush.

I haven't said his name in a very long time.

"Hello, princess," he says.

Once he called me that with love, now there's only ice in his tone.

"What? Why are you calling me?" I ask, trying to keep my nerves at bay. "How did you even get this number?"

"Did you really just ask me that?"

It was a stupid question. The Steeles are reputable in the technological world. They can hack into anything. And Xander's the best hacker I've ever met.

"No. But I do want to know to ensure no one is able to use the same route you did."

"No one can," he says lazily. "The means with which I used to acquire your number are mine and mine only."

"Enough with the small talk," I say, despite the thudding in my chest. "There must be a reason you called me."

"Yes, I'd like to set up a meeting. I'm in New York," he informs me.

"Why did you go through the trouble of hiding your location when you were just going to tell me?"

"Why not?" And I can just imagine the shrug that accompanies that. "5 o'clock tomorrow, the roof of Flatiron hotel. Come alone.'

My eyebrows go up. "There's no way in hell that's happening. Why would I meet you after ten years of no contact? And I'm not at liberty to go anywhere alone. Especially considering the position I'm in."

"Oh yeah, I heard about your promotion. Congratulations. I guess you're not a mafia princess anymore but a queen. I would have sent a flower basket, if I didn't fucking despise you."

His words are like a shard of ice piercing my chest.

"If you despise me so much then why do you want to meet me?"

"My hatred of you is personal. This is about business."

"I'm not coming."

"But you will, Katerina. Because you hate not knowing things. What I have to say to you is important. Come alone," he repeats. "If any guards or protection detail following you around think you can't handle yourself, then they're idiots."

That would be so sweet if it wasn't for the fact that I know he doesn't mean it as a compliment.

I sigh softly. "You knew me ten years ago. I've changed and I'm not walking into a meeting with you without having any information."

"Your loss, princess," he says easily. "But I'll be waiting.

5pm, Flatiron hotel. Leave the guards downstairs and come up alone."

And with those words, he hangs up. I stare into space for a couple of seconds. I am absolutely shaken to my core, so much that Rico has to grab my shoulder to bring me back to reality.

"Was that your ex-boyfriend, Alexander? The heir to Steele industries?" he questions, staring at me inquisitively.

I shake my head, my throat closing up. "I need to..." I gesture outside.

Rico understands and leans over to open the car door.

"Katerina," he says and I can hear the worry in his voice. I practically stumble outside and manage enough dignity and poise to not run into the house. I make it to my room, before locking the door and sliding down to the floor, taking short gasping breaths.

I'm having a panic attack. My hands start to shake as I sit on the floor, trying to count my heart beats. I haven't had a panic attack in years. Ten years to be exact. The last one I had was in relation to Alexander Steele. I guess it's fitting that this one is as well.

It takes about thirty minutes for me to recover. I manage to push myself off the ground, getting to my feet to sit on my bed. I am beyond grateful that my father wasn't around to witness that. Now I just need to make sure none of the men mention it to him. I'll have Rico make the necessary threats.

I know he's outside my door right now. Waiting for me to step out. But I'm not ready to face him. I'm not ready for the inevitable questions. But I also can't hide like a scared little girl. So I get to my feet once again, steeling my nerves as I walk over to the door and open it. Rico's leaning on the other side of the wall. As soon as the door opens, his eyes are on me, searching.

"Just come in," I mutter, leaving the door open and walking over to the bed to take a seat.

He enters, seating on the chair facing me.

"So you haven't heard from this guy since you broke up," he begins. "He calls you today, asks for a meeting and you completely freak out. Forgive me if I'm wrong, but that seems a little fishy, *cugina*. What happened between you two?"

"We broke up," I mutter.

"I've broken up with a lot of girls," my cousin counters. "One call from any of them has never made me as pale as you are right now."

I curse under my breath softly.

"It was a bad break up, Rico. Let it go," I say authoritatively.

His brown eyes continue to peer at me. "You're not going to that meeting alone."

"I'm not going at all," I say tiredly.

He gives me a look that calls bullshit and I sigh.

"Fine, I'm going," I admit.

I'd be dumb not to. I never in a million years would have expected him to reach out to me. And I'm going to find out why.

"And I'm going with you," he states.

I shake my head. "He said to come alone. You can wait for me in the car."

I give him a look daring him to contradict me. But seeing as I'm the Boss he doesn't, instead inclining his head in agreement.

"Good. Now leave please. I'd like to rest," I tell him.

He gets to his feet while I kick off my heels and burrow under my blanket.

"Rico," I say softly before he steps out. "Tell the men that saw…." I trail off.

"I'll tell them you were feeling ill and needed to use the restroom," he says gently.

"Thanks *cugino*."

He offers me a small smile before walking out of the room, leaving me alone. I fall asleep soon after. Sleep has always been a means of escape for me. When shit doesn't make sense, I sleep. It's my coping mechanism. By the time I'm up tomorrow, my head will be clearer and I'll be able to figure out my next course of action.

I WAKE up refreshed the next morning and get dressed, heading out for the day with a cup of coffee in hand, eyes clear, head sharp. My journey to the car is however derailed by my father stepping into the path. I offer him a small smile.

"Where have you been, Papa?" I question, looking him in the eyes. "You weren't home last night."

We're nearly the same height with him only an inch taller than me. But in my heels I'm taller. His height doesn't really matter though. Not when he's one of the most feared men in New York and one who built his empire from scratch. My dad can be ruthless, intimidating. All qualities I try to emulate.

He's dressed in running shorts and a tank top. My dad is in his fifties but he looks younger. And since he left his position as Don, he's been much more relaxed. More than I've seen him in years.

"When I returned you were asleep," he says. "And stop questioning me like you're my guardian. My movements are none of your concern."

"I'm just worried you're doing something dangerous," I mutter.

Since I became Don, the dynamics of our relationship have been heavily shifted. Now that he doesn't have so much responsibility he's been inclined to pursuing other hobbies. Hobbies I'm not sure I'd like if I was made aware of them.

"I'll be fine," he says, before looking me over. "How are you, *mi amore*?"

"I'm fine, why are you asking?"

"Oh, one of the men was telling me that you were ill yesterday. If you're still ill, you should be in bed resting."

My fist clenches. Despite Rico specifically telling them not to, they still tattled to my father. It's like they're intentionally undermining me. My father might not be doing so intentionally, but the men are sending a clear message, the more they do so. They don't trust me, they don't accept me. I'm willing to bet it's because I'm a woman.

Still I bat the thoughts away. It's a problem for another time.

"I was feeling a little nauseous last night, Papa. But I'm okay now, thanks for asking."

His brown eyes don't leave my face but after a second, his expression eases.

"Alright. You'll let me know if there's any trouble right, Katerina?"

"Of course," I say, the lie leaving my lips easily.

There's probably nothing that would make me go to my father for help. Doing so would be a show of weakness. He knows it, I know. Whatever's wrong, I'll handle it myself.

"Have a nice day, *mi amore*," he tells me, stepping aside.

He's humming a tune as he walks away while I head for my car. Rico's already there, waiting for me. His eyes roam over my face, searching for a hint of yesterday in my expression. He won't find anything but steel. Once he's assured himself that I'm okay, he opens the door for me.

"Where to first?" I ask him.

"Headquarters. I need to tell you something in private. And then we need to deal with some other issues."

He opens the car door and I enter. Thirty minutes later, we're at my family's most protected building apart from the house. The building is like a vault and contains all of our most prized information secrets. It's where all our affairs are handled, different rooms for different problems.

When we arrive, Rico and I take a seat in my office.

"I looked into the Steeles, to find out some information on them."

I cock my head to the side. "You mean you *tried* to look into them," I correct. "Steele industries is a technological giant in the corporate world. They have robust encryption protocols and are continuously monitoring their network traffic. Basically, they're a fortress with a hell of a lot of security codes to prevent any of their data from ever leaking. They have firewalls and codes, most of them built personally by both Alexander and Graham Steele. There's no looking into them. Any information they don't want out, doesn't get out."

Rico blinks before rolling his eyes.

"Took the words right out of my mouth," he says sarcastically. "But seriously, if we can't find anything on them, then you're walking into this meeting blind."

I shrug. Rico's eyes narrow. "And you're not worried," he says.

"It doesn't matter. By 5pm today, I'll know what I need to know."

I'm absolutely terrified. Alexander assured me it was business but there's no way he can keep his personal feelings aside during a meeting with me. Neither of us can.

When the time for the meeting arrives, I head for the hotel with my head held high. I'm in complete control, intent on not losing my cool. As soon as I step onto the rooftop however, my steps falter. I spot him immediately.

My stomach churns as I stare at him for a few seconds before he looks up. There's a dark scowl etched onto his handsome face as he sits. Eyes on his phone, fingers scrolling. He's in a casual three piece suit sans a tie. His dark hair is as full as I remember, although it's straighter instead of wavy. His eyes, the same striking green that haunts my dreams. He's grown more muscular, his jawline as sharp as ice.

The expressionless face is new though. The Alexander I remember used to have an openness to him that was endearing. The man seated gives off a vibe that feels like a 'fuck you and stay away' to the rest of the world. My heart tightens.

He's changed.

He looks up then and I'm frozen in place. I fell in love with that man when I was 19 years old. And then I destroyed us.

CHAPTER 8
Alexander

She's actually here.

When I spoke to her yesterday, a part of me believed she wouldn't show up. Katerina's never done anything she didn't want to. Strong-arming her is impossible and yet she showed up. I'm pretty sure it's because of guilt.

She stands far from me, still staring. My eyes roam over her, cataloguing every detail of her face, spotting any differences or changing. I had every inch of her memorized once before. I thought I knew everything about her. I was dead wrong.

Her curly blonde hair flows past her shoulders, rounded full lips that I know for a fact are pink but she's painted them a deep red color today, making her appear even more dangerous. She has a petite nose, straight and I know for a fact that her nose is pierced, although I wouldn't be surprised if the piercing's closed up by now out of unuse. I was the one that dared her to get the piercing after a drunken night out in college.

Katerina's 5'7 with average sized breasts and a cute little ass. She has a scar on the inside of her palm, that's as long as a needle. When I first saw it she informed me it was from an incident of her falling from her bike. When the truth came out, she revealed she'd gotten the scar from getting injured playing with knives as a kid.

That's how our entire relationship was. For most of it, she lied to me with her every breath. By the end of it I was too in love with her to even imagine letting her go, despite it all. But she left anyway. In all the time I've been alive, I don't think I've ever met any woman as beautiful as her.

I've also never hated anyone as much as I hate her.

Slowly, I rise to my feet and she finally walks towards me. She's wearing a cream two piece outfit, a shirt and a flared skirt. Her hips swings as she approaches, brown eyes never wavering, not a hint of emotion behind them.

She stops at the table in front of me and there's a tense moment as we both stare at each other. Finally I clear my throat.

"Hello, Mrs. Mincetti. It's a pleasure to meet you," I say, stretching my hand for a shake.

Her eyes narrow, she doesn't make the same move on her part. I retract my hand and smirk.

"Yeah, it was hard to get the words out too," I mutter, lowering myself into the chair. "Sit down, Katerina. We need to talk."

There are no need for pleasantries. Not between us. She cocks an eyebrow, probably debating between obediently sitting or standing just to prove a point. The point being that she takes no orders from anyone.

Damn strong willed, stubborn ass woman. I used to love that about her. Now all it fills me with is irritation. Finally, she takes a seat across from me. The area is empty, with only the worker manning the bar in sight. I can always call for a waiter to bring us anything but we're not here for refreshments, we're here to speak.

"Why did you call me, Xander?" she asks, getting straight down to business.

I raise her finger for her to pause, shaking my head.

"Xander's reserved for my close family and friends. You can call me Alexander or Mr. Steele."

Her jaw clenches. "Alright, *Alexander*," she states. "How may I help you?"

"I'd just like to start by saying that if there was any chance in the whole world that I could do what I wanted without going through you, I would do it. Neither of us wants to be here. Me much less than you. But I'm in a critical situation. Also, I'm not here to ask for your help, I'm here to make a deal."

She shifts in her seat, slight intrigue in her eyes.

"What deal?"

"First things first, it seems like you're getting a little power hungry, princess. You've been going after some people, particularly a few senators in D.C. Senators who are close to my family. I need you to back off."

Katerina smiles. It's a smile devoid of any warmth. It doesn't even reach her eyes. I suddenly remember the sound of her laugh, the way her eyes would crinkle. I spent a long time thinking about that, missing the sight of it. Longer than I'll ever admit.

"That's not happening," she says simply. "Next."

Instead of arguing or trying to sway her, I move swiftly until the next topic. There'll be time for that when all the terms have been laid out.

"My company's launching a new branch here in New York. At the same time it's also launching a product meant to change the face of technological security. I can't go into the details but it's good stuff, expected to make us millions."

"And this concerns me how?" she questions, appearing bored.

"You're familiar with Colton industries?" I questions.

"Perhaps."

"Well they're my family's biggest competitor and word on the street is that they're planning to launch that same product about a week before we do."

"So? May the best man win," she says on a shrug.

I roll my eyes. "Yeah that would work. Except they stole the plans for the project and are going to mooch off our hard work and marketing it as their own. We can't let them do that."

"Aren't you guys a tech company? How do you get your plans stolen from right under your nose?" she asks frowning.

"Excellent question, princess. The simple answer is that the Colton's are rats. They have something I own and I want it back."

She stares at me for a second. "And what does all that have to do with me?"

"Your family's one of the biggest investors in Colton's industries. Your father owns about twenty percent of the shares."

"Yes, and?"

"And seeing as you're so chummy with those assholes, I need you to get me in so I can destroy their plans to launch the project," I say, laying it all out plainly.

She doesn't even look fazed.

"No," she says evenly. "No to stopping my plans with politicians. No to helping you betray one of my family's allies. No to all of it. If that's all, I'll be going now."

"Stay seated, Katerina," I say lightly.

Her eyes narrow into a glare. "You do not tell me what to do."

"No, I don't. But you're going to sit down and listen to me because you owe me this much. After everything you've done to me, you fucking owe me."

"So what? You're going to guilt me into agreeing to your stupid suggestions?"

"I would, if I even thought you were capable of guilt. You aren't capable of basic human emotion, Katerina. I would know."

A shadow passes over her eyes at that, but I don't even try to decode it. Instead I'm grabbing my phone and opening a file to show her.

"Your family has about 3 million dollars in an offshore account under your father's name. There's a paper company in your name used for laundering money as well, right?"

Katerina stiffens.

"I got all that within the five minutes I sat here waiting for you, princess. Imagine what I could get if I actually worked on digging up your family's dirty secrets."

"You're blackmailing me," she says tone hard.

"I prefer the term, 'incentivizing'," I correct.

"Whatever bullshit name you call it doesn't matter. It's not going to work. I can't be blackmailed, do you have any idea who I am?"

"No," I answer honestly. "I dated you for months and I have no clue who you are. But who you are doesn't matter to me. It's what I want that matters, and you're going to give me what I want."

I place my phone in my jacket pocket and look at her.

"I came to New York, intent on finishing my tasks so I can get the hell out. There's no part of me that wants to inhabit the same city as you. So give me what I want and then I'll leave. It's as simple as that."

"Nothing is ever so simple," she says vehemently.

I shrug before getting to my feet.

"You like diplomatic negotiation right, Katerina? You're great at making plans that end up being beneficial for you. I'm going to give you twenty four hours to come up with one and then tomorrow you can plead your case and then I'll see what I can do. Last I heard, you did pass the bar exams, right? Although I'm not sure what use someone like you has for a law degree."

"Making sure assholes can't take advantage of me," she says through gritted teeth.

"Really? Well there aren't any assholes here. Just a businessman, looking to cut a deal," I state. "I'll see you, tomorrow."

I start to walk away without a backwards glance. I'm more than proud of myself for keeping composure throughout that meeting, despite the thudding in my chest.

I thought it would be easy to see her again. I was wrong. Standing before her was one of the hardest things I've ever had to do. The last time I saw Katerina, she was crying and begging me to leave. She was breaking up with me. And then she disappeared for months.

The next I heard from her, there was a baby on my doorstep and after, nothing. Radio silence. It kills me that she's been living all this time without a care. Because from the looks of it, she wasn't affected at all by me or the mention of our past.

Everyone told me she was a cold hearted bitch. I guess I just had a hard time believing it until I saw it.

Later that night, Nate and I are in the living room of the penthouse we'll be staying in for the duration of our stay in New York. We only just arrived in the city a couple of days ago. We've never lived together, just the two of us and I think he's excited by the prospect. He didn't put up too much of a fuss when I suggested moving here.

I think Nathaniel's happy as long as we're together and I completely share the sentiment. He's curled up on my side, watching some kind of cartoon where the characters are shooting laser beams at each other. He lets out a soft giggle at a part but I'm barely paying any attention, my mind on Katerina and our meeting today.

A couple of minutes later, Nate's poking my stomach.

"You okay, dad?" he questions, green eyes staring at me inquisitively.

I look down at him and nod once. "Sure I am."

He makes a face. "I feel like even if I asked you when you were absolutely not fine, you would have still said you are."

"That's because I always have to be fine for you," I say on a chuckle.

"You don't have to be though. I'm not fine all the time, and you shouldn't either."

I think about his words for a minute, digesting it. I'm about to ask him specifically when he's not fine but he quickly brings up something else before I can.

"I like the new school," he says. "A lot of cool kids. One of them is an inventor."

"So, you're making friends?"

He shakes his head. "Just observing from afar."

"You should try to talk to kids your age, sport. You might have something in common with them, which is how you build relationships."

"Dad, the only friends you have are me and Aunt Kayla," he points out with a small smile.

"Not true," I lie, although it's hitting me that my son might be emulating my hermit tendencies. "When I was in school, I had a ton of friends. I was a literal belle of the ball."

He laughs. "You can't be a belle, dad. You're a man."

"It's an expression and that's not the point. The point is that you're only young once and you have one chance to make meaningful relationships and connect with people."

He's quiet for a couple of seconds, taking in my words.

"Fine. I guess I'll try to talk to the inventor kid," he finally says.

"What's his name?"

"Daniel. He's also really good at art. He draws really well."

"He sounds cool."

"He is and he has a lot of friends too. I guess you could say he's a belle of the ball. Like you were," he smiles.

"Yeah and you can be too. Take baby steps and get to know Daniel. Alright?"

He nods in agreement, but there's an expression on his face that tells me he still has more to say.

"Go on, sport," I prompt.

"You met my mom in school too, right? When you were the belle of the ball?" he questions curiously.

Like always, when he mentions his mother, my heart clenches and then falls. Outwardly though, I'm able to manage a small smile, my expression pleasant.

"Yeah, I met your mom when I was in college. You want to hear about her?"

He nods. "Yes, you can tell it to me in bed." He grabs the remote to switch off the tv. "My bedtime's passed anyway."

You'd think I'd be the one enforcing the time he has to go

to sleep. But Nate's always been a stickler for rules. My perfect, obedient boy. He leads me into his bedroom that's been decorated just the way he likes it. Painted a dark blue color with posters of his favorite shows, on the walls. There's a giant robot from a show he likes in the room, which we had transported from D.C. I made sure he had everything he needed to be comfortable.

I wait on his bed, while he goes in to brush his teeth and change into his pjs. When he returns he climbs in, getting comfy under the blankets. I seat above them right beside his little body. His eyes are wide awake and curious. He always gets excited when I tell him about his mother.

"Your mom was the prettiest girl I had ever met," I begin, like I always do. "She was really smart too, assertive, she never let anyone walk over her. The first time we met, she was in the middle of scaring another girl off."

"So mom was scary?" my son questions.

"She could be sometimes. But she was also kind. She was only 18 but she had already established several charities to help people in need. That's one thing she was passionate about, charity. She also like to skate and read. Her nose was almost always in a book."

He smiles, "Like me."

I've probably told him all this at least two dozen times. And yet each time, he acts like he's hearing it all for the first time.

"Dad, why did you fall in love with mom?" Nate asks.

I think about that question for a second before replying. "It was impossible not to fall in love with your mom, honey. She could be a little rough on the edges at times, and she never really let anyone in. But once she did and you got to know the real her, you couldn't help but fall in love with her."

"She sounds amazing. I wish I had met her," he says softly.

"Yeah, sport, me too."

He gets another story about his mom out of me, before his eyelids start to fall closed. Soon enough, he's fast asleep. I place a kiss on his forehead, before exiting the room. I head for the bar in the house, grabbing a bottle of wine.

On nights like this, after talking about his mom I find myself needing it in order to help the aching in my chest.

KATERINA ARRIVES at the meeting point at exactly five pm the next day, donning her usual cold expression. She barely even looks at me as she sits down. As she does, my eyes are drawn to her fingernails, particularly her pinkie finger.

She used to have a bad habit of biting her fingernails when she was nervous. She also hated it and tried hard not to stop. If she's doing it now, it means she's nervous which makes me extremely curious about what she has to say.

"Hello, Katerina," I greet in a show of politeness.

She inclines her head in reply.

"I'm assuming you've thought about my offer," I prompt.

"What you're asking for is completely unreasonable and under normal circumstances, I wouldn't be considering it, blackmail or not."

"But..."

"But owing to our unique relationship, I have some terms that need to be fulfilled before I can help you."

I arch an eyebrow, waiting for her to continue.

"First off, you said the project you're planning to launch is meant to change the face of technological security. I want my family to have access to it," she starts.

I'm not surprised by that so I don't react to it. Simply nodding and gesturing for her to continue.

"And I'll stay away from the D.C Senator your family has ties to. Only him, I'm not stopping all my plans for your benefit."

"I wouldn't expect you to," I agree. "What else?"

"I'll help you with the Colton's but you have to figure out a plan that ensures that it's not traced back to me. I'm not losing an alliance with their family because of this."

"I'll work on an airtight plan," I assure her. "Is that all?"

She looks her lips, her eyes growing a little shifty. A smirk involuntarily reaches my lips as I wonder what else she has to say. Her terms so far haven't been more than I expected. Katerina inhales softly, giving me an inclination that what she wants is something big.

"I-" she hesitates. "I want to see him."

For the longest moment I just stare at her, uncomprehending. Then I'm taking in the look on her face and the implication of her words. I'm unable to stop a burst of laughter from escaping. Of all the things I thought she would ask, I wasn't expecting that.

"I'm sorry, what?" I ask, uncaring that I sound cruel.

Katerina's jaw is clenched as she repeats herself.

"My son, Alexander. I want to see my son."

I scoff, my hand going to my hair as I run it through once.

"Unfortunately that might be a little impossible, princess. Especially considering the fact that he thinks you're dead."

Her eyes widen and her face immediately grows paler.

"What?"

CHAPTER 9
Katerina

Nine years ago, I made the hardest decision I've ever had to make. Leaving my son in the care of his father. Because I had no choice. It sounds like an excuse, and maybe it is but I did my best. I fought, I thought of every possibility where I could keep him with me, but in the end I had to let him go. There were so many moments leading up to me leaving him, so many things involved. Maybe a part of the decision involved my own selfishness but that doesn't really matter. When I left him, a part of me died.

But at least I knew he was safe. I knew he was loved and he had his father.

I just never considered the fact that he would grow up thinking I was dead. My hand starts to tremble, my heart as well. I don't care that I'm in front of the one person capable of using my weaknesses against me and winning. I don't care that I probably shouldn't be showing this much outward emotion.

One of my first lessons when I started learning how to be

a Don was to be stoic all the time. Never to show weakness, pain, suffering. All of that flies out the window. I suddenly can't breathe, air is trapped somewhere in my chest, my throat tight. A weight starts to settle in my stomach.

Very slowly, I look up at Alexander's face. My eyes sting as I realize he really has changed. I'm on the verge of a panic attack and he looks like he couldn't care less. He's still icy cold. And that more than anything shocks me back into feeling somewhat normal. The weight on my chest starts to loosen, albeit slowly. He doesn't say a word through it all.

A voice in my mind curses me, calling me weak.

I already know I am. It's just a matter of getting stronger. But that's not going to start now.

"You told him I was dead," I finally manage to say, unable to keep the shakiness from his voice.

Alexander leans forward to grab the cup of coffee I am just now noticing. He takes in a long sip, his expression thoughtful.

"Correct me if I'm wrong, Katerina. But shouldn't you be grateful? Better he think you're dead than the fact that you abandoned him," he spits. "I would have never let my son think that. And in a way I did you a favor. He bears you no ill will. In his mind, his mother was an amazing woman who died when he was only a baby."

"You lied to him," I say softly.

"I protected him," he counters. "I'm sure you wouldn't even begin to know how it feels, but as a parent, that's my number one responsibility, making sure he's not in pain."

I exhale softly, needing to get a grip on my emotions. Deep down, I understand what he's saying. Logically, it makes sense. It was the right thing to do. But that doesn't make it hurt any less. In his mind, his mother is dead. I'm dead to him.

"Do you need a couple of moments?" he asks, green eyes hard. "I'm sure it's a lot to take in."

"No," I shake my head. "And my terms still stand."

He pauses in the process of taking another sip of the coffee.

"What?"

"I want to meet him. Just once. He doesn't have to know who I really am."

"That's not happening," he says, eyes flashing.

"Alexander."

"No. You're not his mother. You have no relation to him. The only thing you did was give birth to him but that doesn't make you his mother. Do you understand?"

My fists clench. "Then we don't have a deal."

He gets to his feet angrily. "You know a part of me really hoped you weren't as horrible a person as I thought. But you are. You're using my son as a bargaining chip to fulfil your own wants. He's not an object you can just pick and choose whenever you feel like it. He's a child, a little boy, my little boy. You have no right to demand to meet him."

My throat dries. I start to speak, to try to explain but he doesn't wait to hear what I have to say. He walks away heading for the elevator. I get to my feet as well, hurrying after him and managing to get there just before the doors close. He pretends not to notice my presence.

"You think I'm a bitch," I start. He doesn't reply. "I am. I'm a terrible person for what I did to you. And what I did to Nathaniel-"

His eyes meet mine sharply. "Don't fucking say his name. You have no right."

I only just found out his name a couple of years ago. The Steele's made sure there was no mention of him anywhere before that. I was going crazy trying to catch a glimpse of him, to know one thing about him. When he was five I even went to D.C to see him. But I didn't make it very far.

He was exposed to the public not long ago. He started accompanying his father in functions and they didn't seem intent on burying news articles about him anymore. Since then I've seen pictures, videos of him on his aunt's Instagram. Every single one making my heart hurt. I've tried my best to be strong.

But those short glimpses haven't been enough. I just want to see him, look into his eyes. Even if it's just once. I know I don't have a right to it. But I can't help wanting it regardless.

Alexander's looking at me now, green eyes filled with fury. I swallow softly, trying to give off some semblance of control.

"You have every right to be angry," I start.

"Don't patronize me, Katerina. This conversation is over."

I take a step towards him and place my hand on his arm. The touch is searing, the first in almost a decade. "Please," I say softly, uncaring how desperate I sound.

In one split second, he's wrenching his arm away and shifting our positions so I'm pressed against the wall. My breath leaves me in a rush. I try to push back but he's bigger and much stronger than me. I blink up into his eyes and swallow softly. His body presses into mine, his chest warm against my heaving breasts. The musky scent of his cologne invades my senses as he renders me unable to move.

I straighten my spine, making sure to look him in the eyes, despite how stunned I am by the turn of events.

"If you go anywhere near him, Katerina. I'll end you."

A chill runs through me at the words, at the brutality in them. He's changed so much. But I also need to remember who I am.

"Calm down, Alexander. And let me go," I order, raising my hand to push him away.

He captures my wrist in his hand and raises it up the wall, effectively rendering me immobile. My stomach start to churn. Out of nerves from the proximity. I swear I turn into the biggest idiot when he's around. And I can't believe he's still able to affect me this much.

Just when I'm about to kick him in the balls or something, anything so he'll back off. He releases me on his own, taking a step back, then another until his back is on the opposite side of the elevator doors. It dings at the exact moment as we arrive on the ground floor. The doors open but he doesn't immediately exit.

"He's in New York," I say softly. "Isn't he?"

His expression doesn't change but he doesn't reply which is enough confirmation.

"I don't want to hurt him. The last thing I want to do is hurt him."

Xander looks me up and down and scoffs.

"You already have, Katerina." He starts to walk out but then turns around halfway to say. "This isn't over."

Of course it isn't. It's nowhere near close to being over. If he knows me well, he knows that I never give up when I want something. And right now, I just have to plot a course of action, figure out how to get what I want.

I'm the boss of the Mincetti family. And while I may have made some mistakes, I refuse to be cowed.

When I exit the elevator, I do so with my head held high. No trace of the woman, begging for a chance to see a son she abandoned. Rico's standing in front of the car with my guards. He steps forward as soon as I make an appearance, eyes roaming my face.

"We saw him leaving. He looked angry as hell," Rico

states. "And you look like you've been through hell and back. What happened?"

"Can we just leave, Rico?" I ask weakly. "We'll talk later."

"Of course, Don. Where to?"

I briefly wonder if going home right now would be a good idea. Especially with my dad around. As soon as I appear, he'll have questions about where I've been. Questions I can't answer because he can't know anything about the Steeles.

"Let's go to Sophia's house. I want to see my little niece."

Truthfully, I want to hold Nova to me and imagine she's my little baby. The one I gave up. But on the flipside, being around her and my sister, sometimes makes me feel so fucking sick. Nova has a cousin she has no idea about. My sister has a nephew. A nine year old, little boy called Nathaniel. And he's perfect.

I've never met him but I know without a doubt that he's perfect. And I love him so much in spite of it all. I wish his father would understand that.

Alexander used to be so understanding. Willing to look past my flaws, willing to forgive me. I can't blame him for losing that ability. Not after what I did and the effect of my actions.

We arrive at Sophia's home and meet them in the middle of dinner. My sister gets to her feet, her expression worried as she takes in me and Rico.

"What's wrong? You never stop by unannounced," she says.

"I missed you and Nova," I tell her softly. She flicks an eyebrow up but doesn't say anything as she moves to hug me.

Sophia has always been better at both giving and receiving affection than me. She's also great at putting herself out there, despite the possibility of being hurt. I don't possess that ability. At the first hint of trouble, I close up, feel the need to run and hide.

My little niece climbs down her booster seat rushing towards me. The only person remaining seated at the table is her father who watches the scene quietly. I crouch down to hug Nova.

"Hi, my little angel," I greet.

"*Zia* Kat," she says happily, placing a tiny hand on my cheek. "Happy to see you."

I smile, feeling my chest warm. Coming here was definitely the right idea. For the first time since I met Alexander earlier, I feel a sense of normalcy. Sophia insists we have dinner with her family, gesturing for Rico and I to take a seat at the table. I look towards Anthony as soon as I do, arching an eyebrow.

"You're suspiciously quiet," I note.

"I know when not to poke fun at you, *cognata*. You look rough," he states.

"Careful or I might think you actually like me."

"We wouldn't want that," he says with a small smile.

"Papa likes Zia," Nova says, adding her two cents to the conversation.

I smile. "Of course your Papa likes me, Nova. He's a big old softie."

She giggles just as Sophia reenters with Rico behind her, holding two plates of food. We all settle in to eat and I feel more at ease than I have in days. This is the only place, I truly allow my worries to disappear. Where I feel the most comfortable. With the people I love the most.

But all good things must come to an end. After dinner, Rico and I have to leave. We say our goodbyes, with Sophia heading upstairs to tuck her baby into bed. I don't miss the look she gives her husband as she leaves.

Anthony follows us outside, stopping me a few feet from the car. "Hey, listen if there's something wrong, you know you can always ask for help, right? I mean sure, you can be a little scary and a little annoying but we're family. And we protect each other."

"You're only doing this because Soph asked you to, aren't you?" I tease.

"Sure she did. But I'm also doing this because I care."

I smile, placing my hand on his arm reassuringly.

"I promise, if there's something I can't handle and if I need your help, I won't hesitate to ask."

"Your sister's worried about you," he informs me.

"She shouldn't be. Let me do all the worrying. You guys just be happy."

"How about you try to be happy too. Huh, *cognata*?" he asks,

"We'll see."

I can't be happy. Not if I don't get to at least meet my son. I just need to see him. Just once. When he was in D.C, protected by his entire family, unreachable, I managed to convince myself that I had no choice to stay away.

But now that he's in my city. So close to me. I don't think I can stay away. Not anymore.

"Make sure the warehouses are in strategically hidden positions across the city," I'm saying to Rico. "We can't risk an FBI raid right now and loose the entire shipment so we have to keep them hidden until they're ready for exportation. Okay?"

Rico doesn't reply. He's staring at me from across the table, dark eyebrows furrowed. I sigh softly, clasping my hands together.

"What?" I question.

"You still haven't told me what went down with Alexander Steele," he states.

"Nothing much. Our conversation reached an impasse and we couldn't continue. And exactly why are you so interested in him. I told him, this has nothing to do with our business. He requires my help on something and we're negotiating the terms of the agreement."

"What terms?"

"I'm not saying."

His jaw clenches. "You know I trust your judgement, Katerina. You're smart as hell, smarter than most people and I know you know what you're doing. But in the past few days, I've watched this man affect you more than anyone else ever has. You can't blame me for being curious."

No, but I really wish he wasn't. Especially not since he could very well find out the truth.

"I know but I promise there's nothing wrong. I won't let him affect me like that anymore."

"Feelings aren't a button you can just turn off and on, Katerina."

My eyes narrow. "I'm sorry, did I ask for a lecture?"

"No," he says, sighing defeated, "You were telling me about keeping the shipment hidden from the FBI. I'm listening."

We go back to discussing business. When I woke up today, I decided that the only way to truly get what I want from Alexander, is to separate my emotions. We're conducting a business deal, and sure it has something to do with an issue that's vastly personal. But if there's one thing I'm good at, it's negotiation.

As long as I can keep my head in the game and my heart out of it.

CHAPTER 10
Alexander

A muscle ticks in my jaw as I stare at the man standing in front of my desk. His eyes hidden behind thick black framed glasses widen as I get to my feet, rounding the table. I stand in front of him, slamming the documents in my hand on the desk. He jumps at the sound.

"What's your name?" I question.

"T-Th-Thomas, sir," he stammers.

I study him for a second, wondering exactly how he was hired and who was in charge of the hiring process at this branch.

"Thomas," I repeat. "I'm going to believe there's a reason you have this job. But between you and me, a keen attention to detail isn't one of them."

He manages to look me in the eye, swallowing softly.

"I'm sorry, sir."

"You're sorry?" I grit out. "Imagine these files were released to the public. A huge mistake like that could be detrimental. It only takes a single word, one sentence to jeopardize the hard work of several people. Do you understand?"

"Yes, sir. I'll rewrite it all and return it before the end of the day."

I nod once, gesturing for him to leave. He doesn't waste a second before rushing out. I look up and notice someone leaning against the wall, watching my employee as he runs out. My eyes narrow at the sight of Graham.

"What the fuck? When did you get here?" I question.

He smirks, "Around the time you started to berate that poor guy," he replies, stepping forward. "Ease up will, Xander? You know you have a nickname at HQ? Wanna know what it is?"

"I'm sure you'll tell me," I say dryly, my mood souring completely at the sight of him.

Unexpected visits are Graham's specialty. He likes it because it throws people off.

He grins, "Medusa. That's your nickname, big bro."

"Isn't Medusa a woman?" I ask frowning.

"Yeah but the name came up due to the fact that the employees think you have the ability to petrify a person with one look. Take a look at ol' Thomas. My man was about to pee his pants," he says on a chuckle.

I roll my eyes. "How exactly are you even privy to stupid employee gossip?'

"I have my sources. Plus, someone in the family has to be close to the masses."

"Whatever. Why are you here?" I ask, taking a sit at my desk.

He sits down in front of me as always without invitation.

"I'm here to see my big brother. Ensure he's settling down well."

"Bullshit. You wanted to come find out how things are going? Looking for damning information to take back to dad?"

"Maybe," he smiles. "Unfortunately, all I've got is that you're particularly skilled in making the workers scared shitless. Excellent leadership qualities, Xan."

I grit my teeth. "If you're done, how about you get out?"

"Not so fast. How are things going with your baby mama?"

I freeze, something flaring in my chest at the terminology. I look up into my brother's eyes.

"Do you want me to beat the shit out of you?" I ask.

"Ha. Like you could," he replies.

"You're such a child," I mutter, massaging the bridge of my nose. "Can you please just fuck off?"

"Nope. I'm staying in New York for a while. I'm bored and I have a feeling things might get interesting."

I feel a headache starting to bloom. "Are you really that jobless? Father hasn't provided you with any tasks. Or does he still not trust you after you last fuck up?"

"That's none of your business. Tell me how you're handling Katerina Mincetti."

"No," I answer gruffly, picking up a document to look over it and also ignoring him in the process.

"I can help you know? From what I remember, she kind of liked me."

"Of course she did. Birds of a feather and all that," I murmur. "I'm not sharing anything with you, Graham. Get out."

He doesn't move, but he also doesn't speak. Seconds pass and I decide to pretend he's not in the room at all. Time ticks by as we both sit in surprisingly comfortable silence. After several minutes, I look up and he's scrolling on his phone.

"What is it exactly that you want?" I question.

He shrugs. "Like you said, I'm not quite in our old man's good graces yet." he suddenly smirks, eyes lighting up,

"Remember when we were younger. I was 12 and you were 13 and he asked us to play a game of cards against each other. Remember how I won?"

"I remember you cheated," I state, frowning.

"Yeah I did and then you told father, expecting me to be punished or some shit like that. He didn't punish me though, he told you that there's nothing wrong with getting your hands a little dirty so long as you get what you want. Cheating's fine, just don't get caught."

"Any reason you're telling me this?"

"Yes. You're dealing with a woman in the outfit. Despite everything, she's the head of an organized crime syndicate. And the woman is also kind of your Achilles heel."

"Try not to make comments on matters you don't understand, Graham," I say through gritted teeth. "It's unbecoming.

"But I do understand though. I know everything, just as I know you'll inevitably fail. I'm not sure if father's intentionally setting you up or if he truly believes you can handle her but you're deluded if you think he'll give you what you want."

The worst part is, I get what he's saying. He has a point. But still, I don't have to sit here and listen to him.

"Again, what motivations brought you here? It almost sounds like you came here to warn me but I'm not deluded enough into thinking you actually care."

"I do care though. I care about you messing up so I can swoop in and still your glory."

My eyes narrow. "Seeing as that's not going to happen anytime soon, how about you just leave?"

"No," Graham says, slowly rising to his feet. "I wasn't kidding about sticking around. I won't interfere in your plans, but I also won't stay still while you fuck up everything up."

"Thanks for the vote of confidence," I mutter, refusing to let him see how angry his words are making me.

"Talk to me again when you've successfully handled Mincetti."

He walks out of my office and I'm leaning back in my chair staring into space. What both he and my father don't get is that there's no handling Katerina. If our last conversation is anything to go by, she's not going to be backing down, and there's no way to control her, not even by threatening her.

Our last conversation also tells me that there might have been some truth in Graham's words. She can be my weakness because that conversation escalated into something volatile faster than I could breathe. She drives me crazy and not in a good way. I hate how much she affects me but considering it's all in relation to my son, there's not much I can do to stop it.

I let out a soft groan of frustration before opening my laptop to check on the programs I've been running. It's cloaked with multiple VPNs bouncing my signal all over the world, every second in real time. Which means I can't be tracked digitally or hacked into, allowing me to look into whatever it is I want to without worrying that anyone will find out.

Opening a cloaked window I tune everything else out as I feed in some keywords, easily breaking past the Mincetti's family's mainframe and firewall. I'm not sure exactly what I'm looking for. Blackmail material, probably. Even though it makes me feel like a horrible person. I feel like I'm sinking down to the depths of Graham and Katerina. Two people I know who would do anything, use anyone to get what I want.

There's another hidden truth though. Another reason for hacking into the Mincetti's. There's something that's been bothering me for years. Nine years ago, Katerina left the country and headed over to Moscow, almost immediately after she broke up with me.

I know something happened. Buried by either her or her family, I can't say. I also know she would never tell me if I asked her outright. I'm not supposed to be curious, I'm not even supposed to care. But if what I find out leads me to even a silver of understanding her motivations and reasons why she did what she did. Then...

I don't even know what the fuck I hope to achieve.

I arrive home later that night to find my son and his uncle on the couch, eating a bag of chips, eyes fixed on the TV. I'm momentarily surprised to find Graham lying there so casually, especially after the shit he pulled earlier today.

"You're like a leech that just won't go away," I mutter in greeting, pulling my suit jacket off and unloosening my tie.

Nate looks up at the sound of my voice, his eyes lighting up.

"Hey, dad."

"How was school today? And where's your babysitter?" I question.

"School was fine. And Tara left. Uncle Gray asked her to leave," he informs me.

My eyes land on my brother who's doing his best to look innocent and unassuming.

"Who even let you in here?" I ask.

"The kid did."

My son looks from me to his uncle, his expression pensive.

"Please don't fight with Uncle Gray, dad. He said he's in the city for a couple of days and doesn't have a place to stay so I told him he could just stay here with us."

My muscles tense. I look at my brother again and there's a light smile playing on his lips.

"Your uncle can get a room at a hotel," I say carefully. "He's not staying here."

"But we have an extra room," my son counters innocently.

I run my hand through my hair in frustration. I swear one of these days I'm going to kill my brother.

"Graham," I begin. "You can stay in a hotel, right? Or better yet, just go back home."

My brother looks at me, stroking his jaw as he pretends to think it over.

"I could. But I think I'm gonna stay here," he finally says, breaking out into a grin. "The kid wants me to. And it's pissing the hell out of you, so I'll take that as a win."

I glare at him, he glares back. A phone in the room starts to ring and Nate climbs off the couch heading for the dining table and grabbing his phone.

He picks up the call. "Hi, Aunt Kayla," he says enthusiastically.

I sigh softly before moving to sit on the love seat. Graham shoots me a wink that makes me want to punch his smug face. I swear his frontal lobe has never fully developed. No wonder he gets along so well with a ten year old.

"Yeah, dad's home," Nate continues to say over the phone. "Uncle Gray's here too. He's going to stay with us."

I don't hear what my sister says on the other line but suddenly Nate's stepping in the middle of the living room and putting the phone on speaker.

"Listen up, dear brothers," Kayla's voice rings out. "I hear you're going to be co-habituating for a couple of days and there can be no fighting, understand? Nate's a sensitive kid and he doesn't need all that bad mojo in what's meant to be a stress free environment, okay?"

Nate nods, looking at both me and his uncle. "I'm a sensitive kid," he repeats.

My lips twitch and Graham laughs outright.

"Alright, buddy. I'll be on my best behavior, Kay," he tells our sister.

"Xan?" Kayla prompts.

"Fine! He can stay. But you're on breakfast duty."

Graham snorts. "Sure, if you want to see the penthouse burn down."

"Thirty years old and you still can't cook. Exactly what are you good for?" I ask.

"Boys..." Mikayla cautions.

"Whatever. I'm tired. Nate order pizza," I say to my son. "Bye, Kay."

"Bye. I'll come join the party as soon as I get permission from dad," she informs us.

Mikayla's 25 and should absolutely be allowed to go wherever the hell she wants, whenever she wants. But owing to the fact that she's the only girl, my dad has a much tighter leash on her. He can be extremely protective and she's had to deal with the weight of his overbearingness.

I head into my room to change. By the time I return, the pizza has arrived and we all settle in for dinner. Graham and I pointedly ignore each other, leaving Nate to carry on the conversation. When he gets to the part about finally making a friend, I perk up.

"Daniel and I have a lot in common," he informs us. "And he's funny and smart too. He has a little sister called Catherine and he lives in a big house with his mom and dad."

"He sounds like a good kid," Graham points out, eating a slice of pizza.

"He is. Yesterday, some boys were making fun of another boy and Daniel got right in the middle and told them to back off, or he would beat them. It was funny because Daniel's much smaller. Those boys were in the 6th grade and they were mean but Dan still stood up to them."

"He seems like a brave kid," I say.

"He is. And he's really cool too. He has all these toys that he brought to school."

We listen to him ramble on about his new best friend for the rest of the night until he has to go to bed. I'm glad he was finally able to make one. I was getting worried. I guess the change of environment did him a lot of good.

After tucking him into bed, I get in a couple more hours of work before turning in for the night as well. My thoughts involuntarily go to Katerina. We haven't made contact in three days. Mostly because I haven't reached out to her and there's no way she can reach out to me. Which must be driving her crazy.

I just need some space. To regroup, reform my defenses. I still remember the look on her face when I told her Nate thinks his mother is dead. She seemed heartbroken. It was the most emotion I've ever gotten from her. At least when it comes to her son, she has a heart. I'm just not sure how far it goes and I'm unwilling to find out.

Which is why I'm finding it hard to say yes to her request. My father warmed me to keep my son far from her and I plan to. But a part of me can't help but think about what's best for him. He was four when he came home and asked me why he didn't have a mum. Seven when he asked me if I couldn't just make him a new mom. We've all tried to fill that hole in his life but it'll always be there.

Then again, Katerina isn't asking for a chance to be part of his life. She just wants one meeting. From where I'm standing, she still hasn't gotten her priorities in order.

I'M at the office the next day when I receive a call from the front desk on the first floor.

" Mr. Steele, there's someone here to see you," the woman informs me.

I arch an eyebrow. "I'm not expecting a visitor.

She sounds a little apprehensive as she speaks, "I informed her that she would need an appointment, sir but she's insistent and refuses to leave."

"Who is it?"

"She says her name is Katerina Mincetti."

Of fucking course.

I run a hand through my hair once. "Send her up," I state, before hanging up and dropping the receiver.

Three minutes later and she's walking into my office. A loud exhale leaves me as my body tenses at the sight of her. She's not just walking, she's sauntering into my office like she owns the place. It's one of the things I used to admire about her. Her lethal powerful grace.

Her eyes meet mine as soon as she's inside and for just a second, I can't look away. It's a look filled with intensity. Although I can't pinpoint exactly what intense emotion it is and how I'm contributing. She's wearing pants today, her outfit business casual. My eyes drift down her body for a second, unable to help myself before I'm looking back at her face.

It feels like all the air's being sucked out. I don't get to my feet, simply raising an eyebrow.

"What are you doing here, Katerina?"

She places her hand on her hip as she stares me down, "I had to get your attention somehow."

CHAPTER 11
Katerina

Four days of no contact. I knew he was angry. He had every right to be angry and I tried to be patient. I'm well aware that I'm the one with the disadvantage in this situation. But still, there's only so much time I can spend waiting.

His eyes roam over my face like they always do, searching for something, although I have no idea what. He seems satisfied though as he leans back in his chair. His muscles flex as he crosses his arm. I get the feeling he's trying to give off the picture of ease and calm. His black hair is slightly rumpled, which means he's run his hands through them a few times today. Something he tends to do when he's frustrated or angry.

"Trust me, you have my full attention now," he says in a dry tone.

"Good, because I had no way of calling or texting you. And you going dark on me for days after that last conversation is just cruel."

One eyebrow flicks up. "I'm cruel for going dark on you

for a few measly days? Katerina, you disappeared for fucking years."

That hits me like a bolt to my chest.

"You're right. I shouldn't have said that. But is this really why you're here? For revenge? To punish me?" I ask in frustration.

He gets to his feet, stalking around the desk before leaning down in front of it. He crosses his arms over his chest.

"Believe it or not, I have no desire to punish you. I couldn't care less about you."

Well, that hurts. But its pain I deserve.

"Okay," I nod. I walked in here intent on not getting into a fight or arguing with him. He holds all the cards right now and if I have to play docile lamb to get what I want then so be it. "I get that too."

His eyes narrow. "You're being way too agreeable."

My hands go up over my head, "What do you want from me?"

"I already gave you my terms, princess. You're the one unwilling to accept."

"Oh you mean the unfair deal where I gain next to nothing?"

He shrugs. "Take it or leave it. But I'm not giving you what you want."

I take in a deep breath, glad that his office has blinds and the door is shut. We have privacy but I'm not sure what else to say, I look around, cataloguing the room. It's huge and new. The entire building is, considering it has only just commenced operation.

There's a plush set of couches in the center of the office and I walk towards them, taking a seat. When I look back at Xander, he seems slightly amused. He pushes off the desk and takes a seat on the couch farthest from me.

"There has to be something I can do. Please, I just want to see him," I say softly after a couple seconds of silence.

"And then what?"

"What do you mean?"

"You just want to meet him once and then you'll stay away from him? Never approach him again."

I stay quiet. I can't answer that question in the affirmative. He offers me a smile, it's not in any way friendly.

"That's exactly why I can't say yes, Katerina. If I do then it's just giving you an opening to worm your way into his life. And then you abandon him again."

My jaw clenches. "I would never do something like that again."

"And I'm just supposed to take your word for it? The answer is no. Nothing's going to change my mind."

I swallow softly, changing tactics.

"This is all because you don't trust me," I say gently. "What if I found a way to prove to you that I've changed? That I'm not that person anymore."

"It isn't just about trust," he says sounding frustrated. "You sit there, talking about change and I barely even knew who you were before."

"You can get to know me. Ascertain for yourself exactly how my presence in your son's life will affect him."

He arches an eyebrow. "You mean one meeting. I'm not letting you into his life, Katerina. No way in hell."

Baby steps.

"Just please, give me a chance. I'm literally begging you, Alexander. You might not know me and you might not be able to trust me but you and I both know I never beg."

"Yeah but I hold all the cards now. You're at my mercy."

I make a face at that. "Not a fan of that wording, but whatever you say."

His eyes get that mischievous gleam they used to get when he was younger. But in the next breath, it disappears, leaving icy cold behind.

"So, how have you been?" he asks conversationally.

My eyebrows furrow in confusion.

"You said you'd give me a chance to get to know you and see if I can trust you with my son. This is my way of doing it."

My lips curl upwards. "By asking how I've been?"

"I've heard it's a marvelous conversation starter. Come on, tell me. Did you graduate Harvard?"

"Yes. I'd have thought you'd would have found out everything about me over the years. Keeping tabs on me to ensure I stay away."

He shakes his head. "I wanted nothing more than to forget you so no. Once you disappeared, I tried to reach you for weeks. When it was clear you weren't coming back, I gave up."

I wish that didn't hurt as much as it does.

"Okay," I inhale softly. "So yeah, I graduated Harvard. Then I went to law school, became a lawyer. It was all very fulfilling."

That's a lie. Passing the bar felt like going through motions that were expected of me. I never really wanted to become a lawyer. But my father used to mention growing up how it was always a good idea to have the knowledge of the law on our side during the course of our business. So I sacrificed, I decided I'd be the one to take on that responsibility.

"Liar," Xander breathes.

I stare at him in surprise. "What?"

He shifts in his chair. "You do this thing when you lie.

You don't know? There's this slight uptick in your jaw, barely noticeable. But I noticed a long time ago. Back then I thought it was just a weird quirk. But thinking back on it, you only used to get it when you were telling me lies."

I blink, looking at him for a long moment. The silence stretches and becomes uncomfortable until he clears his throat.

"Anyway, my turn. I'll tell you how I've been, although I didn't do anything nearly as *fulfilling*. As I'm sure you already know, after I graduated, I joined my father's company, worked my way up slowly. My old man wanted us to know the value of hard works and refused to let us take any shortcuts. So I started as an intern, got officially hired and things progressed from there. I'm the vice president now."

He seems to be downplaying what I'm sure was a lot of effort to get where he is. His father's a hard proud man, worse than my Papa, especially when it comes to his expectations of his children.

"I'm sure it wasn't easy," I tell Alexander, offering him a small smile.

"Yeah well. I did what I had to do to provide for myself and Nate."

My breath hitches at the sound of his name. I clear my throat, daring to ask a question.

"Can you tell me about him? Please?"

"Twice in one day, princess? You sure you're a big bad scary boss?"

I roll my eyes. "Will you tell me or not?"

"Fine. I'm not going to give you too much information but he's a great kid. He likes to read, he's good with numbers and he also has a particular talent when it comes to taking apart devices and rebuilding them."

"Rebuilding them?" I ask confused.

He leans forward, eyes shining with pride. "When he was seven, I came home to find a 3D printer in pieces. I was pretty surprised. He looked a little worried I'd be mad. I wasn't. But the next morning when I woke up, he'd found a way to put it all back together."

"That's crazy," I murmur.

"I know right?" Xander chuckles. "I had his IQ tested soon after. It's pretty high. Not quite genius level but pretty damn close."

My heart swells with pride I have no right to be feeling.

"Since then, I've helped to cultivate his talents. Bringing home different machines to see how he'd work with them. He hasn't shown an affinity for hacking, yet. But he's good with computers, taking them apart at least."

I nod, thinking back on all the moments I must have missed. Now that he's forthcoming with information, I realize I have no many questions. So much I want to ask but I can't. If I push too hard, he'll push back and I can't afford that.

"The Colton's are having some form of gala in about a week. It occurs annually," I suddenly stay.

He tilts his head to the side, "And?"

"And owing to our partnership, my family has been consistently invited for the past few years. I've never gone but I figured this year I'll show up and maybe I'll bring a date."

He frowns. "They'd recognize me in a heartbeat, princess. And in case you forgot, the whole point of this is to not get caught and ensure it can't be traced back to my family."

"Yeah, I know that. But the gala, is also a masquerade," I tell him with a smile.

He arches an eyebrow, and then his mouth is lifting into a smile as well. A genuine one.

"What kind of tech company thinks it's a good idea to

throw a masquerade party? Those are security nightmares," he states.

"A nightmare for them, an opportunity for you," I point out.

His smile widens. "So you're going to help?"

"Of course. I'm trying to build trust or at least some semblance of it. And that starts with doing this for you."

The phone on his desk starts to ring. He offers me an apologetic glance before standing to pick it up. He speaks to the person on the other line for only a couple of seconds before dropping the call. He looks at me.

"I have a meeting, princess. But I'll text you so we can work out the details of our plan. Is that okay?"

I nod, getting to my feet. "Of course, thank you. And I promise not to barge in here next time."

"No need. I'll be giving the front desk a picture of you and having you banned from the premises," he says, giving me a smile that doesn't quite reach his eyes.

The words are teasing but I get the feeling he's not completely joking. I also understand that was his way of telling me not to come here again.

"Got it," I tell him. "See you later, Alexander."

"You can go back to calling me Xander," he informs me. "Alexander sounds weird, especially coming from you."

Our eyes meet from across the room and I blink at the sudden lightness in them.

"Bye Xander," I say softly before walking out.

WHEN I INFORM Rico that I'll be attending the Colton gala, he has more than a couple of questions. But it isn't until I tell him that I won't be needing any security for the night that the questions become a full on inquisition.

"What's going on, Katerina?" he asks, his expression suspicious.

"Nothing. I am allowed to attend a party on my own, am I not?"

"You are, but you wanting to go there without any protection is suspicious."

I look up, fixing him with a hard stare. "If it was my Papa making such a request, you wouldn't question him for a second."

Rico has a retort to that ready. "Sure but you're not Eduardo, you're my cousin. And ever since Alexander Steele arrived in town, you've been acting weird. I want to know why. Because I'm a hundred percent sure your wanting to attend the gala has something to do with him."

I let out a soft breath of frustration. It's not like I blame him for having so many questions. He's right, I am acting suspicious. But only because I'm keeping so many secrets and I have no idea how to even begin to unpack them.

He has no idea that I'm working against the Colton's. Rico's supposed to be my second in command, but I'm keeping things from him that could very well be detrimental to the family. Then again, I can't risk him finding out that I have a son. That would be catastrophic. Which means I have to keep it all hidden, no matter how much I hate it.

"Rico, can you please just let it go?" I ask tiredly.

A muscle ticks in his jaw. "Fine but I'm not the person you're going to have to contend with. Your father's partly the reason you have so much security in the first place. If he finds out you're going to that party alone, he'll have questions."

My father's more open minded than most people in our world. Female Dons are extremely uncommon but he's never made me or my sister feel like less just because we're women. He always used to say that from the moment I was born, I was his heir. And I did my best to be worthy of that. To be worthy of the title. He passed it on to me, albeit under duress but with a promise that he wouldn't interfere. He'd let me be the leader he raised me to be.

But it seems I need to remind him of that. I can't rule if my father is continuously pulling the strings in the background.

CHAPTER 12
Alexander

"I'm coming along," my brother announces a couple of hours before the masquerade party.

My hands which had been previously chopping some onions, fall to a stop as I look up at him. I still can't believe he's still hanging around. But unfortunately, one week later and he hasn't gone back to D.C. He looks completely at home in sweats and a tank top, siting on one of the elevated stools in front of the countertop as he watches me. I'd been doing well these past few days, ignoring him and his presence.

After a couple of seconds, I resume my chopping, sure he can't be talking about what I think he is.

"Yo, Xan," he says, waving a hand in the air in front of me. "Did you not hear me?"

I grit my teeth as my gaze meets his.

"Where do you think I'm going, Graham?"

"The Colton's are having a masquerade gala later today. I saw your personal shopper bring in a mask yesterday. One plus one, equals two." he informs me.

"I'm so proud you're capable of basic math," I quip.

"How hard was it for you to figure that one out?"

He glares at me. "Don't be an asshole, Xander. I'm trying to help out."

"You've never helped anyone in your life without standing to benefit from it," I point out.

"True," he agrees. "But if whatever your plan is somehow successful, then I'd like to bask a little in that glory. Come on, there's no way in hell you don't need help."

I move away from the countertop, turning my back on him as I begin to check through some drawers. I'm looking for a whisk, while also thinking over his suggestion. When I return, he's staring at me expectantly.

"There won't be anyone home to watch Nate."

He shakes his head. "I already called the nanny. And I got my mask delivered earlier."

I peer at him. "Why do I have a feeling you'll go there anyway, regardless of what answer I give?"

That makes him smile.

"You know for someone who doesn't like me much, you sure do know me well," he drawls.

"Whatever. We leave at 8pm."

He nods and I start reworking the details of my plan. Despite how much he pisses me off, Graham actually can be useful. Especially in delicate situations like this.

The time comes to leave and we're heading out of the house and into my range rover parked in the garage. When Graham tries to get in front, I shake my head.

"Get in the back. We're picking her up," I state.

His eyebrows climb. "I really don't appreciate being relegated to the back like a petulant child, big bro. Especially not for a woman that abandoned her son."

I roll my eyes, before climbing in. "Get in the back," I

repeat. "And don't say shit like that tonight. I mean it, Graham."

It's the last thing we need considering what we're about to do. I expect him to argue some more but surprisingly he obediently goes to the back. We drive for only a couple of minutes before we arrive at the designated meeting point. A conspicuous hotel. Once I'm parked, I send her a text telling her to come outside.

It only takes about two minutes for her to appear. Once she does, every muscle in my body tenses. My heart stutters to a stop as she walks towards the car. In the back, Graham lets out a whistle.

"Damn, Xan. Say what you will about your baby mama, but that woman is seriously beautiful."

I don't even turn to glare at him for what he called her. I'm too busy staring. She's in a long, flowing dress made with shimmering blue fabric and adorned with delicate lace and sparkling sequins. There's a long slit on the side of the dress, reaching up to her mid-thigh. The dress is also sleeveless showing a large expanse of beautiful golden skin and as she gets even closer, my eyes linger on her cleavage before going back up to her lightly made up face.

When she arrives beside the car, her gaze goes to Graham first. She turns to me, eyebrows raised, brown eyes flaring. I'm a little tongue tied so Graham speaks up.

"Hey, Katerina. How have you been?"

She stares at him through narrowed eyes before looking back at me. With her fierce gaze on me, I clear my throat, finally finding my words.

"There's a slight change in plans," I inform her. "Graham's coming along with us."

She look unamused. "You can't just change the plan like that without informing me."

"There wasn't any time to do that. He won't cause any trouble, I promise. He's going to help."

Or at least I hope he is. Graham could very well be working his own agenda this evening but I don't have the time to think about that. Katerina sighs.

"Not like I can do anything about that now," she says, opening the door.

"Please, dial down the enthusiasm," Graham says sarcastically. "But you look gorgeous, Katerina. Five years and you haven't changed a bit."

My eyebrows nearly hit my hairline with that statement. I whirl around to face my brother.

"What the fuck are you talking about?"

The last time he saw her should have been about ten years ago when we broke up. Graham smiles, but he doesn't reply. When I look at Katerina, her hand is on her head as she stares straight forward.

"Can we just go? Now's not the time to talk about this," she mutters.

I look at the both of them again, feeling my jaw clenched. Still I start the car, driving us in the direction of the gala. We go over the plan one more time on the way. Just before we arrive, I look at Katerina once more.

"You look beautiful," I manage to say. "But did you forget we're supposed to be blending in?"

We agreed we couldn't afford to draw any attention to ourselves. It's why Graham and I are in simple black suits. Plus, we also have roles to play.

Her gaze meets mine, "This is me blending in. It would look weird if I wasn't in an ostentatious outfit."

She has a point. Anyone that knows her know she likes dressing up. It's one weird thing about her. You'd think a girl in her world, wouldn't care too much about stuff like that. But

Katerina's always loved fashion. When we dated, I can't count the number of runway shows she dragged me to. I met her sister at one of those.

"Fine. We're one minute away. Masks on," I tell both of them.

My mask is lying on the console beside me. I grab it one handed before fitting it onto my face. It's a simple mask, black and gold with sharp angles, only covering my eyes and nose. I manage to tie it at the back. When I look back at my companions, they've worn their masks as well.

Grahams' mask is longer, covering most of his face with feathers and vibrant colors. I roll my eyes at the sight. Of course he picked something like that. I swear neither of them understands the term blending in. Katerina's mask is blue to match her dress with an elegant filigree design and intricate tiny crystals adorning it.

We are definitely drawing attention as soon as we walk through the doors of that party. We all step out after parking with Graham immediately going to Katerina's side. He offers her his arm and after a moment's hesitation, she loops her hand through it. My jaw grinds at the sight. I follow them both as we head to the entrance.

We're stopped for identification. Katerina pulls out a gold emblazoned enveloped with the words VIP written at the top. The guard's eyes flick from her to Graham and I.

"They're my bodyguards," she informs them, her tone ringing with authority.

That seems to be enough for them because they step back allowing us to walk in. I roll my eyes as soon as we're out of sight.

"They need to hire a better security company," I mutter, because a part of me was sure as hell they'd at least require us to remove our masks before entry.

"I'm a Mincetti," Katerina says, replying to my statement. "They were never going to question me for too long."

Graham speaks up then, "Remember when your last name used to be Petrov? Fun times," he grins.

I fight the urge to face palm and also hit the back of his head. Katerina stiffens momentarily but recovers briefly.

"I definitely didn't miss you, Graham," she tells him.

"Careful, you might actually hurt my feelings."

I decide to cut in then, stepping forward. "You're meant to scope out the perimeter, Graham. I'll walk in with her."

He shoots me an annoying smirk before letting go of Katerina and walking on ahead, entering the party before us. I look down at the woman beside me.

"Are you going to tell me what he meant by seeing you five years ago?" I ask curiously, unable to get that out of my mind.

She shakes your head. "Ask your brother."

I notice a tremble in her hand and although I can't see her face, I realize she's more on edge than usual.

"Are you okay?"

"Of course. Why wouldn't I be?" she asks, absolutely lying.

"Katerina..." I start.

"Let's just get tonight over with, Xander. Please?"

And then she's looping her hand through mine like it's the most natural thing in the world. I feel her touch, searing even through the material of my clothes. When her breath hitches softly, I know she felt it too.

I pull at the bowtie at my neck, wondering at my maddening attraction to her. Even now, despite everything.

"Ready?" I ask her.

She blows out a soft breath. "Let's do this."

We walk into the large hall and the party that's already

underway. An orchestra plays soft music unobtrusively in the background in a corner of the hall. There's a small clear area, evidently the dance floor. People mill about with champagne glasses and appetizers held on silver plates. At the end of the hall, there's a long table, adorned with several different kinds of dishes and server. A buffet.

As expected, we draw a few stares as soon as we walk in. Ethan Colton stands near the entrance door, sipping what looks like scotch from a glass tumbler. He's not wearing a mask. As soon as his eyes land on us, they gleam with recognition. He approaches us almost immediately. Which was expected, considering Katerina's mask barely covers her face.

He's around the same age as my father, although a short, stout man with balding brown hair.

"Miss Mincetti," he says respectfully, holding her hand and lifting it to his lips to place a light kiss on the back of her palm. "I'm honored that you accepted my invitation."

"I was in desperate need of a night out and thought this was the perfect event," Katerina says warmly.

"Well then I hope you enjoy yourself," he says, eyes going down to the slit in her dress.

He spends a second too long staring, making me grit my teeth. He's old enough to be her father.

Look away, asshole.

Katerina's completely calm and unruffled beside me. I'm about to say something when Colton's eyes meet mine.

"And who is this?" he questions.

"My bodyguard," she replies simply.

He doesn't question her, simply nodding. "I'll leave you to it then. Enjoy the party, Katerina. Perhaps you'll save me a dance."

My vision turns a little red at that. Katerina must sense the shift because her hand tightens around my arm.

"No, thank you, Mr. Colton. I'm not a big dancer."

He simply offers her a smile I think he means to be charming before walking away to entertain his other guests.

"He's still as slimy as I remember," I mutter, pulling an earpiece out of my jacket pocket. "Why the hell did you let him do that?"

She looks at me calmly. "I'm not going to make a scene in the middle of a party. Mr. Colton will understand his place soon enough."

Hearing her say that causes chills to run through me. Sometimes I genuinely forget how dangerous she is. The earpiece connects so I can speak to Graham.

"What's up?" I ask him, still staring at Katerina.

"Colton has two guards following him and watching his every move. I'm not sure any of us can get close enough to get access to his phone," my brother informs me,

Frustration fills me at that. I relay what he said to Katerina and she frowns.

"Maybe I will have to take him up on his offer of a dance," she says thoughtfully.

"No," I snap. "We'll think of something else."

Our plan is pretty fucking simple. Get a hold of Colton's phone so I can attach a device that immediately transmits all the information on it to my system, while also giving me access to Colton industries mainframe. It's a product that's still in development. It has a couple kinks that we still need to work out. Like the fact that it tends to completely fry the phone it's used on a couple hours after use.

Not my problem though.

"I could cause a distraction," my brother says. "You just have to get close enough. His phone is in his right jacket pocket."

"Okay. When?" I ask.

"In about thirty minutes. At the rate he's drinking that scotch, he'll be tipsy in no time. Why don't you and Katerina try to relax and have fun for a little bit?" he suggests.

"Fine. Thirty minutes," I remind him before switching up the earpiece.

When I look back at Katerina, her eyes are roaming the party, taking it all in.

She notices me staring and says, "I hate parties."

"I know, princess. Too many people, right?" She nods in agreement

She's always been uncomfortable around loud crowds. Which is how I know she did have some feelings for me back then, because she let me drag her to way too many parties.

A waiter passes and I grab two glasses of champagne off his tray, handing one over to her. She accepts it gratefully and I'm hoping she'll relax as she starts to drink. I notice several eyes on her, probably people who know who she is but they don't approach. I think they're scared, maybe not of her, but her family name. It's fascinating.

"How is it that you're uncomfortable around so many people, but you also manage to lead a mafia organization?" I ask curiously.

She blinks up at me, probably wondering why I'm suddenly bringing it up. Or maybe she's surprised I can say it so easily. I'm not delusional, I know who she is.

"Leading isn't that hard in my line of work. I spend more time around blood and guns than I do people," she says, eyes fixed on me.

I can tell she said it to make me uncomfortable, but I am unfazed.

"Ah, that makes sense."

"Although the job's not as fun as I thought it would be," she continues saying. "It's a lot of paperwork when I'm not taking care of unsavory matters. I'm constantly behind a desk."

"People in position usually are. I thought it's what you wanted," I say softly.

"I do, but…" she trails off unable to finish her sentence.

"Do you want to dance?" I question.

She raises an eyebrow at the sudden change in conversation.

"You hate dancing," she says.

I'm a little surprised she remembers that.

"True, but I think we're drawing even more attention standing in place. If we're not going to mingle, we might as well just dance," I say sensibly.

"Fine. But if you step on my toes, I'll stab you."

That makes me chuckle. I lead her towards the dancefloor. There are a few couples already there. We take our place at the edge. I suddenly feel hot all over, as one of my hands snake around her back while the other holds on to her hand.

The tips of my fingers, skate across her back, right above her ass. Sparks shoot across my skin at the contact. Katerina becomes very still.

"Can you not touch me like that?" she asks.

"Touch you like what princess?" I smirk.

She doesn't reply as I pull her closer, leaving only an inch of space between us. Her eyes widen.

"Xander. This is not how a bodyguard would dance with me," she points out.

"Sshh. Don't think about it," I say, enjoying the feel of her body in mine too much to care about all that right now.

My face nuzzles the top of her head as we begin to drift across the dancefloor, our steps completely in tune. The song playing is slow, the melody entrancing as I hold her to me and everything falls away.

I find myself wishing the world would fall to a stop then. Or maybe I could go back to a past when I didn't hate her.

My feelings are so conflicting. There's no denying my attraction to her. I loved her once before. But she also betrayed me and hurt me more than anyone else did. And yet right now, I'd give anything for us to be okay. For none of it to matter.

Katerina places her head on my chest as we sway to the music. She's completely relaxed so I'll take that as a win. But I also can't help but wonder why she was so tense in the first place. Something must have happened before she joined us.

The thirty minutes Graham gave us are almost up but I continue holding her to me, unwilling to let go. Unwilling to stop. My heart is racing and a part of me is terrified she can hear. When the song finally ends, she takes one step away, her eyes on me.

She opens her mouth and I'm not sure what I was expecting. But the words she speaks are definitely not that.

"I killed someone today."

CHAPTER 13
Katerina

I had an epiphany a couple minutes ago as we danced.

Xander's the only man I've ever allowed myself to love. And now that he's back in my life, it's become increasingly clear that those feelings never truly disappeared.

Every look, every touch, every smile, it all makes me feel too much. And I can't be put in that position. Not again. I can't feel like this, because the last time I did, it had disastrous consequences on everyone I loved. Which is why I need to stay away, keep some distance. Which is also why I just blurted that out.

He blinks at me, once, twice.

"Okay…" Xander says confused.

"He probably didn't deserve it," I continue.

The disco light dances across the mask covering his face.

"Why are you telling me this?"

"I don't know," I lie.

"Did you have a choice?"

I nod once. "I did but I still chose the option that ended with me putting a bullet in his head."

Finally, finally, he flinches, eyes growing wide. The man I killed was young, I don't even know his name.

Earlier today my father arrived at headquarters. Behind him, two men dragged another who was barely conscious. According to my father, the man has cheated him out of a lot of money while they had been gambling. A bad habit I hadn't realized he had relapsed into. But that wasn't the point.

The point was that my father wanted me to shoot the man. In front of everyone who had gathered to watch. All the capos who still didn't completely believe I was worthy. I don't think my father was trying to undermine me. But he had probably heard the same whispers I had. That I was weak. In his own sick, twisted way, he thought he was helping.

The man didn't deserve death. Cheating at a couple of card games wasn't a good enough reason to shoot him. But my father knew I would do it. He was trying to force my hand. So I did it. And after I pointed the gun at my father's head and threatened to kill him too if he came to our headquarters again. There was a ripple in the room at that, shock from the men. My dad had been momentarily confused, then it turned to amusement.

He announced that his daughter had banned him, sounding so fucking proud about it. And then he just left. But the damage had been done. The blood of the man I killed seeping across the floor.

"What was the other option?" Xander asks after what feels like forever.

"What?"

"The other option if you hadn't killed him," he clarifies. "What would it have entailed?"

"I don't know. I would have probably lost everything I worked for until this moment."

"Then you had no choice," he says finally, easily.

My eyes widen. At the simple understanding, at the way his eyes don't seem to hold any judgement. The opposite actually. I'm about to ask why he doesn't seem repulsed, when his head suddenly cocks to the side. The earpiece he's wearing blinks red once and I watch as he listens to his brother.

"The distraction's happening now," Xander murmurs.

We both step off the dancefloor, moving a little closer to Colton and waiting to see what happens. A couple of seconds later, one of the waiters trips and there's a loud crashing as all the contents on his tray are spilled on the floor. A woman shrieks as a shard of glass slices into her leg and starts to bleed and just like that, chaos begins.

"Your brother is certainly innovative," I say slightly amused.

Xander huffs out a breath. "I guess this is as good as any other plan. Stay here," he tells me, reaching into his jacket and stepping away. People are yelling and the air grows denser as the crowd tries to step forward and back to both catch a good look and escape the scene.

My eyes are fixed on Xander as he navigates them easily until he's right by Colton's side. His hands deftly reach into his jacket pocket where his phone is. It all happens in a matter of seconds. He attaches the device, removes it and makes his way back to me, eyes twinkling with satisfaction and mischief.

"That was surprisingly easy," I say as the room begins to grow calmer.

"Don't say that," he cautions. "Whenever people say that bad things happen."

I roll my eyes but can't help a small laugh. His eyes are fixed on me, an expression I can't discern on them, mostly due to the mask.

"Come on, princess. Let's get out of here," I tell her.

"Not yet. I need to have a conversation before I leave."

He follows my line of sight towards Colton and nods once. "I'll go find Graham. Meet us at the car?"

The older man starts walking towards the bar and I follow, slipping through the crowd carefully. When his brown eyes land on me, they widen and then his mouth stretches into a slimy smile.

"Miss. Mincetti. I'm sorry about that little display. I'm not sure what happened."

"At least everyone is fine," I say, setting my purse down on the bar.

"Yes," he murmurs, eyes fixed on the swells of my breasts.

I wrinkle my nose in disgust, wondering exactly how to put him in his place.

"I must say, Katerina. You grew up into such a beautiful woman. I remember when you used to play around as a little kid. And now," he says with flourish, shifting closer and placing a hand on my arm.

A shiver rolls through me. Very different from the ones Xander seems to be able to draw from me with barely any effort. I smile, amused and when I shift even closer to him, Colton's smile widens into a grin. The grin dies a quick death when I deftly pull out a blade from its strap under my thigh. I place the point against his stomach.

"Careful, Mr. Colton. The next time you touch me without my permission, this knife will be buried inside of you. Do you understand?"

He gulps before nodding eagerly. I offer him a bright smile, withdrawing the knife and hiding it back inside the strap beneath my dress.

"We'll be in touch. I have an excellent idea for a partnership between us."

"I can't wait to hear it," he says, voice dull and eyes wary. After one last smile, I turn around, making my way out of the party.

I am so sick and tired of people underestimating me and walking all over me.

When I arrive at the car, I find Xander and his brother in some kind of stare down. Xander's glaring and Graham looks equally as pissed.

"For fucks sake, if you want to know so bad then ask her!" Graham yells.

I arch an eyebrow as I move closer. Both of their gazes immediately shift upward towards me. I take them in for a moment. They look extremely alike, both brothers. Even their mannerisms are the same. But they've never really gotten along, not that I blame them for that. Especially considering Graham's character.

"What's going on?" I ask, trying to diffuse tension.

"He wants to know where we met five years ago," Graham replies, pointing at his brother.

My breath seizes for a second at that. I look towards Xander, trying to think of something to say.

"This isn't really the right place…" I begin to say.

He pulls out the keys, unlocking the car. "You'll tell me on the way. Let's go," he says, tone bordering no argument.

I roll my eyes. He's certainly become even more arrogant in the years past. Still I follow him inside, Graham climbing into the back seat. His expression has cleared and he looks amused again. He thrives on situations like this.

Meanwhile my heart is racing as I consider exactly how I'm going to tell him the truth. As soon as we're away from the premises of the party, we all take off the masks. They come off and Xander's glancing at me.

"I'm waiting, princess," he prompts.

I inhale softly. "I saw Graham five years ago in D.C. At your home."

His eyes swivel towards me for a second in surprise and he takes his eyes off the road. But only for a second before he's looking back in concentration.

"Maybe I should drive. Not really interested in getting into an accident because your baby mama's delivering shocking news," Graham suggests from the back.

"Shut up, Gray," Xander mutters.

I turn to glare at him for the name he referred to me as. Even though it's true, I feel uncomfortable being relegated to just that.

"What were you doing in my house?" Xander questions.

My chest tightens as I reply. "I wanted to see Nate," I whisper.

His face doesn't ripple at that but I notice his hands tightening around the steering wheel. He doesn't speak so I continue.

"I tried so hard to stay away from him but that day I just broke and decided to fly to D.C. I drove to your house without a plan. I had no idea what I wanted to do. I just," my breath hitches. "I wanted to see my son. I drove all the way towards the front of your gate and then I just couldn't do it anymore. I parked at the side of the road, asking myself what I was even doing there in the first place. I was about to leave, but then a man came out of the house and walked to the side of the car. He said he was your father's assistant and that your father had requested my presence inside the house."

Xander's jaw clenches. "You were in my home five years ago?"

"Yes, I followed the man in and he led me towards the back. I think he was trying to ensure no one saw me. He led me to your father's office and then he left."

"What did he say?"

My eyes fall shut as I remember the conversation. Richard Steele's a pretty scary man. My father's a former mob boss and yet I don't feel nearly as intimidated as I felt that day in his presence.

"Well he was pretty angry. There were some threats, a lot of underhanded digs at my character. He promised to destroy my family if I ever showed up there again."

I was younger then and honestly not in the right frame of mind. I was just missing Nate. I wanted nothing more than to hold my son. So I made a mistake. I should have thrown a knife at Richard's smug face. I regret not doing that sometimes.

"How typical of our father," Graham says and I can hear the smile in his voice.

Xander's hands shake, his eyes growing darker with rage.

"He asked me to leave so I did. I didn't really care about his threats, not really. But it was the right thing to do. It's not like I would have actually been able to face you or Nate," I say quietly. "Graham saw me as I was leaving the house."

"Yeah, you should have seen her, Xan. She looked like a kicked puppy," he says on a laugh.

My jaw clenches. I swear he acts like a little toddler. Xander still doesn't say a word. He doesn't speak the entire way to the hotel. I wait patiently, knowing it must be a lot to digest. When we arrive at my stop, he looks back at his brother.

"Wait here," he orders Graham before getting out. I follow suit.

He stands in front of me at the entrance to the hotel, watching me for an uncomfortable amount of time.

"Why was it the right thing to do?" he finally asks.

"What?"

"You said it was the right thing to do. Not seeing your son. Why? If you missed him so much, why did you abandon him?"

"Xander," I start to say gently.

"Just fucking tell me why, Katerina. I'm sick and tired of this shit. You want me to trust you. To believe in you, then you need to be honest. Something happened ten years ago. I'm not stupid, I know there must have been a reason. You left a baby on my fucking doorstep without any explanations, Katerina. I thought you were dead or dying. I thought something was seriously wrong."

Something was wrong. But I can't tell him. I wouldn't even know where to begin.

I open my mouth to speak but nothing comes out. Frustration lines Xander's face. He looks away from me, running a hand through his hair.

"Do you remember our breakup?" he asks.

Of course I remember. That moment is practically ingrained in my mind. We'd been dating for a couple of months when he asked me to come home with him and spend thanksgiving with his family. My family isn't too big on celebrating thanksgiving so I agreed like an idiot. For some reason, I never thought to look into the Steeles.

I had been deluding myself up until that moment, telling myself our relationship was nothing too serious. I was already in love with him but nobody's better at lying to themselves than I am. I thought it wouldn't matter and I didn't want to invade his privacy. I already knew his family was rich, he told me a lot about them, more open than I ever was in the course of our relationship.

What I hadn't been expecting however was that his family was a corporate group that specializes in technological advancements. They have an expanse of data open to them and an elite team of hackers. It only took Richard Steele two hours to find out my real identity. And then all hell broke loose. Literally.

I can still remember the look on Xander's face when he realized I had lied to him. My last name wasn't Petrov, at least not really. I was a Mincetti, daughter of a mafia Don. He had no idea how much the nickname, princess actually suited me until that moment.

"I was in shock after the truth came out," Xander starts to say. "It was a lot to take in. Believe it or not, I didn't care about who you really were. I cared more about the fact that you lied to me. Your family wasn't a problem."

I smile sadly. "It would have become a problem eventually."

"So you took the coward's way out," he says eyes flashing. "After my father kicked you out, you called me and asked to meet up. I thought you wanted to explain. Instead you broke up with me, in the cruelest way possible. Do you remember what you said, Katerina?"

His eyes are hard and unflinching. I swallow softly, my hands curling into fists.

"Say it again," he commands.

I shake my head.

"Say it."

My eyes fall shut and I try to blink back tears.

"I told you it was all a game to me. That I never loved you, I was just bored."

"You said our relationship meant nothing." His voice is so icy cold as he speaks, reliving that moment.

God I made so many mistakes. I was just an idiot. If I could take anything back it wouldn't be the moment I dropped Nate at his doorstep. It was that moment, when I got scared and broke up with him. Because it seemed easier. Because that moment was the catalyst for everything.

"You know the worst part? Despite hearing all that, I was still in love with you. Like a fucking idiot I thought we could make it work. And then you disappeared and I didn't hear from you for months."

My breathing's a little shallow. Xander's breathing heavily, he's staring at me like he's waiting for something, anything.

"You hesitated," I finally say, my voice soft.

He cocks his head to the side in confusion. "What?"

"I heard your conversation with your father. The day the truth about me came out. He asked you to follow him and I was so worried, I followed you both, staying outside the door as he spoke to you. He asked you to choose. Between me and your family, your position in your family's company. And you hesitated. I didn't want to be the reason you lost everything," I say softly.

I watch as his eyes grow wide, as he remembers.

"Did you hear what I said after?" he bites out.

I close my eyes and nod. "You said you choose them both and that you wouldn't let him stop you from going after you wanted."

"Exactly!" he snaps. "I chose you regardless of it all. I would have gone to you. I had just found out you lied to me for the entirety of our relationship and yet I wasn't going to abandon you. But you did it to me. Why?"

"I'm a horrible person-"

"That's not what I fucking want to hear," he cuts in angrily. "Did you know? That you were pregnant when you broke up with me?"

I shake my head. "No, God no."

If I had known then none of this would have happened. I would have stayed with him. The pregnancy would have given me a reason to stay.

"I didn't find out I was pregnant until weeks later," I tell him.

"Alright, fine," he says exhaling softly. "But when you found out, why didn't you come back?"

"I couldn't," I say, floundering for something better to say. "It was too late by then."

"Why was it too late?" he asks.

I don't reply.

"Dammit, Katerina!"

I flinch at his tone and he groans, looking away. My eyes well up with tears.

"I can't say it. Please don't make me say it. It doesn't matter. Not right now. I just, I'm tired of hiding. I miss my son so badly that I can't breathe sometimes. I can't keep living with the knowledge that he's still alive and I have no way of reaching him. I just want to see my son," I say, a tear sliding down my cheek.

His eyes narrow onto it and lets out a deep sigh.

"I'm going to go now," Xander says.

"Xander."

"I need to think about all this. I'll let you see him," he says and I let out a breath of relief. "Not now but soon. I just need to figure out how to do this. What I want to do."

"Okay," I say nodding eagerly. "Thank you, Xander."

He doesn't say anything else. His eyes meet mine once

more, alight with a heart stopping intensity. And then he's walking towards his car.

I breathe in shakily, trying to calm myself. I'm about to walk into the hotel and change before calling Rico to come and pick me up.

I gather my dress in my hands and turn towards the entrance. But then someone practically melts out of the shadows and out of the dark. My heart falls to a stop as Rico appears, pushing off the wall. I nearly scream.

He stares at me, expression hard and eyes filled with fury. My heart starts working again, pounding against my chest.

"Rico," I start unsurely.

"You have a son?" he asks.

And just like that, all the walls I've tried to build come crashing down.

CHAPTER 14
Alexander

The world spins as I look up at the ceiling in my office, my mind miles away. I haven't gotten any work done since I got into the office. I'm too rattled, too confused. My head's a mess. It has been since the gala two days ago.

I haven't spoken to Katerina, I've barely spoken to anyone apart from Nate. We finally took care of the Colton issue so that's one problem checked off my bucket list. One I got access to the company's mainframe it was easy to track the information about the product. From there it was a series of sequences and carefully placed viruses, destroying everything. They're lucky I didn't go after their other shit. I wanted to, if not for anything but the way that bastard had stared at Katerina. But it would have been a bad idea.

And irrational. My every thought when it comes to her is irrational.

I still can't believe I agreed to let Nate see her. Days later and I'm half sure it's a bad idea but then there's a part of me that can't help thinking about what she and Graham revealed.

She came to see him. Even if it was once, five years after he was born, she came.

That more than anything lets me know she cares. But it still doesn't make me feel reassured enough to expose her to Nate. I have no idea how he'll react, what truths to tell him.

How do I let a nine year old know that his mother's alive when he thinks she's been dead all this while?

I also can't stop thinking about the other thing she said.

You hesitated.

I had no idea she had listened in on that conversation. No clue that she heard the ultimatum my father gave me. And despite how much I want to deny it. I did hesitate. Because after so long struggling for my father's approval, it was hard to throw it all away.

But I would have. For her. I would have done it for her.

I'm suddenly jolted from my thoughts when the door into my office slams open. My dad walks in, the physical embodiment of anger. I raise both my eyebrows, slowly getting to my feet.

"When did you arrive, father?"

He doesn't reply, shutting the door behind him. He approaches my table and slams something down onto it. A picture. There's two people in it, a man and a woman, wearing masks. Two very familiar people in each other's hands. My stomach churns.

That's Katerina and I at the masquerade party two days ago.

I look up at my father. "What's going on?"

"You incompetent fucking child, do you have any idea what you've done?!" he yells.

My fists clench. I'm thirty one years old, my father calling me a child is an insult that cuts deep. But that's how he's always been. Using malicious words to tug people down. It's a wonder I've survived living with him for so long.

"Instead of yelling how about you tell me what's wrong?" I ask calmly.

"You're asking me what's wrong. Look at that picture, Alexander."

"I'm looking," I say dryly. "But I don't see a problem. Yes, it's me and Katerina but our faces are covered. It's nothing to be so angry about. You're the one that asked me to work with her to get to Colton. I did that."

Who the hell even took the picture?

My father looks on the verge of pulling his hair out of his head. Seriously, he's completely overreacting. I tilt my head to the side.

"Is the picture about to be released to the press? If yes, there's plausible deniability, because our faces aren't in it," I say reasonably.

He scoffs, "You have no idea what you've done."

"Then explain it to me!"

He heads for the side of my office instead, grabbing a bottle of whiskey from the fridge. He pulls out a glass and pours some in, before heading back towards me. He takes a sit without a single glance and I watch as he drinks a huge swig of the drink.

"Congratulations, Alexander. You've ruined everything I've done these past nine years. You just ruined your life and your son's life as well."

My fists clenches as my blood runs cold. "What does this have to do with Nate?"

He nods towards the table. "That picture was taken two nights ago. And earlier this morning, I got a call from a reporter in New York Daily informing me that a story's about to break about one of my sons. Naturally I assumed it was

Graham. I thought he'd gotten into some stupid scandal here once again. But it wasn't. No, they informed me it was so much worse."

"What's the story?" I ask in a low voice.

"Apparently, the person that called in with the tip and took the picture only wanted to spread a rumor that you were dating the head of a crime syndicate. But the reporter took that story and ran much further than that, digging into the past."

Something knots in my gut, "How far back?"

"Well considering there have always been suspicions and conspiracy theories about who Nathaniel's mother could be, this reporter took it upon himself to find out. It wasn't hard for him to dig up the fact that both you and Katerina Mincetti went to Harvard. And after only a few calls to some of your former classmates, he found out you also dated. Do the math, Alexander."

"He knows she's his mother?' I ask in a whisper.

"He knows everything!" he yells. "The story's going to break tomorrow about your relationship with her and the fact that you two had a love child."

I feel like I'm going to be sick.

"I know I fucked up," I start, taking in a steady breath. "But there's still time. We can bury it. Pay off the reporter, anyone that knows. We can fix this."

He gives me a pitying look as he takes another gulp of whiskey.

"Did you forget whose party that picture was taken at?"

My heart drops. "Colton knows?"

"Yes and because you were apparently dumb enough to get your picture taken at his party, he's aware you're the reason his plans for the product release are suddenly going haywire. He knows you were at his party and he knows the Mincetti girl helped you. He wants revenge."

"Fuck!" I breathe.

"And while I might have a hell of a lot of influence in D.C, in New York, Colton has more power and he's intent on ensuring the story gets out. I talked to the reporter already, offered him a lot of money not to break the story, he refused. Said he already had a better offer. There's no stopping this, Alexander."

Yeah I'm definitely going to be sick.

"That woman," my father says. "Has always been your weakness. You don't think clearly when it comes to her. I had hoped you'd have grown a pair. I thought you were smarter but you're still the same boy that was so in love with her he couldn't see up his own ass. You're a disappointment, Alexander. And I had such high hopes for you."

I grit my teeth but don't reply but my mind whirring as I try to come up with a viable solution.

"This ruins everything," he continues. "How are the board supposed to trust you as CEO when your reputation is in tatters because you're publicly known to have a relationship with a crime syndicate? And I'm supposed to just give you my company? No way in hell is that happening."

"I don't fucking care," I say finally finding my voice.

"What?"

"I said I don't care," I repeat. "Do you know how hard I've worked to gain even a little bit of respect from you. You're a controlling narcissist and a fucking asshole. All you care about is your pride. Do you even give a damn about your children? Don't answer that because I already know you don't. You pitted me against Graham in every aspect as we grew older, you placed a tight leash around Mikayla's neck her entire life. You don't even see the length of your own inadequacies because you're too busy judging everyone around you!"

A muscle pulses at the side of his forehead.

I continue. "I'm done. Ten years ago you asked me to choose between my position in the family and what I wanted. I'm choosing to prioritize my family. My son and his mother. I don't care what you do. I don't give a fuck about my reputation. I'll take care of my problems on my own."

He stares at me, sympathy laced with anger.

"Like I said, a fucking disappointment."

I'm about to say something else when the door to my office opens again. Graham walks in, fear in his expression. My father laughs into his cup.

"The other disappointment has arrived. How does it feel to have ruined your brother's life, Graham?"

My head snaps up as I look at him. "What the fuck are you talking about?"

Graham looks at me, green eyes wide with fear. He starts to speak, fast.

"I didn't mean for it to escalate so badly. I just wanted a small story about how you're in a secret relationship with the head of a mafia group. Just to damage your reputation a little. I didn't think they'd dig into the past and find out the truth. I swear it, Xander. I never meant for Nate to get hurt."

My heart practically drops. And here I thought he and I were making some progress over the last couple of days.

"One son is at the center of all the trouble, another's the catalyst that led to it. The both of you are, idiots," my father pronounces.

His voice is really starting to grate on my nerves. I need to get out of here. I grab my jacket and my phone and start to walk towards the door.

"Where are you going, Alexander?" father questions.

"To pick up my son," I grit out.

And hopefully figure out a way to explain all the shit that's about to go down. Graham's still standing by the door. He opens his mouth probably to deliver another stupid apology but I can't even listen to him. Blood roars in my ears and before I stop to reconsider, my hand is rearing up and I'm punching him in the face.

He staggers backward, holding onto his jaw. "You're a fucking bastard, Graham."

I walk out of the office without looking back. It's 2pm and Nate won't be done with school until an hour later but I figure this is probably as good a time as any to pick him up. He's in the middle of class when I arrive after getting to permission to let him leave early.

When he sees me, there's a bright smile on his face and my heart falls with the knowledge of what I'm about to reveal to him. I lean down to hug him.

"Hey, sport."

"Hi, dad. What's wrong? Why did I have to leave early?" he questions, pulling away.

I grab his lunch box from his hand and intertwine our fingers as I lead him out of the school.

"Well I got done with work pretty early today and I thought you and I could go out and get some ice-cream."

"Really?" he asks, green eyes gleaming. "Let's go. I want mint-chocolate chip. And three scoops instead of two."

"Woah, slow down, buddy. I said I'd buy you ice-cream, not give you diabetes."

He laughs. "What's diabetes?"

"It's a sickness you can get if you eat too much sugar. It can get pretty serious."

He sighs. "Okay. I guess I'll eat two scoops then."

"You guess?" I ask, a little amused as we arrive at the car.

I help him into the backseat, ensure that his seatbelt is on before heading for the driver's seat.

"I'm glad you didn't have a lot of work today, dad. It's been a long time since you took me out to eat ice-cream," he says making my heart clench.

Work keeps me away from him far more than I'd like. And while Nate never really complains, I know he gets sad when I'm too busy. I make myself a promise that I'll make more of an effort to spend more time with him.

That's if I even still have a job after all this.

We get our ice-creams, him happily chomping down his as I suggest we take a walk around the park nearby. It's quiet and there's not a lot of people. The perfect place to talk. We find a bench and settle down on it. I smile when I notice the drizzle of ice-cream on his shirt, pulling out a napkin to help clean it off.

"You know your mom's favorite ice-cream is mint-chocolate chip too, right?" I ask him.

Katerina would love knowing that. They share so many similarities, little ones, big ones, things they have in common. He looks like her too. His nose, his mouth. He has my eyes and hair but his face resembles his mother.

"Seriously?" he asks wide eyed. Then his eyes narrow. "You said is, instead of was, daddy. It's bad grammar."

"What?"

"You said my mom's favorite ice cream is mint chocolate chip. But she's dead so it should be was. Our teacher taught us that in class a few days ago."

My chest tightens. Fucking hell.

"You're right, sport. It would be bad grammar to use is instead of was," I mutter, my eyes getting fixed on a spot above his head.

I can't do this. But I know I have to. It would kill me if he had to hear this from someone else apart from me.

"Nate," I say gently. "How would you feel if your mom was still alive?"

He shrugs. "I'd be happy. I miss her sometimes. Even though I didn't know her. I still miss her."

I let out a shuddering breath.

"I am so sorry, sport. But there's something I have to tell you. And I need you to listen carefully."

CHAPTER 15
Katerina

It only takes a second for everything in your life to come crashing down. Only a couple of days for my life to change irrevocably.

I'm not too surprised though, my sins were bound to catch up to me eventually.

I spent the last two days trying hard not to think about Xander and what he promised me. But every nerve in my body is bunched up in anticipation with every moment the thought of seeing my son crosses my mind. I wouldn't even know what to say to him, where to start. I don't even know what the meeting would entail. If Xander will decide to tell him the truth or not.

It's only 5pm but I'm lying in bed, after spending an entire day at work too distracted by my problems to really focus. There's a knock on my door and I'm surprised when Rico walks in. His jaw is clenched tight, his eyes shadowed.

Him walking into my room is surprising enough. He hasn't said a word to me in two days, not after I told him everything. The entire truth, even what went down with Sokolov. He listened and then he just shut down. It's made me even antsier because I have no idea what he's going to do with what he's learned. He has every right to be angry but I wish he would just talk to me.

"We have a huge problem," he announces in a hard voice.

I sit up even straighter, my heart starting to race. "What is it?"

"Tomorrow morning, a story's going to be released in the press. About you and Alexander Steele," he tells me.

My eyes furrow. "Rico, what are you talking about?"

He's about to say more when my phone starts ringing beside me. It's Xander. Now I'm officially worried. I look at Rico once before picking up the call.

"Hello?"

"We have a problem," he says, bypassing a greeting.

"So it would seem," I say, my mouth curling downward. Can they just tell me what's wrong so I can try to fix whatever problem this is? "What's is it?"

"They know, Katerina. They know about Nate."

My heart stops. I swear one moment its beating and the next, nothing.

"Who?" I manage to ask.

"Well as of tomorrow morning, everyone will know."

He then goes on to tell me everything. How a picture of us was taken and then sold to a reporter. The reporter digging further and finding out about our past relationship. Him filling in the blanks and concluding that Nate is my son.

By the time he's done, my heart's started working again. But now it's racing. So fucking fast.

"Oh God," I whisper, my breathing growing choppy.

Everything starts to disappear behind my eyelids. My hands start to shake as my heart begins thumping loudly in my ears. A drop of sweat rolls down my spine. Somewhere far away, someone's calling my name. Rico. Rico's climbing onto the bed. But I can barely make him or the words he's saying out.

I double over with a gasp.

"Katerina!"

Somehow, his voice manages to penetrate the haze. I blink, coming back slowly. His voice is still in my ear, light commanding words.

"Breathe, Katerina. Just relax, breathe," he says softly.

I latch on to the sound of his voice, letting it trickle down my throat and into my body, warming me from inside as tremors shake my frame. Finally, I exhale a gasping breath.

"Good girl," Xander says over the phone.

I'm surprised I didn't drop it. I blink, once, twice.

"Just breathe, princess."

"I'm back," I say shakily.

"Okay, good, good. I'm sorry for laying that on you. It's a lot."

"I can, I can fix this," I tell him, finally looking at Rico who's on the bed beside me. "Bury the story."

He shakes his head. But Xander's the one that replies.

"You can't bury the story. Colton's behind this. He's intent of making sure it gets out."

"What?"

Rico speaks up then. "I intercepted the man that was going to deliver a message from Colton to your father. Asked him to give you a couple of minutes to gather your thoughts. But Eduardo's going to know soon, Katerina. Things are about to get ugly."

I'm nodding at his words but in reality it's not really computing. I'm still having a hard time believing everything's going to shit so fast.

"Katerina," Xander says over the phone. "Nate wants to see you."

"What?"

"Nate wants to see you," he repeats. "I told him the truth earlier today. And he wants to meet you."

My hand goes up to my mouth as my eyes widen.

"You need to go," Rico tells me, gauging from my reaction what Xander said. "Leave now before your father finds out."

"Xander," I say softly.

"I'll send you our address," he states easily. "Be careful, Katerina."

He hangs up after and I get to my feet unsteadily. My cousin's looking at me, gaze not as hostile as it's been the past two days.

"Under normal circumstances, I'd say you should go to Sophia first and explain everything before she finds out the truth. But I know your son takes priority right now. I'll go to Sophia."

My eyes well up with tears. My sister is never going to forgive me. Even if everyone else somehow finds a way to forgive me, she won't.

"Be strong, Kat. You can't fall apart. Not right now," Rico says.

I nod once, taking in a huge breath as I try to gather my courage. "Thank you, Rico."

"I'll have someone bring around a car. Get changed quickly."

He leaves and I quickly put on some clothes. And then for good measure, I pack a small bag of things that are necessary. My laptop, another change of clothes. Knowing my father, I won't be able to return home for at least a couple of days.

He's going to be furious. He might actually kill me.

But I can't think about that. Not now. Not when I'm about

to meet my son for the first time. I gave birth to him nine years ago. And I'm about to meet him for the first time today.

My mind is miles away as I drive towards the address Xander sent. I'm surprised I get there safely. When I arrive, I only have to state my name at the reception before I'm allowed up to the penthouse. I'm a complete and total wreck the entire ride up.

The elevator door opens, giving me a view into their home. Xander's standing right in front of the doors when I arrive. His eyes trail over my face immediately, cataloguing my expression. I'm sure I look like a hot mess. He doesn't look too good himself, his hair looks like he's all but pulled it from his roots.

And yet when he smiles at me, it momentarily feels like everything will be okay.

"Hi," I say unsurely.

"Come in," he gestures with his hand.

I walk into the house my eyes immediately colliding with a spectacular view of the city. The far wall of the room is nothing but glass, a long endless wall of glass. I take in the dark clouds in the sky, the skyline of the city, the view nearly magical.

The interior of the house itself is large and spacious and homely. It has a large living area with a long plush couch and a loveseat. There are various tones of grey and blue in the room. The far end of it has a long electric fireplace with art hanging on the walls.

My eyes take in the artfully decorated penthouse to distract me from the impending meeting. My heart feels like it's about to explode. The marble floors are black, streaked with gold and contrasting nicely with the entire décor. There's an open kitchen with a dining table that can easily fit six people and stools scattered across the island.

There's a staircase curved to the level above and I'm guessing it leads to the bedroom. When I look back at Xander, his eyes are still on me, watching me carefully.

"It's a nice house," I say for lack of something better to do.

"Yeah, Isabella took care of everything," he informs me.

I remember Isabella's his stepmother. She seemed like a nice woman. Although I only met her once at the thanksgiving dinner that ended horribly.

"Nate will be done soon. He's a little nervous," Xander tells me, eyes shining with sympathy.

I nod in understanding, feeling a tremble go through me. He notices, just like he tends to notice everything. It's a little annoying.

"It'll be okay, Katerina."

"Somehow I doubt that," I murmur.

Then we hear light footsteps padding down the stairs. My lungs seize and I hold my breath almost involuntarily as he finally appears.

The first thing I notice are his eyes. His big green eyes that stared at me with so much wonder in them when I gave birth to him. Now they regard me warily, unsurely. He continues to stand at the foot of the steps, both of us staring at each other.

He has freckles dotting his nose. Adorable little freckles and a head full of light brown hair. It's curly, just like mine, just like his dad. But what really kills me is the fact that he looks like me. My hands go over my mouth as a sob escapes me.

I am going to lose it.

Nate takes slow careful steps towards me until he's right there, looking up at my face.

"Hello," he greets politely, gently.

And because I've lost complete and total control of my mind, all I can do is gasp softly.

"Hi," I finally say. "You've gotten so big."

I mentally face palm. *Of course he's gotten big, Katerina. The last time you saw him, he was a baby.*

"Thanks, I guess," he tells me with a shrug, the action reminding me so much of his father. "Dad told me you're my mother."

"Yes. My name is Katerina."

"Katerina," he says testing it out. "It's nice to finally meet you."

I just stare at him, unsure where this conversation is going. He's too calm about all this. I thought he just found out I was alive today. I look at his father and he seems just as confused as I am.

Then when Nate speaks again, my heart breaks. "Where have you been all this while?"

Forget breaks, it practically shatters. The tears I've been trying to keep at bay start to flood past my eyelids. I slowly lower myself onto my knees so that I'm eyelevel with him.

"Nate," I say softly. "I am so, so, sorry. I could spend the rest of my life apologizing to you and it still wouldn't be enough. I'm your mother but I wasn't there for you. I left and I never should have left. Leaving you was the hardest thing I've ever had to do but I did it because I had no choice."

He listens quietly and then he speaks.

"But you're here now?" he asks.

I nod without hesitation. "I'm here now. I won't go anywhere again. I promise."

He nods too, very slowly. But then he doesn't say anything. My hands shake as I work up the courage to ask something else.

"I'm very sorry, Nate but can I just give you a hug? Just one hug, please."

He looks towards his dad and I don't know what Xander does but then he's looking back at me and nodding again. I pull him into my hands and for the first time in nine years, I feel like I can finally break.

"Oh my baby," I say as tears fall down my face. "My beautiful, perfect boy."

The last time I cried so much was when I left him on that doorstep. And because he really is perfect and the sweetest person on earth, he hugs me too, his small hands going around in circles as he tries his best to comfort me.

My body shakes and racks with sobs but I hold him through it all. And he lets me.

CHAPTER 16
Xander

When I walk up to the terrace the cool night air gently brushes against my face. The city lights twinkle below, casting a soft glow on the surrounding buildings. Katerina's silhouette outlines the backdrop of the night sky as she stands in front of the railing. Her long blonde hair practically dances in the breeze.

"Rico I'm fine, I promise I haven't been crying," she says, her voice soft but firm.

I'm sure he would believe her if it wasn't for the little sniff after that sentence.

"I'm fine," she repeats. "When have you ever known me to fall apart?"

The short answer to that would probably be never. But considering what I just watched minutes ago. Her breaking down as she hugged her son for the first time, I'd say that's changed. Katerina's world is extremely different from mine. I can't say I know much but what I do know is that it's a world that preys on weakness, failure.

Living with my father, growing up with him was hard.

But I can't even begin to imagine the life she must have lived. And while I don't think she hates her upbringing, she seems very comfortable actually, I do know that whatever I went through must have been child play compared to the expectations she's had to live with.

"What's going on back there?" Katerina questions. "With Papa? Have you gone to meet Sophia?"

Whatever he says on the other end makes her shoulders slump. I watch as her hand grips the railing tighter.

"He'll calm down," she murmurs. "He has to."

She falls quiet again for a couple seconds before speaking.

"Yeah, I'll probably head over to a hotel or something. Call me when you get to Sophia's. And Rico? Thank you."

The call ends and she lets out a soft breath. I decide to make my presence known, walking forward until I'm right beside her. She looks up at me for a second before looking back towards the night sky.

"Hey," I say. "Were you just talking to your cousin?"

"Yeah, Rico. I should probably introduce you two sometime."

"I'd like that."

"How is he?" she asks.

"Nate's good. Already in bed. It's late and he's had a rough day. He fell asleep as soon as I tucked him in."

"Okay," she nods, still facing forward.

"So what's wrong? You look like the embodiment of distraught."

She smiles but it doesn't quite reach her eyes.

"Oh nothing's wrong. Apart from the fact that my father has sent out men to find me, and drag me back home by my hair, kicking and screaming if they have to," she informs me.

My jaw tightens. *What the fuck?*

Katerina continues. "Oh and my sister still has no idea what's going on but she will soon and once she does, she's probably going to hate me."

That gives me pause, "She didn't know?"

"No. No one knew," she says softly. "I didn't tell my family about Nate."

I don't say anything for a couple of seconds letting that digest. What could she possibly have been hiding? Why didn't she tell anyone? Not even the people she trusted.

"Don't worry, I'll leave soon," Katerina states, looking up at me. "I just need a couple more minutes."

My eyes narrow. "You're not going anywhere."

Her mouth opens slightly. "What?"

"We have an extra room. You can sleep there, while we figure everything out."

"But-"

I shake my head before she can counter me.

"Katerina, you don't have anywhere else to stay. And you're already here. Plus, it would be in poor fashion to kick a woman out at 11pm in the middle of the night."

That finally makes her smile. She gives me a look.

"You're doing a horrible job of hating me."

I shrug. "I can go back to doing that in the morning. Let's just sleep tonight, okay? I know you need to rest."

She inhales softly. "Thank you. For everything. Thank you for letting me see him."

Her eyes get a glassy sheen and she looks away, running a hand through her hair.

"Of course, Katerina."

I lead her back inside, towards the bed I already asked to be cleaned up. She looks around for a couple of second before looking at me.

"Tomorrow morning, I'll make some calls. Do my best to mitigate the fallout from the article. It's an exclusive so if we can keep others from reporting on it, things shouldn't be too bad."

"We both know that's not going to happen, princess. If a story's out there, it's out there."

"But, it's just not fair!" she says, her voice rising an octave. "I hate what this is going to do to Nate, to you."

"Honestly, I think you have a lot more to worry about than both of us," I point out.

She sighs, looking away.

"Go to sleep, Katerina. We'll figure out our plans for world domination tomorrow," I tell her.

She rolls her eyes but her lips twitch.

"Good night, Xander."

"Night."

I walk out of the room, climbing up the stairs. After checking up on Nate and ensuring he's still asleep, I head over to my bedroom. It feels like every nerve and neuron in my body is fired up, running, my brain whirs as I try to figure out my next course of action.

I wasn't lying when I told Katerina that she would probably have to deal with the worst of the news. Especially considering her family had no idea. Which is still insane to me. She and her sister are pretty close. Why would she not tell her?

Now I'm even more curious. I need to know why Nate's birth had to be such a huge secret. I need to know what she's hiding.

THE FRYING pan sizzles as I prep it for breakfast. It's simple, not too over the top. Just some eggs, toast and bacon. Nate comes bouncing down the stairs as soon as the smell of food fills the house. He takes his seat at the table, waiting for me to finish preparing our meal.

It takes a couple of minutes for Katerina to appear. She steps out of her room in a long t-shirt and loose shorts. My eyes trail down her legs for a second but then I'm distracted by the look of panic Nate shoots my way.

Ah. He didn't know she stayed the night.

"Katerina needed somewhere to sleep last night, sport," I explain. "I offered to let her stay here. Is that okay?"

She stands uncertainly at the threshold between the living room and the kitchen, her eyes fixed on Nate. My son looks down at the table and nods.

"Yes, it's fine. Good morning, Katerina," he says in a low voice.

Very slowly, she walks inside. "Good morning. Did you sleep well?"

"I did."

The air is slightly tense, awkward, which is to be expected. Last night after the long hug she gave him, it was pretty quiet. Neither of them seemed to know what to say and how to navigate the situation they've found themselves it. Quite frankly, I'm not sure how to help. They have to figure it out on their own.

Katerina needs to figure out how to have a relationship with her son.

"That's nice," she says softly.

Nate points at the chair opposite him, "You can sit there. Daddy sits at the head of the table."

"Okay," Katerina says, moving to take her assigned seat.

Her expression suddenly turns lightens. "You know in my home, I usually sit at the head of the table."

Nate's eyes widen. "Really? Why? In my grandfather's house, he sits at the head of the table. And here, dad does. You're a girl though. Why do you get to sit there?"

I chuckle softly under my breath.

Katerina answers him earnestly. "That's because I'm the head of my family. Girls can be in charge as well."

Nate's eyes widen further and I'm a little discomfited that the concept is so foreign to him. Katerina doesn't seem to mind. She seems a little amused actually.

"Is it because there's no boy that can sit at the head of the table?" he asks curiously.

"No. My dad is still alive. And I have an uncle and a male cousin who's practically like my brother. All of them are well suited for the role but it was given to me, because I was just as capable, even more so."

Nate nods slowly, thinking over her words.

"What about your mother?" he questions.

I still for a second. Damn, he really needs to stop being so perceptive. I watch as different emotions run across Katerina's face. Her mother has always been a sort of touchy subject. All I know is that she died, a long time ago. But it's clear the scars resulting from the death run deep.

"My mom passed away a long time ago, sweetie," she tells him gently.

"Oh," his face scrunches up. "I'm sorry."

"It okay. I had my Papa, my uncle, my cousin and my sister growing up."

"You have a sister?" he asks and she nods. "What's her name?"

"Her name is Sophia. She also has her own family and a cousin I'm sure you'd love to meet."

"A cousin?" Nate asks wide eyed.

I'm sure this is a lot of information. It must be hard for him to process the fact that he has a whole new family he had never even heard of until the day before.

"Yeah, her name is Nova. She's an adorable little two year old."

Nate grows quiet for a couple of seconds, letting that digest. Katerina stares at him for a minute, her expression shifting into guilt. I guess she realizes how overwhelming it must be for him. I finally finish preparing the food, dishing it all out in three separate plates. I place their food in front of them. Katerina looks up at me gratefully.

"Thanks, Xander. I really appreciate it."

"It's just some toast and eggs, Katerina. Relax and eat," I tell her with a playful smile.

She rolls her eyes but does as asked, biting into her meal. Nate is already shoveling his food into his mouth when I sit down. We're all quiet for several seconds.

"Dad, why didn't I go to school today?" he asks through a mouthful of food.

I look at him and arch an eyebrow. "Considering present company, how about we try to display some more respectable manners during our meal? That means chewing and swallowing before speaking."

He pouts at that making Katerina laugh.

"It's okay, I don't mind."

Nate makes sure there's nothing in his mouth before speaking again, "So why didn't I go to school?"

Katerina and I share a look before looking back at him.

"Well, sport the next few days are going to be a little tumultuous-"

"What does tumultuous mean?"

"Rough," I clarify. "We're about to have a rough couple

of days. You know how sometimes our family's in the news? Well, we're going to be in the news again. You, me and Katerina."

"Why?"

After keeping the secret about his mother from him for most of his life, I'm intent on making sure he has all the facts when it comes to matters concerning him. That means explaining the situation and making sure he understands what's at stake. He's old enough to do so.

"Because everyone is about to find out that Katerina is your mother and it might come as a bit of a shock."

"Oh, I get that. It was shocking to me too," he states. "Why does everyone care though?"

I take in a deep breath before looking towards her for help. Her lips twitch.

"Because, sweetie, my family's a little famous in New York. So the news will cause an uproar. It might be better for you to stay at home for a couple of days until it dies down."

He pouts. "But I won't get to see Daniel in those days. I want to go to school," he complains.

Before he can throw a tantrum, I hurriedly soothe him.

"Maybe Daniel can come over to our house and play with you one of these days? I'll try to get in contact with his family and see if that would be okay."

He nods eagerly at that. "Okay, dad. "

Thankfully, the rest of the meal goes by without any other problems. After we're done, Nate disappears to play in his room. I make both Katerina and I a cup of coffee and we head to the living room, taking a seat.

"Is it just me or does this feel strangely domesticated?" I ask after a couple of seconds.

"Honestly, I'm leaning more towards uncomfortable. But

sure, domesticated works," she says on a shrug. "I think it feels weird because it's so normal."

"You've never being good at normal," I point out.

"Neither have you," she shoots back.

"Anyway, it's a brand new day. What's your plan? I know you already have one."

Instead of replying she takes a sip of her coffee, her expression thoughtful.

"Realistically speaking, the news is going to affect your family's' company much more than it's going to affect my family's business. My biggest problem now is how to reattain trust and respect I've worked so hard to get from the men who work for my family but I'm sure I'll figure that out eventually."

"How about your family? Shouldn't they be your biggest problem?"

She sighs softly. "My dad will cool off in a couple of days and when he does, I'll try to explain everything to him. As for my sister... I'm sure Rico would have told her by now. The fact that she hasn't called me or reached out to me is extremely telling. I don't know if I should call her or go and see her."

"What would you say? How are you going to explain it to them?" I question. "Because I'm pretty sure you know 'I didn't have a choice' isn't going to cut it anymore. It's not just me right now. It's Nate, your family. It's time to come clean, Katerina."

Her expression doesn't waver. It's clear she was expecting it. Expecting me to ask. But I can tell she's dreading it. A light tremor goes through her hand. She carefully sets the coffee mug on the table in front of us, before looking back at me steadily.

"I'm going to start by saying that I know that there's no

excuse for my actions. But when all of this happened, I was young and stupid. A 19 year old with no clue what she was doing. I was also in a place of hurt and again, I know that's not an excuse but if I could take it all back I would."

My breath leaves me a in a rush.

"I'm listening, princess."

CHAPTER 17
Katerina

This is the second time I'm telling this story in the last few days. And I know without a doubt it won't be the last time. Still, out of everyone else, the person who deserves to know the truth the most is him. Xander stares at me expectantly as I begin to speak.

"There were a lot of factors involved. But it all started after our break up. After I left D.C, I went back home to New York, needing some sense of normalcy, a distraction, anything to take my mind of you. Which is why when my father offered to send me to Moscow on a business trip, I took it. It was my first time going there on my own and the trip entailed trying to amend his relationship with a particularly nasty Boss who was intent on causing us some trouble. But he trusted me to handle it. The Boss was an old man called Sergey. Sergey Sokolov. And while he might have been an asshole, brash, dangerous, his son was so much worse," I say quietly.

"His son?" Xander asks.

"Yes. His son's name is Maxim Sokolov and to put it simply, he's a psychopath. Anyway, when I first arrived in Moscow, I didn't know all that. I knew Sergey was a little terrifying but I was prepared to handle him. I had a plan. What I didn't plan for was his son. Almost as soon as I arrived, Maxim set his sights on me."

There's no other way to say this, so I resolve to say it as bluntly as possible. Like ripping a band aid off, except the pain this is going to leave behind will be so much worse, persistent, unflinching.

"Despite how scary he could be, he could also be pretty charming and he wasn't exactly ugly. I was naïve, and lonely and sad, so I allowed myself to be charmed into his bed."

Beside me, Xander stiffens. "You what?"

A tremble goes through my hands. I clasp them and place them on my lap.

"It was a mistake, Xander. I was feeling lonely, I was young, in a county on my own without any support. I had just broken up with you and it was hard. Maxim paid attention, he was kind of sweet. He acted as a buffer between his father and me and he helped me out. I was living in their home because of the negotiations. Maxim played the part of a good host that was concerned for my well-being. A part of me knew it was all an act but in the face of everything I was going through, I refused to see it. One night I got drunk. Drunk enough to sleep with him. It was only one time but unfortunately that was all it took. Two weeks later, I was having breakfast with their family when I suddenly felt nauseous. I rushed out of the room to puke. Maxim called a doctor immediately, who didn't hesitate to proclaim I was pregnant."

Xander's so still, I'm not sure he's even breathing. My heart is pounding so loud I can feel it in my ears. I still remember how I felt that morning. I was lying in bed, Maxim a few feet away, speaking to the doctor. That fucking doctor who didn't have the decency to tell me in private. Maybe if he had, things wouldn't have gone so wrong.

"I didn't believe it at first. I asked to be left alone. It took a lot of fighting but I was allowed to leave on my own. I left the house and went to buy a pregnancy test. When it came out positive, I went to a hospital and asked for a scan, which is where I was told how far along I was."

A muscle jumps in Xander's jaw.

"How far?" he asks slowly.

"Seven weeks. Nate's yours, Xander. He could never be anything else but your son," I say softly. "I wouldn't do that to you."

He exhales, "Continue."

"When I returned to the Sokolov's, Maxim was ecstatic. I arrived to find him telling his father the 'good news', I was pregnant and carrying his child. I was shocked he would have thought that. I pulled him aside and tried to explain. I reminded him that we used a condom the night we slept together, then I tried to tell him how far along I was but he wouldn't listen. Which is when the monster started to come out. He got angry and questioned why I was trying to keep him away from his baby. I tried to leave the house but he wouldn't let me. He dragged me and locked me in his room."

Even now, I can't help but shiver at the thought of the days I spent there. He wouldn't let me out despite how much I screamed and pleaded for him to do so. He wouldn't listen to reason. It was terrifying. I hadn't realized until that moment, who he really was.

"I managed to escape though," I say in an undertone, unwilling to revisit how terrified I was locked in that room. "One of his men helped me and as I soon as I got out, I ran. As far away from the Sokolov's as I could. But I also had another problem. I couldn't go back home."

"Why the hell not?" Xander bursts out. "You should have come home immediately. You should have come to me!"

My eyes fall close. "Maybe. But in that moment all I could think was that I was 19 and pregnant and I had no doubt just ruined my father's relationship with his business partner. The Sokolov's were out to get me but more than that, one thing was clear, if my father found out about the baby, he might have killed me."

Xander's eyes meet mine. "You could have come to me," he repeats.

"It wasn't that simple! How was I supposed to get out of Moscow? The moment I went to an airport, the Sokolov's would know. If I managed to leave the city, then my father would know as soon as I arrived in New York. I was stuck between a fucking rock and a hard place. Literally, neither of those options seemed reasonable."

"You preferred staying a city with psychopath than going home and facing your father?"

"Xander, I was pregnant. It's different for women in the outfit. We're not treated the same way. Sure, my father is different. He raised us to be strong, powerful. But he was also an Italian Don that would have seen a premarital pregnancy as an insult, a slight to his reputation. Sophia was literally forced to marry her husband because of that. And I'm so glad that my sister was already in love with the man she had to marry but back then I was in a completely different position. Your father practically kicked me out of your life, I broke up with you, ended our relationship after keeping my identity a secret. And then there was Sokolov to contend with. It was such a mess."

"So what did you do?"

"I had to stay in Russia. I informed my father of the situation but I lied and told him the Sokolov's were intent on killing me because of a misunderstanding. He wanted to come immediately and get me out but that would have led to a lot of bloodshed and a war we would have lost. We didn't have that much power in Russia. I convinced him that I would be fine hiding out in the country. Only for a couple of months, while the Sokolov's calmed down. Just for everything to settle down. And in the meantime I would also help him build alliances while I was there. I told him I could go undercover, do some underground work, and dig out information on the inner workings of the Bratva in Moscow. In the end, I managed to convince him that it was in our family's best interests for me to remain there. Which is how I was able to hide my pregnancy. I stayed in Moscow for eight months. I gave birth to Nate there. And as soon as he was born, I found a way to leave."

"The psychopath just let you go?" Xander asks gruffly.

I shake my head. "No, till the moment I left he was still intent on chasing me down. I was lucky to escape honestly. As soon as I arrived in the U.S, I went to D.C, to your house. I couldn't take Nate home. If I did, who knows what my Papa might have done to him. So I left him and then I returned home and acted like nothing happened. A month or so after I left Moscow there was news that the Sokolov's had been involved in some kind of shootout. Both Sergey and Maxim were dead and I was so glad. I thought it was all behind me."

"You thought?" he grits out.

"He's not dead," I say quietly. "I only just found out recently. Maxim survived somehow and now he's in control of his family's business. He's still alive."

"Fucking fantastic," Xander swears, getting to his feet. He runs an agitated hand through his hair. I can only stare up at him warily. "You're telling me there's a criminal psychopath out there somewhere who actually thinks Nate is his son and could come knocking down your door at any moment."

"It's been nine years," I say, daring to hope. "If he hasn't come here in nine years then he won't be coming now."

"That's sounds like wishful thinking, Katerina. Things like this just don't go away, fuck!" he yells.

Then he looks upstairs, worried that Nate might hear. He lets out a breath, looking at me.

"That was one hell of a story, Katerina," he says in an even voice. "I'm not even sure where to begin to unpack that."

I stay silent, unsure what he wants me to say. Xander looks away from me, staring at a point far away.

"At least it all makes sense now. Your motivations. But I still think you should have come to me."

He's angry. And he has every right to be angry.

"I'm sorry, Xander. I did what I thought was best."

"I know," he says quietly. "So what now? Putting aside the Russian psychopath. Your father now knows the truth, what do you plan to do about that?"

"It's different now," I tell him. "I'm Don. I'm in charge."

"You're hiding out in my home currently, princess. I'm having a hard time believing you're in charge."

Well that certainly cuts deep.

"I'm not hiding," I grit out. "I'm trying to figure out the course of action. I have no way of predicting how my father will react in this situation. I don't know what he's going to do."

"Would he hurt Nate?" Xander asks.

"No. He would never. Nate is his grandson. Family's the most important thing to us. I'm more worried he'll insist on seeing him. I'm not ready for Nate to meet my Papa. He can be a proud man, brash as well. And right now, I'm sure he's very angry. I don't want Nate anywhere near him."

"Damn right," Xander mutters. "I'd rather my son stays far away from him if I'm being honest."

That gives me pause. "Xander, he's still Nates' grandfather. Eventually, maybe not soon, but eventually, he's going to meet his grandson."

"Your father's a criminal and murderer."

"So am I," I counter. "In case you've forgotten, I come from a family of those. I've also killed people. I run a crime syndicate."

He looks away. "You're different."

It hits me then, something I've never truly realized. Xander looks at me through rose tinted glasses, he has no idea, how deep the darkness goes. How much it consumes me every day. He might think he does, but he doesn't.

"No, I'm not," I say softly. "I'm a product of my upbringing, Xander. That's never going to change."

We both fall silent for several seconds. Until he breaks it.

"You think the articles out by now?" he questions.

"Probably. I left my phone in my room."

"Same. But we should go check it out. I'm sure mine is already blowing up by now."

I'm sure that's just an excuse to get away from me. I let him have it.

"Yeah, okay. I need to make some calls too."

I watch him leave as he walks away, heading up the stairs. Once he's gone from my sight, I head inside as well. As soon as I open the door to the room, my phone is buzzing. It's a call from my father, which I immediately ignore, instead choosing to check out the article. The headline jumps out, making my jaw clench.

Heir to Steele Industries and his Sordid Affair with a Mafia Princess.

How unoriginal, I think with distaste. And I'm not a fucking princess anymore. I'm a queen. I skim through the article, my blood heating at the mention of Nate and how he's alleged to be mine and Xander's love child. The article is obviously written in a way that it serves as a smear campaign, against both mine and Xander's reputation. But I never had much of a reputation in the first place. I'm just angry that they're trying to drag his name through the mud. And I'm so fucking angry that Nate has to be involved as well.

The reports cites several sources who provided him with information on the timeline of our relationship. The names of his sources are redacted of course, but I fully plan on finding each and every person who spoke and make them pay.

I'm still going through the article when my phone buzzes once again. It's an incoming call from Rico. I pick up immediately. He's literally the only person I'd be happy to talk to currently.

"Hey, *cugino*," I greet.

"Good morning, Katerina. Did you sleep well?" he questions.

I hate sleeping in beds apart from my own. It makes me uncomfortable. It took some tossing and turning last night but I managed to fall asleep eventually.

"I slept okay. What's the progress report?"

"Well, your Papa has calmed down enough and is waiting for you to come home and explain yourself," he informs me.

"He'll be waiting a while," I mutter. "I will return to the mansion tomorrow."

Rico's momentarily silent. "You think that's a good idea?"

"Probably not. But I just-," I hesitate. "I want one more day. Xander's being so cooperative and nice, I'm scared that if I leave, he won't let me back in and I have so much I want to say to Nate, so much I want to ask. I'm not ready to leave my son."

He sighs softly. "I get that, Kat. But he can't keep you away from your son. If you want to see him, then you will see him. You're Don, no one keeps you away from what's yours."

"That is entirely the wrong approach and will most certainly not be happening. He raised the boy for nine years, *cugino*. Legally speaking, he has more rights than me."

Rico snorts. "Who said anything about rights?"

"Ethically speaking, it would be callous of me to think I deserve anything more than what he's willing to give," I retort.

"Fine. You can take care of that issue on your own. How are we cleaning up this mess?"

"After explaining to Papa and calming him down, I need to take care of Colton. He's the reason all this happened after all."

"Of course," Rico says in agreement. "And for what it's worth, I don't think you should be too worried about your Papa. He made you Don, Katerina. You outrank him, which means you can do whatever the hell you want."

"I wasn't worried," I state.

"Sure," he chuckles. "Amway, I got to go."

"Wait, Rico," I state. "What about Sophia?"

"I'm sorry, Kat but you're going to have to give your sister some time."

"How did she take it?"

"Not well. She didn't say much, and as you know with Soph, silence is big indicator of how she's feeling. I didn't tell her the whole story, I figured I'd leave that to you. I just told her you had a good reason for the choices you made."

"Okay," I say breathing softly. "Thank you."

"No problem. So when should I come pick you up?"

"Tomorrow. I'll text you Xander's address."

"Alright. And be careful with that man. I don't know him and I don't trust him."

I find myself saying something, I don't say often and have definitely not said in relation to someone who isn't a member of my family, "I trust him."

CHAPTER 18
Xander

The elevator opens surprising me as a 5 foot 7, dark haired menace steps out of it. I stare at my sister for a couple of seconds.

"Surprise!" she yells, waving her hands in the air. Her eyes roam the apartment for a second. "Nice house. Where's my little troublemaker?

"Mikayla, what are you doing here?" I question. "And why wasn't I notified before you came up?"

She smiles that mischievous smile that always puts me on edge.

"I told them I was your sister," she replies.

My jaw grinds. "And they just believed you?"

"I showed them my ID so they could confirm I was a Steele. I just wanted to surprise you."

"Great. Color me surprised," I mutter.

After Katerina's revelations earlier this morning. I'm on edge, my mind constantly waging a war of opposing sides that I don't fully understand. I don't even know what to feel. Anger, betrayal, guilt, sympathy, it's all a jumbled mess.

I thought I would find peace once she told me the truth.

But honestly, peace is the last thing I feel as I try to figure how to navigate everything. It's a lot.

My sister blinks, "What's got you in a sour mood?"

I don't reply, walking towards the kitchen to grab a drink of water. My sister follows, her heels clacking against the floors.

"Seriously, I knew you'd be brooding in light of recent events but dad said you were mouthing off and being rude and that you left the company. He also said you walked out of your office with your head held high. He's quite angry with you. But when I heard what you did I was so proud, Xan. You finally stood up to him."

My chest heaves as I sigh. "Yeah, I did. It felt great. You should try it sometimes."

She grins. "Maybe I will."

"When did you get to New York?" I ask, leaning against the counter after pouring some water in a cup.

"I arrived with our dear father a few days ago. We've been staying at a hotel in Manhattan. I would have come to New York sooner actually. But as you know he controls my movements and would not allow me to take the jet unsupervised and without leave from work. Have I told you how much I hate that job?"

"Several times," I say.

Mikalya works as a manager in one of our branches, helping to develop and design products. The only problem is that she's never had an affinity for anything technology. She has always veered towards fashion actually but my father has never considered that a viable career option.

"Anyway I wanted to come here as soon as we arrived but dad insisted I wait for a while until things settled in light of your scandal. But I knew you'd appreciate the help today."

"Thanks," I say gruffly, placing my hand on my jaw. "Have you seen your other brother?"

I can barely keep the rage from my voice at the thought of Graham. Mikayla's face falls.

"I heard what he did and I am really angry with him, Xan. He should have never done that. He crossed a line."

"Graham's crossed more lines that I care to count since he was born. I don't know why I thought he could ever be different."

Mikayla sighs. "I spoke to him over the phone. He really regrets what he did, Xan. He feels really guilty."

"If he shows his face in front of me, I'll kill him," I mutter

"You don't mean that."

I give her a hard look, conveying just how serious I am. She looks away, lets out a soft breath before looking back at me.

"Alright fine. Enough about that big doofus. Let's go back to you. Why are you so upset? And where is Nate?" she questions.

I'm opening my mouth to reply when we both hear light footsteps coming down the stairs. A couple seconds later, Katerina appears in the doorway to the kitchen. I swear my sister grows pale as she takes her in. Mikayla always one for the dramatics lets out a soft gasp.

"Xan isn't that..." she trails off.

It occurs to me that she probably had no idea I was in contact with Katerina. Or that she had come to be a part of my life again. She also probably didn't know that father sent me here to New York and contributed to our reconnection.

"Yeah, about that," I say clearing my throat. "Kay, this is Katerina. Katerina, you remember my sister Mikayla, right?"

They both look slightly uncomfortable. Katerina stays on

the edge of the doorway. Finally, Mikayla recovers, stepping forward. She smiles widely.

"It's so nice to meet you," she says in delight. "You might not remember me much. I was only fifteen the first time we met and it wasn't exactly under pleasurable circumstances."

"Of course I remember you. It's nice to see you again and you've grown even more beautiful," Katerina says sincerely.

Mikayela shakes her head. "Are you kidding me? Look at you, you're a goddess and you're glowing. You have got to share your skin care routine with me. Oh and I love that shirt..."

I stop her rambling before it goes any further. "Kay," I say firmly. "Tone down the enthusiasm."

She turns around, shooting me a dirty look before looking back at Katerina who still seems a little uncomfortable despite the soft smile gracing her lips.

"I am so sorry about what my family has put you through," Mikayla states.

My eyebrows furrow and Katerina's mouth falls open slightly.

"I'm pretty sure that's my line," she mutters.

Mikayla shakes her head. "My father played a part in the circumstances we've found ourselves in today. And I know in my heart that you would have never stayed away from your son for so long if you didn't have a choice."

Katerina's eyes widen even further at the simple understanding. I suddenly feel like a horrible person. The situation isn't exactly black and white but watching my sister come to that understanding goes a long way in trying to sort out my feelings. Because she's right. My family also had a hand in what happened. We contributed.

"Thank you, Mikayla," she says unsurely.

My sister claps her hands together before turning to face

me. "Now, I'm getting really tired of asking where that nephew of mine is," she states.

"He's upstairs," Katerina informs her. "We were hanging out but he asked for some apple juice so I came down here to get him some."

"I'll go and give it to him. He'll be so happy to see me. And Katerina I really hope we get to talk more sometime. I have a feeling we can be friends."

She heads for the fridge and grabs a small juice box. Facing me on the way out, she mouths, "You owe me an explanation."

My lips twitch.

"That might be the nicest interaction I've ever had with any of your family members," Katerina says as we watch Mikayla leave.

"Yeah, Kay has a pure heart. She'd never blame you for your actions."

She's also extremely trusting to a fault. It's one of her best and worst qualities.

"And do you? Blame me?" Katerina asks quietly.

I look at her, feeling a muscle tick in my jaw. "You're not exactly blameless, princess."

She nods. "Still angry then."

"I'm not angry," I state, causing her to arch a disbelieving brow. "I'm not angry, just confused because I don't know what to feel. What do you expect me to feel?" I ask in frustration.

"I can't tell you what to feel, Xander," she answers, shaking her head. "Your every emotion is valid. And I know I've caused you a lot of pain and grief. I'm just glad, that you finally have answers. That I was able to explain. I know it's selfish of me, but at least that weight's being lifted off my chest. It's one less secret I'm keeping from you."

"How many more secrets are there? How many more layers can you possibly have?"

I watch the rise and fall of her chest through the material of the shirt she's wearing. To top of it all off, I can't seem to take my eyes off the expanse of the skin of her legs showing owing to the shorts she's wearing. Everything she does affects me. It's maddening.

Katerina walks further into the kitchen, stopping just a few feet away from me.

"Do you remember our first date?" she asks suddenly.

"Of course I remember," I reply.

I could never forget that.

"I told you that first date that knowing me wouldn't be easy. My life revolves around challenges, and sometimes it hurts. I made it clear to you from that start that it would be easier if you just gave up. Because I'm not a conquest and I'm not just any other woman that would be falling at your feet. I'm so much more than you could begin to imagine. I had a lot of wants and aspirations. And none of that included falling in love. Not with you or anyone else. That was supposed to be our first and last date. I laid it all out for you, clearly," she states.

"Yeah I thought about what you said throughout the date. And you remember what I did when I dropped you off back at your dorm?" I question, moving closer.

Her breath hitches when I stand in front of her, only inches between us. Her scent surrounds me, intoxicating, maddening.

"You kissed me," she whispers.

"I kissed you," I murmur. "And you let me. Because you knew, just like I did when I first met you. That there's this invisible string, always pulling me to you. And I have no idea how to cut it, Katerina."

Her tongue darts out, licking her bottom lip. "I don't think you can."

My eyes fall shut for a moment. "I thought I was rid of you."

"I've never been rid of you, Xander," she says softly.

My eyes open, met hers with an intensity that sends a chill through me. My heart pounds against my ribcage as I stare at her.

Do it, the voice in my head is insistent, leaving no room for hesitation.

My hand reaches up, grazes her jaw. "I still hate you," I say into her beautiful brown eyes.

"I know. But you also want to kiss me," she retorts, brown eyes fierce, teeming with desire and something else. Uncertainty. "Do it, Xander."

She's always so strong, I guess I'm allowed to be weak in the face of her. So I listen. To the voice in my head, to her. My head lowers slowly, my heart continues to thud in anticipation. My mind whirs with disbelief as my mouth meets hers. And then everything stops.

It's like a jolt of electricity. A pathway into my mind, bringing up everything I thought otherwise buried. The passion that used to consume me, fills me to the brim.

Kissing her used to feel like a drug. And years later it's still as potent as ever.

CHAPTER 19
Katerina

I'm a big fake. A poser. I have been all my life. I struggle with so much. Imposter syndrome, anxiety. Most of the time I feel weak, inadequate, so much less than perfect. So much less than what I'm supposed to be. I hid it though. I constantly tell myself and everyone around me how strong I am. I build walls, I keep the truth hidden, and my insecurities are shoved so far back in my mind. So far that sometimes I pretend they don't exist. But they do.

The one true simple reason I fell for Xander was because he made me feel seen. In a way no one else has before. I'm not sure how he did it but when I met him, it was like he could look at me and pull out every hidden thought, all my fears seemed like nothing when I was with him. He's the only person that's ever made me feel safe and protected. I didn't have to speak, he just understood.

Everyone wishes for someone like that. I had him and then I lost him. And now standing here as his arms wrap around me and his mouth molds with mine, I can't help but think about how much of an idiot I was.

So fucking stupid. How could I have let him go? When he

feels like this. Especially because he feels like this. Something in my gut aches, my pulse races and my heart pounds so hard it's fucking painful.

His lips are warm against mine. My knees buckle under the intensity of that warmth. His left hand drops to catch my lower back, pressing me flush against him. Our lips communicate in a dance I'm not sure our minds understand. Ebbing and driving against each other as if even the thought of being apart would kill us both.

I press my palms against his chest, fisting his shirt and tugging him tighter. My fingers trail the contours of his chest. When his tongue pushes past my lips, swirling across mine like he's desperate for a taste, I let him. I sink further and further into him, sinking into his body, surrendering myself completely and he kisses me harder.

My hands rise up to his hair, gripping it tighter as he kisses me. A gasp escapes my mouth when he bites my bottom lip before sucking the sting away. I can't stop kissing him, I don't want to stop. If I stop it'll be over. I don't want it to be over.

"It fucking hurts," he says against my lips.

"I know," is all I'm able to say before he's kissing me again, furiously, his lips searing.

Xander tugs one of my legs up and around his waist, pressing against me. I can feel his hard length, pressing into me. I haven't had sex in a long time. Intimacy has always been hard for me. Except when it's with Xander.

When it's Xander, it's as easy as breathing. I get a moment of reprieve, a moment to breathe when his mouth moves to the corner of my lips, kissing and biting his way down softly. He sucks on a sensitive spot on my neck making me shiver. I feel his pleased smirk against my skin. I grip his arms about to beg for more when there's the sound of footsteps climbing down the steps.

It's like a bucket of ice cold water dousing our bodies. Xander practically rips his body away from mine, jerking away as if scalded. I blink, trying to come to terms with our surroundings, remembering we're still in the kitchen, in his home where our son lives.

We hear voices nearing, Nate speaks to his aunt rapidly, telling her about a school project of his. When they enter the kitchen, they pause in their steps. Mikayla looks from me to her brother, her eyes taking in our stance and the distance between us. There's no masking my heavy breathing. Her eyebrows climb slowly, realization dawning in her expression.

Nate however seems oblivious. He walks in, blinking innocently.

"Is something wrong? Dad? Katerina?" he questions.

I shake my head but his father doesn't speak, staring at a far space on the wall. A muscle ticks in his jaw. The tension in extremely palpable.

Nate's dark eyebrows furrow in confusion.

"How about we head back upstairs, my love? Your parents seem to be in the middle of something," Mikayla sates.

"No," Xander snaps immediately. "We're fine."

And before anyone else can say a word, he storms out of the kitchen. I watch him leave, feeling a searing pain in my chest.

I might have just ruined everything.

Xander hasn't spoken to me since our kiss in the kitchen. He had dinner with myself, Nate and Mikayla, last night but he barely said a word. I caught Nate sneaking glances at his father, worried about him. It's all my fault. Not only did I barge into their lives, I'm starting to upend it.

And if that kiss is provoking such a visceral reaction from him, then it's clear it never should have happened. I just wish he would talk to me. I have to return home soon to face my problems. I've avoided it all for long enough. Rico will pick me up soon and I really wish we could at least have a conversation before I go.

There's a knock on my door and I rise to my feet to open it, revealing Nate on the other side. I try not to let my surprise show. I've been here two days and he's never willingly sought me out. He also hasn't pushed me away when I went to talk to him so there's been progress.

We've gotten better at talking to each other. I've told him a lot about myself and he's shared his hobbies as well, likes and dislikes. It'll take a while to build a relationship but I'm willing to get there.

"Hi, Katerina," he says unsurely. "Can I come in?"

"Of course," I quickly say, shifting from the doorway to let him pass.

He walks into the room and after a brief moment of hesitation, he takes a seat on the made up bed.

"You can sit too," he tells me.

I laugh softly under my breath. "Okay. How can I help you today?"

"You said you were leaving today," he starts. "I just wanted to ask when you'd be coming back."

"Oh, I'll be back soon, sweetheart. Maybe not today or tomorrow because I have a lot of work to do but in two days? I promise I'll come then. I wish I didn't have to go though."

He nods. "Okay. I just wanted to make sure."

"Nate, I promised. I won't leave again. Promises are meant to be kept," I say sincerely.

Now that I've met him, there's nothing on earth that could keep me away.

"I know, dad's always telling me that as well," he says with a small smile. "About dad… did something happen, between two of you? Are you in a fight?"

My heart aches and I sigh softly, wondering how to answer his question. I'm glad he asked though. He's initiating conversation and even if it's hard, I want to be able to talk to him.

"Your dad and I have a very complicated history. When I left you, I also left him as well and he's angry about what I did. I deserve his anger though."

"He missed you a lot," Nate says quietly. "When he would tell me stories about you, I could tell he missed you."

My mouth dries. I have no idea what to say to that.

"I missed him too," I tell Nate, deciding to be honest.

He smiles pleased with my reply. "And I missed you too."

"I missed you more than I've ever missed anyone ever, baby," I tell him. "Way more than I missed your dad."

He laughs. "Don't let him hear that. He'll be sad."

"Actually, I think he'll be glad," I say. "And don't worry, Nate, your father and I will resolve our issues on our own. You just have to be happy. I want that more than anything."

"I am happy. I'm happy you're back."

"Can I get a hug?" I ask quietly.

He nods and I shift forward enveloping his smaller frame. He holds me close and I take it all in. His smell, the way he feels, wanting to imprint it in my head forever. I love him so much. And I want to tell him, but baby steps. We'll get there.

He lets go and leaves the room to go and play with his

robots after I promise him one last time that I'm coming back. I finish packing my clothes, staring at the room and wishing I could just stay there. It's been a form of sanctuary these past two nights. A sanctuary I don't want to leave. But I have to.

When I exit the room, Xander's leaning against the pillar on the other side of the door, face expressionless even as I appear.

"Hey," I say quietly.

"You're leaving?"

"Yes. Rico's picking me up in ten minutes."

"Good, so we have ten minutes to talk," Xander states to my relief.

"Okay," I say carefully. "I was wondering if you would want to before I left."

He stares at me, green eyes shuttered. I hate when he gets like this, cold, distant. I can't tell what he's thinking when he does. I wait patiently for him to speak.

"What happened yesterday was a mistake, Katerina. We both know that."

I'd be lying if I said his words didn't sting. But it's nothing more than I thought. What I expected. Of course it was a mistake.

"It shouldn't have happened," I tell him.

"Our situation is already complicated enough and we can't allow things like that to get in the middle of whatever progress we hope to achieve. Plus, we have Nate to think about. He's the priority, not whatever this is between us," he says in an undertone.

"Nate's more important," I say nodding.

"So we're in agreement? The kiss never happened and we're both just going to forget it," he says earnestly.

I want to tell him that he's being delusional and that's not how things like this work. But I let him have it. I think he needs it to have some peace of mind.

"The kiss never happened. Honestly I don't know what you're talking about. Our lips have never even met, hell, I'm pretty sure Nate was conceived divinely or something."

Like I hoped, his lips twitch and his expression lightens. He finally smiles.

"Very funny, princess," he says dryly. "But seriously, I want you in my life. As Nate's mother. I want us to be able to build a relationship that benefits him. So friends?" he asks, stretching his hand forward.

I nod, reaching towards him and placing my hand in his. It fits, perfectly, like he was always meant to hold it. I know he can feel it to. I notice the tensing in his shoulders, but he lets me go and it all dissipates.

"I think we'll be great friends," I tell him, lying through my teeth.

He nods, seemingly relieved. "Come on, let's go wait for that cousin of yours to arrive. I'd like to meet him."

"Okay, but just a warning, Rico's not your biggest fan."

He chuckles. "Yeah? We'll see."

THERE WAS a time I was terrified of my father. He's never once in my twenty nine years of existence laid his hands on me. Has never physically abused me. In fact he loved me as best as he could. Both me and my sister.

Despite him never hitting me, there has never been any doubt in my mind that my father could be a monster if he wanted to. He scared me for several reasons. Because he didn't try hard enough to shield us from the dark parts of our world, especially after the passing of our mother. I was also scared because I didn't want to disappoint him. Most of all, I was scared because my father sometimes reminds me of a chameleon. Always shifting and changing his colors. I've only ever known one, and I worry sometimes that he'll take off the cloak, and show me the parts of him that strike fear into the hearts of the men of the outfit.

Those feelings while still valid, are not as strong as they once were before. They faded the minute I became Don. When I finally got what I've wanted all this time. What I deserved. It's also why I can walk with my head held high into our home. He might have had power in the past, but he conceded it all to me.

"Papa," I call as I walk into the room that has a pool table in the middle of him.

Several of my capos lounge around. Seated, standing in the corners. Their expressions turn hungry as soon as I walk through the door, like they're desperate to watch me fall. My father's in the middle, surrounded by them. He gets to his feet as I walk in, brown eyes filled with rage.

"So you've finally returned. Where have you been the past few days? I asked your cousin but he refused to tell me. Where he gets his fierce loyalty to you from, I have no idea," my father states, rage filled eyes landing on my cousin beside me.

Rico doesn't flinch.

I arch an eyebrow, "It seems to me that a lot of the men in this room could learn a thing or two about loyalty from Rico."

My father cocks a head to the side, gaze assessing, "You sound proud of yourself, *mia cara*. Even after the mess you've made?"

"I have nothing to be ashamed about."

"I see," he says, eyes calculating, looking for a breach in my defenses.

It's a game I've watched him play all my life. I'm a formidable opponent though. Perhaps the one he'll fail to rile up.

My gaze roams the room for a second. "Everybody out," I order. "Except my father, my uncle and Rico, everyone get out."

They don't make a move. The room is silent as they stare at me. Very slowly, my lips curve into a smile. It's humorless, cold. I reach into my purse, pulling out a gun.

"Have you all suddenly gone deaf?" I shout. "Get the fuck out. The last man out of here gets a bullet in the skull. Fucking try me, I dare you!"

That gets then into action. They've watched me kill too many people not to take my threat seriously. The men shuffle out, one by one until all that's left in the room is my immediate family. My father watches quietly, emotionlessly, my uncle beside him.

"Now that we're alone. We can speak. You have a right to anger, Papa. But don't display that anger in front of the capos. It's unbecoming," I state.

Instead of speaking, he lets out a scoff, looking away from me. My uncle speaks up instead.

"We also deserve an explanation, Katerina. What is this news we are hearing? You have a son?" he asks, and I can see in his eyes that he's more confused than anything else.

So I suck in a deep breath before launching into the story, telling them everything. With each word, my heart grows lighter. So much that I start to wonder why I kept the truth hidden all this while.

By the time I'm done however, my father answers that question for me.

"I'm going to kill that son of a bitch, Sokolov," he spits.

Alarm pulses through me. "No. You're not."

"He tormented you, Katerina. He held you captive. He deserves death. And I will be the one to bestow it upon him. Your uncle and I will go to Moscow."

It's sweet that his first thought is revenge on my behalf and not anger. But that is quite possibly the worst idea I've ever heard.

"You will do no such thing," I state. "Nine years and I ensured at great cost that there would be no war and no bloodshed between our families. We will continue to ignore the Sokolov's."

His jaw grinds. I'm positive if he had still been Don when the news came out, he would have reveled in a fight, and consequences be damned.

No one says anything else for several seconds. My uncle stares, my father doesn't look at me.

"Go on," I say on a sigh. "You must have more to say, Papa. Ask me."

His lifts his brown eyes, so much like mine to my face.

"Why did you not tell your family about your baby? You kept him hidden for nine years, Katerina. What led you to make that decision?" he finally asks.

"Because I was scared of what your reaction would be, Papa," I answer honestly. "You ruled our family with an iron fist. And I was worried that fist would come to serve as a blow against me, against my son. So I hid him, I abandoned him, because I thought I was doing the right thing. And because I wanted him to be safe."

Seconds tick by before he speaks again. "I would have never hurt you or my grandchild. And the fact that you would have thought shows that I failed as a parent."

And just like that, my heart aches.

"You didn't fail, Papa. I promise you didn't. I made mistakes. But you did your best."

He nods once but his expression is still hard. I wish i could have trusted him then. But even if I had, I would have still hidden Nate. Because if I had returned home with my son, Sokolov would have heard. And he would have come for us without a doubt.

"When do we get to meet him?" my uncle questions. "Your boy."

I offer them a soft smile. "I can't give you an answer yet, *Zio*. But you will. I promise."

My father huffs out a breath. "Am I allowed to leave now?" he questions.

"Of course, Papa."

He walks out of the room without a backward glance. My uncle follows but he stops to rest a hand on my shoulder on the way out.

"Your father will come around, *mia cara*. Just be patient."

"Thank you, *Zio*."

He leaves as well, leaving me and Rico alone.

"What now?" my cousin asks from beside me

"Now, we get revenge."

CHAPTER 20
Xander

I think there are three defining moments in my life. When I was five years old and my parents were going through a divorce and soon after my father had a new wife and I had a new brother I was meant to hate but couldn't figure out why. My mom filled my head with all these ideas of Graham and my step mother before I even met them. She would always tell me that they were sheep and I was a wolf that had to destroy them. When I met Graham though, it didn't really make sense, because he was just a little boy. A little boy like me. But I was also a little boy and all I knew was my parents weren't together anymore and his mother was responsible.

The second defining moment was probably the first time I met Katerina. Before her I was just a regular college guy that enjoyed partying hard, indulging in every vice I could manage in order to forget the fact that my home life was shit and I hadn't seen my mother in years prior to that time. The first time I saw her, I think a part of me knew she was special, because I felt drawn to her in a way I've never been drawn to anyone in my life. She probably doesn't know this. But she saved me in a way. Helped to temper the anger I felt, I managed to find something to wake up for everyday that didn't involve my family's expectations and my need to be better in my father's eyes.

But the most important moment, the one really served as a turning moment was when I went from a 22 year old about to get started on his life. One who had just managed to convince his father to give him autonomy and a chance to find his own way in his family's company, to someone with a baby and no clue how to raise him. After Nate arrived, everything changed. I had to move back into my family home. My stepmother was instrumental in the change. I'm not sure what I would have done without her. I

I'm a very different man now that I was then. Some would say I matured, but I also think that sometimes life is all about providing opportunities that test who you are as a person. And when you come out on the other side, you're better from it. A version of yourself that manages to heal you. I didn't realize until I had my son, just how broken I really was. I thought I was okay but the truth is I was far from it, but my son helped me get better.

And now everything I do is for him. Which is why I can't want Katerina. Because wanting her is inherently selfish. And when it comes to my son, I can't be selfish.

Mikalay comes to stand in front of me later that night, peering at my face. I arch an eyebrow before placing the can of beer in my hand on the counter.

"Can I help you?" I ask my sister.

She crosses her arms over her chest and I can tell from the expression on her face that I'm not going to be a fan of what she has to say. Mikayla's never serious.

"You know I really look up to you right? I mean you and

Gray are both my elder brothers but you're the responsible one," she states.

I smirk, "I like where this is going, continue."

"And yet, despite you being the responsible one, you can be such a dumbass sometimes big brother."

My lips turn down into a frown, "I'm not liking it anymore."

"You're in love with her," Mikayla says bluntly, brown eyes fixed on my face.

My chest tightens. "No, I'm not," I deny slowly.

"What happened last night?" she questions and I'm about to tell her to mind her damn business when she interjects.

"Come on, Xan. Level with me. If we're being honest, I'm the only person in our family you can talk to. The only person period, considering you have no friends and no social life."

I make a face. "Is this an interrogation or you taking a shot at me?"

"It can be both," she says earnestly. Then her expression turns soft. "Come on. Talk to me."

I sigh. Nate's already in bed. Despite the boisterousness of the city below, the house is quiet, serene and soothing. I should have been asleep but considering I have a lot to think about, I decided to stay up and have a can of beer alone. But I guess those plans are out the window.

Plus, Mikayla's not wrong. She actually is the only person I can talk to.

"We kissed last night," I finally say. Her eyes start to brighten but my next words effectively turn down her excitement. "It was an accident. And it's never happening again."

Mikayla frowns. "Why not?" she asks. "I don't know if you know this, big brother, but I remember when you were dating her. I was only a teenager but I watched you come home happier for the first time in a long time. Before you even brought her home, I noticed how you would talk to her. It was like you were alive for the first time ever and I loved seeing that."

My jaw clenches. "I was young and in love, Mikayla, it happens. You would know, considering you're in love with someone new every other month."

Her eyes narrow. "Don't be mean," she states. "But you're right. I have issues. I'm constantly seeking approval from men because I need to feel a kind of love that's completely different from the one my father supposedly showered on me since I was young. A love that feels free, without constraints or bounds."

I stare at her for a couple of seconds, completely impressed. "How'd you figure that out?"

"My therapist told me," she says proudly and I snicker.

"Right."

"The thing is Xander, despite everything, I'm better off. Graham is better off as well, even if he's too much of an idiot to see how lucky he is. We both have our mother, she stuck by us. I know how hard it's being for her living with our father for so long but she held out because she loved us. But you didn't have that growing up, you didn't have your mother, all you had was dad."

My fists clench. "This isn't a therapy session, Mikayla. I don't need you laying out all my issues."

"Sure but we need to tackle the root of your issues. The love of your life left you and it hurts. She betrayed you and it fucking hurt. But she's back now. And I think this is the universe giving you a second chance at happiness."

That makes me chuckle. "You want me to try for a second chance at happiness? With Katerina Mincetti? Kay, I love you but you're being naïve if you think that's possible. She doesn't even know what happiness is. She's like a robot programmed only to feel things like loyalty to her family, honor. We were together for almost a year and she was never able to tell me she loved me. We're both.." I falter before speaking again. "We're both messed up, Mikayla. We're both fucking messed up. And yeah maybe she was my light once, but she left me even worse off than she found me when she left. I might act like I'm okay but that's because I've learnt to suck it up and suck it all in for Nate. I know you mean well, little sister. But I don't think we should be together. I don't think we can be together."

"But you love her," Mikayla says assertively, eyes daring me to counter her.

"That's not the fucking point!" I say, my voice rising. "What I feel for her doesn't matter. We'll ruin each other. Do you get that? She has the ability to ruin me and I think I could ruin her too. I don't want to do that. Especially not now when she just got her son back. Do I care about her? Of course, I'll always fucking care about her. Which is why I know staying away is the best thing for both of us."

"You're being delusional," my sister states. "You and the woman have a child together. From what I gather, you're letting her back into Nate's life and yours by extension. Which means she'll be around. Like it or not, she will be in your life, in your space, in your axis. The two of you kissed yesterday, I'm sure you tried to fight it but you couldn't. You two can't simply be friends or whatever idea of relationship you have in your mind, Xander. It's not going to work out."

"I'm going to fucking try to make it work out," I grit out.

My sister lets out a soft sigh. "Just think about everything I've said, big brother. Ruminate on my wonderful words of advice. I've been told that they can be life changing."

I roll my eyes at the sudden change in her tone. She steps towards me, rising to her toes to kiss my cheek.

"Dad has asked me to return to the hotel we're staying at tomorrow. We're sticking around in New York but of course he needs to make sure my leash is tighter now that we're here," she mutters. Before she leaves she fixes me with another hard look. "You have a chance to break the cycle, Xan, take it. And yeah, I know she's Katerina Mincetti. But you're Alexander Steele and you're exactly the kind of man a woman like her needs. You're also a certified genius when it comes to computers. You can change her programming."

With those words, she walks out, leaving me with a head even more jumbled than when she walked in. I groan softly under my breath, wondering why life has to fucking suck.

Unfortunately, things aren't much better the next day. In fact my day starts out pretty horribly because I get a phone call from an unfamiliar number starting with the country code for France. My stomach practically sink to its depths at the sight. I don't know anyone in France. But I do know someone who could be there. My worst thoughts were confirmed to be true when I pick up the call.

"Alexnader," she says, voice feminine with a Southern lilt and a sharp cadence.

I should have picked up the damn call.

"Mother," I grumble. "Fancy hearing from you today. Did the sun rise up from the West over in whatever city you've undoubtedly found yourself in this time around?"

"Cut the sass. I'm in Paris. And you're in trouble," she snaps. "I just heard about everything that's going on. Apparently the entire country knows about your son's parentage."

The way she says it, like it's something slimy and wrong gets on my nerve. Thankfully, it's not the last one.

"Yes. A story was released that Katerina Mincetti is Nate's mother."

She gasps, voice filled with horror. "Oh my God. So everyone knows his mother is a criminal?"

"Mother," I grit out.

"What? She is, isn't she? I don't know much about the Italian mafia but they're horrible people. The worst of the worst."

I don't say what I really want to. Which is that they're probably better people than her. Hell, if there's one thing Katerina's thought me about the outfit, it's that they value family more than anything else. Maybe not always in the healthiest of ways, but regardless. I'm sure mothers don't call their sons for the first time in over a year just to berate them and be judgmental.

"Is there a point to this phone call?" I ask boredly.

"Yes. What did your father say?"

"He kicked me out of the company," I tell her. Technically, I left on my own but I know my words will evoke some fear in her heart.

"What?!" my mother screams in my ear. "He can't do that! You're his first born son, Alexander. You're supposed to inherit everything. It's all yours and I'm not going to stand by and watch as that dick gives everything to that woman and her bastard son."

My jaw tightens. "Don't talk about them that way."

I might want to pummel Graham's face currently but one thing I've realized as I grew older was that my mother's treatment of him and Isabella was completely unwarranted. Dad was the problem. The onus of it all.

"You know it's true. And I can't believe you could have

been so stupid. I said it. When I found out about that son of yours I knew he would come to pose problems for you in the future. Why you decided to raise him, I'll never understand. You should have found that woman and given him back!"

And there goes my last fucking nerve.

"I'm hanging up now. Don't contact me in the nearest foreseeable. Maybe if I'm lucky, next time it'll be on your death bed."

The words are cold and callous but if there's someone that brings out the worst in me, it's her. And she fucking deserves it.

"Wait," she says quickly. "Unfortunately you'll be seeing me much sooner than you'll be hearing that I'm on my death bed."

My eyebrows climb. "What are you talking about?"

"I'm coming back, Alexander. It's clear I need to fix this mess on my own and I know just the thing. It's time you got married to a wonderful, respectable woman that your father will approve of. Maybe then we can appease his anger and everything will go back to normal."

Anger pulses in my gut. But I manage to keep my cool. Nate's awake and playing in the game room. I'd rather he didn't hear any of this.

"You want to appease the man you solely refer to as a dick?" I say dryly.

"Yes and like I said I know just what to do. When I return, I'll find you an acceptable wife."

"I don't give a fuck what you do, mother. But leave me the hell out of it. And I'll die before I find anything you do acceptable."

Before she can say anything else, I'm hanging up. I run an agitated hand through my hair. I know without a doubt she's being serious and that she'll be returning. The problem is, while a part of me loathes her for staying away, the other part would very much like it if she never returned.

Because if there's one thing Jessica Steele brings along with her everywhere she goes, its pain and suffering for everyone else around her.

Nate comes into the living room a few minutes later and I have to school my features into a feigned calm. When he smiles at me, I feel something loosen in my chest, glad that despite everything else he's the one good thing I've got.

"Hey, buddy," I say. "What's up?"

He looks a little nervous. "Dad, I wanted to ask..."

"Go on," I prompt encouragingly.

"Can you ask Katerina when she'll be coming? She said she would return in two days."

I smile warmly, reaching up to ruffle his head.

"Of course. So you like her, huh?"

He shrugs, "She's my mom."

And the simplicity of that statement causes my heart to ache. She is his mom. Its blood and it should be able to transcend everything else, but sometimes it doesn't.

"Well good, because I like her too."

His eyes brighten. "You do?"

"Sure, sport. I do."

"So, she's your friend?"

I nod. And he grins.

"Thank you for being friends with her, dad. I thought about it and if you didn't like her then maybe I shouldn't have liked her either."

Well fuck. I didn't even think about how my actions could affect his perception of Katerina.

"You can like her, Nate. No matter what."

He nods and after making sure that I'll make the call, he leaves to go back to playing. One thing the conversation with

Nate proves is that I can't afford to fuck things up with Katerina. I heard what my sister said. And maybe a part of me knows that she's right. But everything is so fragile right now and I stand by the fact that I can't afford for anything to break.

Later that night, I'm on the phone with her. Mostly to ask when she'll be able to see her son. But also to see just how normal we can actually be.

"I'll be busy tomorrow but I'll come the day after. Maybe late evening. I can have dinner with you guys before returning home."

"You could always stay over," I suggest, lying face up on my bed and trying to ignore the way even the sound of her voice has an effect on me.

"I could but I'm trying to establish boundaries," Katerina states. "We are still trying to be friends, right?"

I clear my throat. "Right," I agree. "Good call."

Who knows what I might do with the knowledge that she's right downstairs in a room not too far from me. She's absolutely right. Staying overnight would be a bad idea.

She doesn't speak for a couple of seconds.

"I really do want to go back to how it was before, Xander. You weren't just my boyfriend back then, you were my best friend. I want that more than anything. Scratch that, I need that. I need you."

Her voice is soft, vulnerable. In a way I know she never is with anyone else.

"I kind of need you too, princess," I admit, feeling my pulse start to race.

But there's also the fact that while I may have been her best friend then, I think I was only able to exist as that because I was her boyfriend. I don't point that out though.

"Okay. So no more awkwardness. It's just me and you."

"Yeah, I know," I say clearing my throat. "How are things with your family?"

She lets out a soft groan before telling me about the situation in her home. And I listen, careful not to interrupt, lest she stop. Because it's suddenly hitting me that now that all the cards are out in the open, all the secrets are out, it's possible for us to build a better relationship that the one we had before.

CHAPTER 21
Katerina

My fingers fly across the keyboard as fast as I can as I work to breach the heavily protected mainframe of Colton industries. I've been at it for two days. Yesterday, there was a sudden fire in one of their buildings, destroying millions of tech and important equipment's. Thankfully, no one was hurt considering the fire was started at night and the only people in the building were knocked out mysteriously and carried out.

I gave orders that no innocent life would be lost. All I want is to damage to Colton's so badly that there will never be a whisper of them or their existence afterwards. My next course of action is hacking into their systems but as expected it's proving a little difficult.

All I can think is that Xander would love to help. He'd probably be having better luck than me as well. Growing up, I've always been intrigued by hacking but it wasn't until I met Xander that I actually learned it. He thought me everything I know. When it comes to computers, he's sort of a genius.

I don't know if I want to bother him with this though.

Especially after the call last night, which felt like immeasurable progress, even if it might not be the kind I want. I've been able to collect my thoughts while I've been away from him. Those thoughts however, are still too muddled for me to understand.

I'm not sure what I want.

And yet I know I want him. And I want Nate. And every minute away from them fills me with a sense of trepidation. So once I reach another block, I decide to pack up my laptop, getting to my feet and calling Rico into my office.

He arrives, eyebrows raised in question.

"Let's just go to the penthouse now," I tell him.

He doesn't argue, instead leaving to put things in order. I pack up everything I'll need and then we're on the way. It's much earlier than I told Xander I would be arriving but I figure he won't mind.

"Are you going to be spending the night?" Rico asks when we arrive at the penthouse.

I look at him, wondering at the odd question. "No. Why would I?"

He smiles, "Why not? You already slept over before and it seems to me you and Alexander are building a relationship."

I roll my eyes. "We are but it's not what you think, Rico."

"Uh-uh," he says unbelieving.

"Fine. Why don't you come up with me and see for yourself how normal our relationship is. Perfectly platonic."

"You're a terrible liar, *cugina*."

Still he steps out of the car with me, following me into the building. As soon as we get there, I notice someone at the front desk. When he turns around, my feet skid to a stop.

There's a permeable chill in the air as I come face to face with none other than Christian D'Angelo in the lobby of the building leading up to Xander's penthouse. Rico recognizes him as well and immediately steps closer to me, his stance protective.

"What the fuck?" he says under his breath.

It's not every day two mafia Dons meet each other coincidentally out in public. Plus, I don't know Christian very well. I know he has a good relationship with Roman and the De Luca family but we've never met, our families far apart with no ties whatsoever.

His eyes are a light brown color, his face chiseled in a way I imagine sculptures are. He's good looking, in an extremely off putting manner, almost cold, uninviting. He's well into his thirties with a scruff of a beard around his chin. He also seems to be cataloguing me as I'm doing for him.

When I'm done with that, my eyes are drawn to the person standing beside Christian D'Angelo. A little boy with reddish brown hair and eyes extremely similar to the man standing beside him. I deduce that he's Chrisitan's son. Daniel D'Angelo.

There's a brief pause as we both size each other up from across the lobby. I'm not sure whether to approach him or not. Chrisitan D'Angelo makes that decision for us. He reaches for his son's hand, holding it in his palm as he walks forward until he's right in front of us.

"Miss Mincetti," he says, inclining his head respectfully. "It's nice to meet you."

"It's nice to meet you too, Mr. D' Angelo."

The politeness feels like a farce. Tension coils beneath my spine. I still don't know what he's doing here. This could very well be an ambush. There hasn't been a war in the outfit in years but his appearance here certainly raises some red flags. Considering he's here with his son though. I'm inclined to believe he's not looking for any trouble.

His expression is steady. I get the feeling nothing fazes

him. He gives off the image of the man I'm sure my father wishes I was sometimes.

"My apologies. I didn't think you would be here. If I had known, I would have been better prepared to meet you."

My eyebrows rise. "What are you talking about? And what are you doing here?"

Christian D'Angelo sighs. It's a low soft hum. Beside him, his son is absolutely quiet, appearing bored like his mind is on other things much important than a conversation between adults.

"We're here to see your son actually."

Despite knowing that I should appear stoic in front of him, my eyes inevitably widen.

"I'm sorry?"

His father's words finally get the little boys' attention however. He looks up at me brown eyes bright.

"You're Nate's mom?" he questions. "That is so cool. It's nice to meet you. Nate told me he also just met his mother and I told him that was weird because I've known my mother all my life and-"

Christian clears his throat interrupting his son's rambling.

"What have we said about acceptable conversations, Dan?"

"Right, sorry," the boy says abashedly. "It's really nice to meet you though."

Despite myself, I smile. He reminds me of Nate.

"Nice to meet you too, Daniel."

Christian looks at me, his gaze flicking to Rico who's silent and brooding at my side.

"Why don't we go upstairs? I'm sure you'll get an explanation then."

I nod and we all enter the elevator. Rico presses the button for the penthouse, and I don't miss the way his hands flex, edging towards his suit jacket. I place a hand on his arm, trying to calm him down. I don't think Christian means to harm us in anyway. I just don't like that this meeting caught us by surprise. The ride up is completely silent, only interrupted by the consistent bouncing from the little D'Angelo. He seems incapable of being still, eyes roaming, legs bouncing. His father appears used to it, he paints a stark contrast though. Completely unruffled. I'm guessing Daniel gets his quirks from his mother.

The elevator opens, depositing us right into the massive penthouse. As soon as we appear, there's the sound of little feet approaching rapidly. Nate appears and my heart warms at the sight of him. He doesn't even look at me though, his eyes landing on his friend. Both boys hug and this time my heart warms for another reason as they start speaking over each other rapidly.

We enter the house just as Xander arrives. He's wearing a black Henley sweater that hugs his physique and blue jeans. He arches an eyebrow in surprise as he takes us all in.

"Hey, princess," he greets, eyes falling on me. "I thought you were coming later."

"I finished early and decided to come over. Imagine my surprise when I ran into Mr. D'Angelo downstairs," I say, my tone light but also conveying how not okay the meeting was.

Xander catches on, his eyes narrowing slightly. Then he's looking at Christian.

"Hi, I'm Alexander Steele. Thanks for bringing your son over."

"No problem. If you don't mind though, I'm going to stick around for a little bit. I know the plan was to drop him off but I figured we might all get to know each other."

His tone borders no argument. And I hear the underlying

message. Until he's sure of where we stand, he's not leaving his son alone in a house with me. Smart man.

"Right.." Xander trails off, looking from Christian to me. I realize he might not really understanding the dynamics of the situation. He claps his hands together, "Alright, how about I pull Katerina to the side for a quick conversation? You can talk to Rico for a while, neither of you mind, right?"

My cousin snorts in reply. Christian's lips curl into a frown. I fight back a smile as I follow Xander into the kitchen. He doesn't waste any time before speaking.

"What's going on?" he asks.

My eyebrows furrow. "What do you mean what's going on? What do you think is going on? Do you have any idea who that is?" I ask, slightly exasperated.

Xander appears entirely too calm. "Sure, Christian D'Angelo. Am I missing something?"

"Xander, he's the Don of the D'Angelo family. One of the most feared and respected men in the outfit. And you just invited his son on a playdate to your house?"

Very slowly, I see his expression turn to one of realization.

"Oh," he says then shrugs, immediately shifting back to calm.

"Oh?"

"Katerina, you do realize who you're speaking to right? Of course I know who he is. I know every fucking thing about him and his family. I wouldn't have allowed him here if I didn't."

"And?"

"And what? I verified his identity and I'm aware of what he's capable of. This has nothing to do with your business. Daniel and Nate met in school and became best friends. Nate's been missing his friend the past couple of days so I reached out to Christian who after some consideration agreed to bring him here so they could see each other. We're all very well informed, princess."

"Except me," I mutter.

He sighs. "I'm sorry, I should have told you about it. I was going to tell you when you arrived later and met Daniel. I didn't think you'd run into his father. I'm guessing your families don't get along?"

"Not exactly. We just don't have a relationship, so things are… delicate."

"Well, considering he's not leaving, this is your chance to make things not so delicate."

I arch an eyebrow. "Meaning?"

"Nate's playing with his friend. Why don't you go play nice with the other big bad Don?" he asks, eyes twinkling.

I roll my eyes. "That's not how it works, Xander."

"On the contrary, I'm pretty sure it is. He's not leaving until he's sure his son will be safe. Our son happens to like his best friend and I'm sure he would hate it if his friend couldn't come over to our home again because his mother's on bad terms with his friends family. Alliances are built every day in your world, Katerina. Build one now."

I grit my teeth. It's really not that simple. I came here after a stressful day taking care of a drug deal gone wrong. There was a raid and a cop ended up dead, which is never a good thing. I had to make several calls, placating whoever might be out for bad blood. After compensating the officer's family, I had to dole out punishments to the people responsible. I'm tired and I was hoping to just come here relax and hang out with my son for a while. But obviously that's not going to happen.

Xander must be able to read my thoughts because to my surprise he says.

"I'll carry you along next time, I promise."

My heart short circuits for a little while. I stare at him, wishing with all my heart that things were different. That it wasn't so hard. That I could just fall into his arms and receive the warmth he always seems to dispel, but I can't.

"Okay fine. I'll try to strike up a conversation with Mr. D'Angelo."

His lips twitch. "He's not so bad," Xander says. "Kinda funny in a droll kind of way. I've only spoken to him on the phone but I like him."

"You like everyone," I mutter.

"Have fun with your new best friend," he tells me with a wink. "I'm going to take some snacks up for the kids and then I need to make some calls in my room. I'll come downstairs as soon as I can."

He places a hand on my shoulder, his touch searing before he walks towards the fridge, leaving me to return to the living room where Rico and Christian seem to be engaged in a standoff. They haven't even sat down. I clear my throat once, to signal my return. Rico looks at me and I see relief in his expression.

I turn to the tall, brooding Don. "I believe reintroductions are in order," I begin.

He arches an eyebrow in question.

"Your son is friends with my son, Mr. D'Angelo. Surely, that means we can try to be amicable."

Christian lets out a huff of breath.

"Alright fine," he says stretching his hand out to me. "Nice to meet you, *Katerina*," he emphasizes.

"You too, Christian. Should we take a seat?"

He nods and we settle down on the couches.

"I'll be honest, I've been curious about meeting you. Your reputation precedes you," I state.

He lips turn up in the tiniest of smiles. "As does yours. I wondered at the first female Don we've had in over a decade in the city. Your family is quite formidable."

"Thank you. I do my best. And I'm not sure if you've introduced yourself, but this is my cousin, Rico. He's my second in command. He can be a little rough around the edges and fiercely protective."

Christian looks at Rico, and I'm surprised when something light dances in his eyes.

"I've heard about you too. My capos like to say you're a coward for letting a woman take your rightful position as Don."

I cock my head to the side at that statement. Rico's expression darkens.

"And what do you say to that?"

"I think they're full of shit. There's a reason she's in that position and not you."

"That there is. Katerina has balls of steel, much bigger than yours or mine."

"I doubt that," Christian says on a smile.

Rico chuckles and almost immediately the tension in the room dissipates.

That was smart of him. To pinpoint that Rico was still wound up tight and try to calm him down. He's good with people, which is kind of annoying because I'm relatively not. I'm great at negotiation, using my head but when it comes to connecting with people, I'm far less equipped.

"So Katerina, why don't you tell me how you single handedly prevented a war from breaking out between your family and the De Lucas?" Christian asks.

I smile, "Well I wouldn't say single handedly…"

We spend the next hour trading stories and just talking and while Christian can be a bit dry, he's also intelligent and charming. By the time he leaves with his son, we're able to greet each other good bye with a warm handshake and a promise to keep in touch. I even manage to sneak in a suggestion that we could engage in future business negotiations which he doesn't seem too against.

Once we're gone, I have dinner with Xander, Nate and Rico. And it's honestly the first time I've felt at peace in the time since the start of all our problems. It's also the first good dinner I've had in a long time. The last time I felt so at peace while eating was when I ate dinner at my sister's home.

Thoughts of my sister leads to an uneasy sick feeling residing in my gut. On the way home, Rico and I decide it might be time to check in on her and see if she's ready to see me. Unfortunately, she is not. Anthony follows us back to the car when we're denied entry, his face apologetic.

"She's really not taking this well, Katerina. I've never seen her this upset," he says gently.

Something twists in my gut. "I just wish she would talk to me."

Tony rubs the back of his neck seemingly uncomfortable.

"Yeah, I think she needs to talk to you too. At least for an explanation. But if I'm being honest, *cognata*, this is kind of a huge deal. Take it from me, a person that had to suffer because someone I trusted and loved kept such a huge secret from me for most of my life. She has every right to be feel hurt."

Guilt hits me like a bucket of ice. I swallow a deep breath.

"I know. Just… tell her that I'm here. Whenever she's ready to yell at me, I'll be ready too."

"I will. And take care of yourself. Be safe."

I offer my brother in law a smile. It's times like this that I can understand why my sister fell so in love with him. He's dependable, like a solid rock. Always there for you even when you don't want him to be.

"Yeah, I will. Bye, Tony."

"Bye," he tells me, offering Rico a short nod. "See you around, man."

A part of me keeps wishing Sophia will show up outside and stop me as we leave the house. That part of me is the one that thrives on hopeless dreams and impossible wishes. The one part of myself I can't seem to get rid of no matter how hard I try.

CHAPTER 22
Xander

Two weeks after the story being released to the public, I decide enough time has passed in between that Nate can return to school. I only stopped him from going because I know kids can sometimes be cruel and I was worried about what his peers might say about the truth being brought to light.

My brave son however assured me that he could handle it because he's got a great best friend by his side who will take care of anyone that says anything wrong to him. And if there's one thing I'm glad for, it's that Nate found a friend in Daniel D'Angelo.

My fingers tap against the steering wheel as I drive away from the private school heading quite literally wherever my drive takes me. It's suddenly hitting me that I'm thirty one years old and unemployed. Working at Steele industries is all I've known my entire life. And I'd be lying if I said I didn't miss it. I gave my all to that company. Not only because it was my families but because computers and gadgets is all I've known since I was a little boy. It's all I'm good at. And now that it's all potentially slipped out of my grasp, it's hard not to feel a little lost.

New York's a charming place. It's a city that's always on the move, everyone has somewhere to be, something to do. It gives of an aura that motivates you because it's clear that if you don't find your own path or forge one, you'll be lost in the dirt. It's very easy to lose yourself in a place like this. Everyone's working hard at their dreams. But there's people who have no dreams, people just hoping to survive.

Despite my family's deep rooted issues, I've never worked hard a day to survive in my life.

So what the hell am I doing here?

The answer comes in the form of a phone call from Katerina. It comes right as I'm pulling over at the parking lot of a huge mall. I smile to myself, glad that seeing her name flash across my skin doesn't give me the same feeling of trepidation it would have weeks ago. It's progress.

"Hey princess," I greet.

"Xander, good morning," she says, sounding a little out of breath. I can hear the clacking of keys on the other line. "I was just calling to ask if you already dropped Nate off. You did still take him to school, right?"

"Yeah. We got there around 8," I tell her. "He likes to get an early start to his day."

"Oh," she says softly. "I should have called earlier then. I just got so busy and the time got away from me."

"Its fine," I quickly assure her. "You can talk to him later when I pick him up. Or better still, would you like to pick him up from school?"

She falls silent at that and the clacking on the other end stops for a few seconds. Then it resumes.

"Of course, I'd love that. Thank you. Listen, I've got to go. I'll talk to you later..."

"Whoa, whoa, hey," I say on a chuckle. "Chill for a second. What are you up to?"

She hesitates before answering. "Well, I'm working on something illegal."

"Unsurprising," I murmur with a smile.

"But it's for a good cause."

"What good cause?"

"I'm trying to bring hack into Colton industries. Destroy all their software from within. But it's proving difficult," she informs me.

"You're kidding?" I ask. "How long have you been working on this?"

"About two weeks."

I frown. Ever since the story broke up. I've got to hand it to her, the devil may work fast, but Katerina Mincetti works faster.

"Let me guess, you are also responsible for the explosion that occurred at their factory last week."

"It was a small fire that destroyed all their tech. plus no one got hurt," she says defensively.

Surprisingly, I find myself chuckling at that, "Alright, princess. I want in."

I can tell it takes her a couple of seconds. "In with what?"

"You obviously need my help, Katerina. I know my best quality is my face but I also happen to have a brain that's capable of breaking into any firewall or mainframe. Some would also argue that my personality is my best trait. But that's not the point."

"No, the point is that you have an enormous ego," Katerina says amused.

"The point is that I can help you," I correct. "Plus, I've been thinking of ways to get back at that bastard since everything happened. I should have known you'd beat me to it. So what do you say? Let me help you take him down. For good."

"Don't you have anything better to do?" Katerina questions.

"No actually. I dropped off Nate so my schedule's wide open for the day. It turns out being unemployed might not be what's it's perked out to be. Come on, princess. I'm bored out of my mind."

She laughs. "Alright fine. But are you comfortable with coming here?"

"Where's here?"

"My family's home. It's in the Upper West Side, I could send you directions."

That gives me pause. I've never been to her family's home. And I get the feeling not a lot of people get the chance to be invited there.

"Would that be okay though?"

"Yeah, my dad's not home. It'll be fine. Plus, you get to see where I grew up," she tells me.

"Intriguing," I murmur. "Alright, I'll come."

"Okay. I'll text you the address," she informs me. "And Xander?"

"Hmm."

"Don't be startled by the guns."

With those words she hangs up and I'm left wondering exactly what I'm getting myself into. The drive to her house takes an hour and once I arrive in the neighborhood, my jaw nearly drops. First at the isolation and then at the house itself. All I have to do is provide my name before I'm allowed on to the compound.

At the sight of the huge mansion that's placed in the middle of sprawling grounds, my jaw drops even further. There's a lot of land, several acres of it and the house itself is pretty amazing. My family is wealthy, an old money kind of wealthy but its clear the Mincetti's have almost as much money, maybe even more.

Katerina was right to warn me about the guns because there are men in literally every corner of the house, armed to the teeth. I don't let their stares bother me as I park my car. A man appears as soon as I step out, gesturing for me to hand him my key so he can drive the car into a more appropriate place. I do so and he points me towards the entrance of the house.

When I enter, I'm guided by someone else, a woman this time, probably one of the help. We walk through the artfully decorated home towards a room with a black painted door. The woman knocks once and I hear a faint come in, before the door is opened and I'm allowed inside.

On the other side is, Katerina Mincetti and for maybe the first time I see her as the Don she was always meant to be. Powerful, beautiful, lethal as she sits at her desk, the expression on her face daring anyone to fuck with her. The expression lightens as soon as her eyes meet mine however. She offers me a smile, before getting to her feet.

"Hey, Xander," she greets, moving towards me. "How do you like the house?"

"It's a little…" I search for the right words. "Intimidating?"

Katerina grins. "Yeah, I guess it can be. My dad really went all out when he built this place. But its home too. My home."

"Well you have a wonderful home. Thanks for inviting me."

"You're welcome. Have you had breakfast yet? We can get some food before we start work," she suggests.

I remember she was never one for wasting time. If Katerina has a task she needs to finish it right that second.

"It's fine. I already ate with Nate this morning. Let's just get to work."

She nods, and I follow her back to her desk where her laptop sits already open. She gestures for me to take a seat in her chair and I arch an eyebrow.

"Are you sure I'm allowed to sit here? Isn't this the Don's seat of power or whatever?"

"I promise you won't get shot if you sit there," she says teasingly.

I shrug before lowering myself onto the chair. I roll up the cuffs of my sleeves, staring at the screen intently.

"How long do you think it's going to take me to break in?" I ask Katerina, my gaze still on the screen.

"Knowing you and your prowess, I'd say about four hours?" she guesses.

I grin. "If I do it in two, what do I get?"

"A pat on the back and a job well done?"

I chuckle, looking up at her and into her beautiful brown eyes.

"Tempting but no. I want something else."

"What?" Katerina questions.

"I'd have to think about it. But I'll let you know, princess. Once I'm done," I state.

"Okay, well good luck. I have to go and take care of something for an hour or so. I'll be back soon. There's a button at the side of the desk over there. Just press it if you need anything brought to you."

"Alright. Thanks, princess."

She leaves and I'm left alone. I stare at the laptop for a couple of seconds, my skin buzzing in anticipation of what I'm about to do. Katerina's already done a chunk of the work, sneaking past several encryption codes and faux walls. But it's clear she's having trouble accessing their main system. The firewall is pretty solid, formidable. But I would have expected nothing less.

I'm not sure how much time passes as I look for a weakness. Probably minutes until I find a blind spot and I'm able to enter their system undetected. From there it's all about creating a few lines of code in order to unleash a virus I meticulously crafted. It slithers through the network undetected.

My lips turn up in a smile as I watch the virus spread, each note of the code playing its part in the grand symphony of destruction. Which is around the time I look up, feeling her eyes on me. I didn't even realize she had returned. When I'm in the zone, nothing else tends to matter.

"You look like a villain in a movie," Katerina says. "I'm guessing you were able to get in?"

I grin, 'Come see for yourself, princess."

She stands beside my chair, crouching down to look at the laptop. I pretend not to be affected by her scent, which momentarily clouds my senses. Or her proximity. She stares at the carnage for a couple of seconds.

"So what happens now?" she questions, a smile in her voice.

"With their software compromised, day to day operations will have to come to a halt. They'll face immeasurable financial losses especially since they're a tech company that should not be susceptible to such an attack in the first place. Any and all faith in their products will be lost. Their reputation is officially damaged forever. They'd need to rebuild their software systems from scratch which wouldn't be easy. And the good news is, it'll be impossible for them to trace it all back to us. I'm sure Colton knows it was us, but he has no proof."

She stares at me for a couple of seconds and I find myself wondering what she's thinking, wishing I could read her mind. Then she blinks, looking away.

"So you did it. And with fifteen minutes to spare," she states, showing me the time on her phone.

It took me exactly an hour, forty five minutes to completely ruin a conglomerate. That would be a little terrifying if I wasn't the one with the ability. I lean back in the seat, offering Katerina a cheeky grin.

"You don't have to say it," I tell her. "I know I'm amazing."

She rolls her eyes. "You're also insufferable. So what do you want?"

I think about it for a couple of seconds before replying.

"On a scale of one to ten how busy are you today?" I question.

"Well considering my position, I'm always busy. But I can make time. It depends on what you want."

I get to my feet and stand in front of her. "In light of my recent unemployment, it would seem that I'm jobless and in the mood for some company."

Her nose crinkles. "And you want me to what?"

I take one of her hands in mine, massaging her palm with my thumb.

"Spend the day with me, princess. We don't even have to go anywhere. You can show me around the mansion you grew up, a grand tour of some sorts," I say imploring.

She seems hesitant but then nods once. "Fine. I guess it can't hurt."

Actually, it could. Really, really badly. But it's okay to want things that hurt.

"Great, first off, I want ice-cream. Come on," I say, pulling her hand and leading her away from the office.

She takes the lead once we're outside the office, walking me through the rows of hallways until we find ourselves in a large kitchen, with an island in the middle. There's a middle aged woman inside I'm guessing is the cook, who stiffens at our arrival, bowing her head slightly.

"Hi, Collete. I was wondering if we had any ice-cream," Katerina says politely.

"Of course, ma'am. You could have called and I would have had it brought to you," the woman, Collete says, her eyes still fixed to the floor.

"That's fine. We'll get it ourselves, you can go," Katerina states, dismissing her.

Collete doesn't argue walking out of the kitchen immediately. I poke Katerina in her ribs gently.

"She was so scared of you, which is amusing because you're a five foot seven blonde who once cried while watching Winnie the pooh."

Katerina's eyes widen and she slaps my shoulder. "Shut up, I didn't."

"Baby, you were right beside me on the bed and I remember it vividly."

Her eyes widen even further and it takes me a second to discern the expression on her face. Then I realize what I called her and now I'm the one feeling horrified.

"Fuck," I mutter. "That just slipped out, princess."

She shakes her head. "It's fine. No biggie."

To avoid looking at me, I'm sure, she heads towards the large fridge in the corner of the kitchen, pulling out two tubs of ice-cream. I'm left standing there, berating myself for being such a fucking idiot. Calling her that used to be as easy as breathing. But that was before. A long time ago. I guess I just forgot.

"It comes with the position," Katerina suddenly says while fishing out two plates.

"What?" I question.

"The fear. When I was younger, Collete was the one that took care of me when I was sick. She made sure Sophia and I were always well fed and happy. I wouldn't say she was a mother figure but she was pretty darn close. But in recent years, her affection has become much more muted. Especially since I became Don. It's also necessary. If they don't fear me, then they don't respect me."

"I see," I mutter, moving towards the kitchen island.

I grab two elevated stools so we can sit on it, while Katerina starts to dish out the ice-cream. She places a bowl of strawberry ice-cream in front of me and I try not to make a face at the mint-chocolate chip in her plate. She notices regardless.

"Don't be judgmental about my ice cream," she says waving a spoon in my face.

"I'm trying but I seriously have no idea how you and Nate eat that shit. It tastes like toothpaste."

"Maybe we're the ones with good taste and you just don't get our refined palate."

"Refined palate? Over mint flavored ice cream. That's funny."

She rolls her eyes before taking a bite and I try not to stare too hard as her tongue darts out to lick her spoon. And imagine what else her tongue could be licking or where it could be. Specifically inside my mouth. Or against my cock. My eyes close momentarily as it twitches in my pants.

Fuck, I'm horny.

Coming here was such a bad idea. Katerina seems oblivious though. She looks to the side, offering me a small smile. Her eyes are light and at ease. Her guards are completely lowered. It's moments like this the somehow manage to take my breath away, how easy it is.

She's telling me about her time in law school when Rico suddenly walks into the kitchen. He arches an eyebrow at the sight of the both of us.

"Hey. I was told I'd find you here. I was also told you had a guest," he states. "I see both statements were correct."

"Hi, Rico," Katerina says with a smile. "Xander's here for a visit."

I offer him a short nod, "What's up man?"

He is not impressed. I understand though. Rico's like an overprotective elder brother. I would know considering I'm one as well. He does not like me. I'm sure he likes my relationship with his cousin even less.

"I'm good," he murmurs, gaze trailing over our faces. His eyes land on the ice-cream with a frown. "So what is this, a date?"

"No," Katerina quickly replies. "We're just hanging out. You're welcome to join."

His frown deepens. "Kat, you know he's not meant to be here."

"Why not?" she shrugs.

"Because if your Papa finds out, it'll be a whole issue," Rico states. "Don't forget your priorities, cousin. The situation is already complicated enough."

The last part is said in Italian. Unfortunately for Rico, I understand and can speak the language perfectly. I don't give any inclination that I can though. But judging by the smirk, Katerina throws my way, she knows.

"You need to relax, Rico. I'm allowed to have a little fun, am I not?" she asks, continuing the conversation in Italian.

"Not too much fun. And not with the father of your child. I see the way you look at him."

"Enough. Also, he can understand everything we're saying," she says, gesturing at me.

Rico's eyes widen as they fall on me. I shoot him a cocky wink.

"By all means, continue. It's fascinating seeing you converse," I say in English.

He rolls his eyes and sighs, "You're both annoying and thanks to you, Katerina, I'll be bald by the time I'm forty."

That makes me chuckle. After one last look at us, he shakes his head and walks out of the kitchen.

"Don't blame me for that, *cugino*," Katerina calls out after him.

Once he's gone, we look at each other again before laughing. I watch as she takes a spoonful of her ice-cream.

"He really does end to act like a mother hen," she mutters with a smile.

"You're lucky to have him."

"I know."

When I look at her, my eyes narrow in on the smudge of ice-cream on the side of her lips. I grin before touching the area on my face.

"You've got a little something," I gesture.

She wipes at it with her finger but doesn't get it all. My stomach sinks and I find myself reaching upward. I brush against the soft skin on the corner of her mouth, wiping away the rest of the ice-cream. Time seems to stand still with the movement. Our eyes lock and the air crackles with unspoken desire. There's a lot of tension imbued into one fleeting moment. It's palpable and electric.

I swallow softly, resisting the urge to brush my thumb across her incredibly inviting lips. As quickly as it comes though, the moment passes, leaving me yearning for more. Katerina steps back, clearing her throat and avoiding eye contact.

My eyes fall shut as I run my hand through my hair in frustration, fighting back a soft groan.

Her voice comes quietly a few seconds later, "So what do you want to do next?"

I don't even have to think about my reply.

"I want you to teach how to shoot, princess."

CHAPTER 23
Katerina

My problem with being with Xander, is that he always manages to make every single fucking thing he does attractive. Not only has did he completely destroy an entire conglomerate in under two hours, which was incredibly sexy and reminded me why I fell for him in the first place. Now he's also standing beside me holding a gun and pointing it at a dummy and, hitting every shot on target despite apparently never trying shooting before.

Its bullshit, I don't believe it. I make sure to tell him that.

He chuckles and the sound of his laughter is like music to my ears.

"Seriously, princess. I just did what you told me. It's not my fault, I'm good at following directions. You know just how good I am," he says and I don't miss the hint of suggestiveness.

"Unbelievable," I mutter, looking away from his face. "Whatever, I'm done shooting. Let's head back to the house."

He doesn't argue and we divest of the guns, turning them over to the capo in charge and walking back to the mansion. Neither of us really speaks the entire way there. My mind is still on the fact that he was able to pick up a gun for the first time and shoot that naturally. His technique and posture could use some work but he could be an ace shooter, if he really wanted.

"You know, it's a little annoying that you're just good at everything without having to even try. You're lot like my sister in that regard."

He looks at me and I'm not sure how he can tell but it's like he's able to effectively pick out the sadness that lays behind the last sentence.

"How are things with her?" Xander asks.

"Well, she's still not speaking to me, so not good," I reply. "But I am hopeful that eventually she'll remember all the times I covered for her when she snuck out of the house when we were teenagers and forgive me."

My words are light and teasing but the truth is my sister's silence is bothering me. So much. Xander convinces me to give him the grand tour so we walk through the hallways, with me pointing out each room. Two living rooms, a long dining hall that we typically don't use, especially now that my sister doesn't live here anymore. We have an extensive library, which used to be my happy place when I was much younger, a home theatre, a game room, and staff quarters towards the back of the house. And a basement, that I don't show Xander because I'm worried there could be dried blood or something unsavory clinging to the walls. We don't use it anymore considering we have our headquarters, but when I was a child I would sometimes hear screams coming up from there.

By the time we're done touring the house, I'm exhausted. We arrive in the area that contains my family's bedrooms. Xander's gaze strays to a particular brown door that has my

THE DON'S DOORSTEP BABY

heart rate speeding up. I see curiosity light up in his eyes and grab his hand.

"Come on, I'll show you my room," I tell him, directing him away from the room at the end of the hallway. The room none of us have been able to enter for more than two decades.

I open my bedroom door with a flourish and we walk in. "This is the room I grew up in," I say. "I've redecorated it a lot over the years as I grew up but it's my safe space."

He looks around, eyes resting on the desk cluttered with papers and books before moving towards the closet door and then coming to rest on my bed. It's been made up, I let the help in to clean every morning. I just never let them touch my desk because I don't want them disrupting my work. His eyes linger on my bedside table and he walks over, picking up one of the picture frames. There are three. One of me when I was a child, one of me and Sophia when we were teens and then one with our dad.

"You were adorable," Xander says with a grin as he studies the picture of me.

"Of course I was."

While he continues his snooping, I lie back on the bed, my gaze going up to the ceiling. I'm actually feeling really good right now. Because we're actually doing it. Apart from that moment in the kitchen which we managed to fight against, I'd say we're doing quite well at being friends.

"It probably wasn't such a good idea for you to bring me in here, princess," Xander suddenly says.

When I look at him, I find his gaze fixed on my legs. Specifically the exposed part that's showing due to my dress riding up. The look in Xander's eyes is hungry. They're dark and filled with so much desire, my breath hitches.

It's dangerous and so enticing, I feel my mouth dry. I spoke too soon about doing well at being friends.

"Why not?" I ask, sliding off my bed and moving to stand in front of him.

Bad idea, a voice whispers in my mind. I ignore it.

Xander looks at me and his expression twists in a combination of frustration and desire.

"You know why."

I shake my head, lowering my voice. "Actually, I have no clue."

When he takes a step towards me, I take one back. The last act of preservation I can manage. Xander's faster though, wrapping an arm around my waist to pull me back. I gasp as I find myself pressed against his chest.

"I want to do so many things to you when we're alone, Katerina. And us being in your bedroom isn't helping matters. Do you want to know what I'm thinking about right now?"

I should probably so no. But I am a weak, weak woman in the face of him.

"Yes. Tell me," I breathe.

"I'm wondering just how many nights you've lain awake unable to sleep. How many nights you succumbed and decided to slide your fingers between your folds. Played with your clit, brought yourself to the brink. The more possessive part of my brain is wondering who was on your mind the entire time."

I swallow softly at the vivid imagery he's painted. He has no idea how right he is. I'm hit with the feeling that he was right here with me. All those lonely nights.

"Maybe I wasn't alone," I whisper suggestively.

His jaw tightens and his expression darkens with rage.

"I really don't want to hear that, princess."

"Relax. I said maybe. The truth is, you're right. I have lain awake on my bed, alone and I've touched myself, several times. But the truth is, every single time I've done it. You've being on my mind. Only you," I confess.

Xander swallows, his throat flexing with the movement.

"Show me," he says in an undertone.

"What?" I blink in confusion.

"You heard me, Katerina. Get on that bed and show me what you did."

My thighs clench at his tone and the suggestion. I know I shouldn't and yet there's a part of me that can't deny just how much I want this. So I do as he asked. He walks backward until he's leaning against my desk while I climb on top of my bed and lie down.

"Spread your legs," Xander says.

His tone is light and commanding. I comply, parting my leg so that my dress rides up a few inches and then some, giving him a view of my panties. I keep my gaze fixed on him. His eyes are so dark and filled with lust. My heart is pounding in my chest.

"Shift your panties to the side, Katerina," he tells me, and I do, angling my underwear to the side so my clit is laid bare. "Good girl."

My cheeks heat. I would never be so pliable with anyone else, so willing.

"Now show me," he murmurs, attention fixed on my spread legs. "Put your hands between your legs."

"Bossy," I mutter.

My limbs don't move for a millisecond. I suddenly remember who I am.

He smiles, "Please," he adds. "Put your hands between your legs, Katerina."

My hand settles on my thighs, before slowly moving upward. When I get close to my pussy, his jaw tightens.

"Run a finger up and down your clit," he says softly.

I moan softly as I do so, feeling just how wet I am. My arousal sticks to my fingers. My other hand goes up to my chest. I reach inside, cupping one of my breasts. I massage my nipple with one hand while running my finger continues to play with my clit.

I moan softly, my eyes falling shut.

"Open your eyes, Katerina," Xander's voice effectively penetrates the haze of pleasure. "Open your eyes and look at me."

Very slowly, my eyes fall open. And then my mouth follow suit because someone his dick is free of his pants and he's stroking it in his hands. His eyes are still fixed on me. I wait, heart pounding for his next words of command.

"Dip your finger inside and tell me how it feels."

My skin prickles but my hand is already moving, dragging back and forth against my folds until I gently push inside. I hear a sharp audible groan which spurs me on. I slip my finger in further, just another inch, feeling my walls clamp around it. I whimper softly. His cock is still in his hands, large and pulsing and I can see pre-cum dripping from the head. The whole thing is sensory overload. I can't even begin to describe how I'm feeling right now.

"Katerina, tell me how it feels," Xander reminds me.

"T-tight," I manage to say. "Wet."

I've never seen anyone driven crazy before, but Xander looks like he's on the brink.

"Fuck," he groans. "I can see just how soaking wet you are from here, baby. I want so badly to feel that against my lips. To eat you out until you're fucking screaming my name."

"Please," I beg, unsure exactly what it is I want.

I add another finger, moving them in and out, increasing the pace. My head falls back as I allow myself to simply just feel. I feel my orgasm impending, like a riot rolling through me. Just when I'm about to come, Xander speaks.

"Stop."

It's just one word, but I hear it loud and clear. It's like dousing my lust with a bucket of ice. My hand stills. Frustration builds in my gut as I prop my elbow against the bed to look up at him. I notice his dick is back in his pants again.

"Are you fucking kidding me?" I snap.

He shakes his head, "You don't get to come until I say so, Katerina. And I want to be the one to make you come. Stand up," he says.

I cross my arms over my chest, and glare. "Make me." I don't give a fuck how childish that sounds.

He grins like that's a challenge he'll happily accept. Then suddenly he's standing by my bed, tugging me up until I'm kneeling on the bed right in front of him. He grabs a hold of my hand, the one that had just being inside of me. With his eyes still on my face, he raises it to his mouth and licks it clean. Arousal hits me like a bolt of lust.

"Your taste, Katerina..." he trails off, staring at me in wonder. "It's indescribable."

His gaze drops to my lips and I'm kissing him in the next second. My hands are gripping his chest, his hands are wrapped around my waist. He manages to pick me up, carrying me across the room until he's propping me on the desk. The actions has several books and papers flying to the ground, but I don't care.

Xander tilts my head back, tugging my bottom lip with his mouth. My hands wrap around his shoulders, pulling him closer, between my spread thighs. His hands slip beneath my dress, sliding past my ass and gripping my waist.

The moment turns into one of desperation. Xander practically yanks my dress over my head and in the same breath drops his mouth to my bare breasts. It's all happening so fast, but considering the back and forth that's been going on between us the past few weeks, it's understandable. My hand reaches past the waistband of his pants, wrapping around his thick hard length.

It's a frantic sort of hunger that drives us. I work him with my hand, pumping up and down as he takes one of my nipples between his lips. I cry out when he gently bites it before sucking the sting away.

"Xander," I moan softly.

He doesn't reply, too busy tugging at my panties. There's a slight ripping sound that barely computes as I realize I'm naked, bared entirely for him. For the first time in almost a decade. He pulls away to assess me from top to bottom, taking his time consuming the sight of me. My skin prickles under his appraisal, then I reach out for him and he obliges, kissing me, his pace suddenly slow and sweet.

"I missed this," he says against my lips. "I missed you. I missed us."

"I missed you too," I whisper back. "Please, please, please, fuck me now."

"You sound desperate, Katerina. Haven't done this in a while?"

He's fishing for information. We're about to have sex and he wants to know just how many people I've slept with since I was with him. For the love of God!

"I haven't had sex with anyone else in about three years," I tell him breathing heavily.

Before he can say anything else, I slam my mouth down on his. He groans, reciprocating and tugging me forward until my hips are barely resting on the table.

"Katerina, I don't have a condom," he informs me.

"That's fine. I'm on birth control," I assure him. "And I trust you."

I haven't stopped using it in years. And even if I wasn't, a part of me knows that I would have wanted him inside of me regardless. Because we've waited too long and I can't wait any longer.

"Get naked," I say against his lips and he doesn't hesitate to do so.

I help him take off his shirt and then his pants come off as well. He steps out of his boxer briefs until it's only his cock, standing proud and erect. Xander looks at me like I'm the only precious thing in the world, but I also see something else in his expression, something I don't really understand.

"You don't have to say it. I know it's a bad idea," I murmur as he continues to stare at me.

His eyes meet mine, steady assurance in his gaze.

"Actually, this might be the best idea I've had in a long time, Katerina," he states, placing his hand on my cheek. "I think I'm done fighting this."

Relief rolls through me. Honestly I'm a little disappointed we caved so easily and couldn't keep the friend thing going. But I'm just so glad that he still wants me. That he's looking at me how he used to before.

I expect me to carry me to the bed. He does lift me but instead of moving to the bed, he stays in place. My legs wrap around his waist. We're aligned perfectly, hip to hip, his cock resting against my wet center.

"You ready?" he asks and I have to wonder at his immense strength as he holds me up.

I squeeze my eyes closed and curl my toes as he sinks in the first inch. My mouth falls open. Another inch and a whimper escapes me.

"Oh," I whisper.

Thanks to the angle he's able to bury himself inside me to the hilt. I'm completely stretched to the oblivion.

"Katerina, breathe," Xander commands.

I hadn't even realized I was holding my breath. My grip on his shoulder is tight enough to bruise.

"It feels.." I trail off.

"Indescribable?" he asks.

I nod. He slowly pulls out of me and my walls clench. I feel him shiver.

"Do it again," I plead.

He does, driving back into me, before dragging out again, nice and slow. Again I have to wonder at his strength. He's not only holding me up without breaking a sweat, but is managing to set a pace that's determined to drive me wild. I wrap my arms around his neck and press my naked chest against his.

Warmth explodes through me as he continues his slow pace. I lift my head to look at him.

"Xander, faster," I say.

He groans and I feel us moving until my back is pressed against the wall. He's still inside me but now he's able to grip my thighs as he thrusts faster, deeper. His hand finds its way between my thighs, the pad of his thumb is rough as he plays with my clit.

"I'm so close," I tell him as he continues teasing me.

He keeps on fucking me, his pace hurried and yet it also seems like he's taking all the time in the world. He keeps until pleasure detonates through me. I'm dying, I swear I'm dying.

Xander chuckles and I realize I said that out loud. "You're not dying, Katerina, I promise." He kisses me soft and sweet before whispering against my lips. "Come for me."

Like a puppet, I do. Every sensation bombards me, so

hard that I nearly tap out. It's too much. I'm burning up from within. Xander follows and together, we hold each other up, gasping and quivering as the pleasure rolls through our body. We don't move from our position against the wall. If it wasn't for Xander holding me up, I'd be putty on the floor. We stay like that for several long minutes.

So many words flood the tip of my tongue. But I can't seem to voice anything. Xander sets me back on my feet and we lock eyes.

"Now what?' I finally manage to ask.

He smiles and my insides melt. Xander leans downwards, kissing me hard.

"Now, we do it again," he replies with a grin when he pulls away.

CHAPTER 24
Xander

If I was asked to jump off a cliff to save my son, I would. If I was asked to jump off a cliff to save Katerina, I would.

That simple logic leads to a quiet understanding. But life has never been that simple. And sometimes I feel like I'll never understand Katerina fully. Currently, its late afternoon and we're lying next to each other on her bed. I'm on my side facing her and her eyes are close. She looks like she's asleep but there's a tiny crinkle in the side of her forehead that lets me know she's not. We've been in this position for an hour. After we eventually wore ourselves out.

"Stop staring at me, weirdo," she mumbles after a couple more seconds pass.

My lips pull up into a smile. "Are you ready to stop pretending to be asleep?"

Her eyes still don't open.

"Actually I was hoping you could treat this as one of those one night stand situations and leave before I wake up."

I arch an eyebrow at the statement but decide to play along regardless, "I would, but it's in the afternoon not at night. And I don't think one night stands usually involve as much sex as we just had."

"They do if the guy has a lot of stamina," she replies.

That has my eyebrows climbing. "And you know this how?"

Something bubbles in the pit of my stomach. I know enough to recognize it as jealousy. Katerina doesn't reply my question however.

"Princess," I prod.

Her eyes are still closed. "Don't you have somewhere to be, Xander? It's almost 3 and you have to pick up Nate from school."

"I'm aware," I state. "And I'll go as soon as you look at me."

She doesn't.

"Katerina."

She lets out a soft sigh. "If I look at you, then that makes everything real and I'm not ready for it to be real yet, okay?"

"But if I leave without you looking at me, then how can you be sure it was ever real in the first place?" I counter.

That gets her to open her eyes. My pulse races as my gaze meets soft brown ones.

"I don't want you to leave," she tells me quietly.

Her words are like a searing bolt to my chest, one that can't be ignored. Before I can rethink my actions I'm climbing off my bed.

"Tell you what? What if I asked Mikayla to go pick Nate up from school? The both of them can hang out for a while."

Katerina sits up at that and I see relief in her expression but also some confusion.

"So you're not leaving?" she questions.

I make sure to look her in the eye as I pull on my boxer

briefs. "I told you. I'm done running away, princess. This is here and now. We can't keep living in the past."

She still looks doubtful but I have every intention of proving myself to her. After making the call in which my sister was all too happy to oblige, I'm climbing back into bed beside her. We sit in silence for a couple of seconds, her backs resting against the headboard.

This is hard. There's no denying that. We have so much to unpack, so many things we need to figure out. I remember reading or seeing something somewhere, in a book, a movie where one of the characters asked the other how they could work on removing their armor. The reply was simple, adequate, just three simple words. *One at a time.*

And I relate so much to that in this moment. Because if there are two people who have been living with armor our whole lives. It's me and Katerina. Her much more than me. She lives with so much of it, I'm not sure it would be possible to take it all off. But I plan to help her.

"Answer me this, princess," I start. She looks sideways at me. "What do you wish for the most in the world? Tell me three of your greatest heart desires."

That makes her smile. It's a soft, warm smile, "Since when are you a genie, Alexander?"

"Just tell me," I prompt.

"Alright," she says, "But three things don't even begin to cover all that I want if I'm being honest."

"Too bad, I asked for three," I state. She looks at me imploringly and I find myself caving. "Okay fine. Five things?"

She nods, happy with my amendment. She sits up straighter before beginning to speak.

"One of the things I want is mostly superficial. But I want to go to Paris. My sister and I used to take bi annual trips to

Paris when we were teenagers. We would go shopping in Rue Saint Honore. And after visiting as many luxury stores as we could, we'd go and eat at the most spectacular places. There's a particular restaurant called Le Meurice Alain Ducasse. The food there is impeccable. I loved going there with Sophia but as we grew up, there were less and less chances to travel because of school, college, work, and eventually we just stopped going. She probably doesn't even remember."

I reach for her hand in slight awe because while I've never heard the story before, I believe with all my heart that those trips with her sister were probably her happiest. The only times when she was able to completely be free.

"Thinking about the trip leads me to something else I want and wish for with my whole entire heart," Katerina says, "I want my sister to forgive me. Sophia's my best friend and her absence in my life feels like I've lost a limb. I just want my sister back."

Her eyes are a little glassy as she says that.

"She'll come back, princess," I say offering quiet reassurance. "What else do you wish for?"

The next one must be pretty hard because it takes her a while before she's able to voice it.

"I want Nate to call me mom," she says, her voice low. "Maybe it makes me selfish. I mean I haven't been back in his life for too long and these things take time. But I really do want with all my heart to hear it. Even if it's just once."

My heart tugs at that. I shift closer to her on the bed, placing my arm around her shoulders and drawing her closer to my chest.

"It's not selfish to want that, Katerina. It's human. He'll call you mom eventually. He just needs a little more time, princess. And I promise you'll hear it as many times as you want. Maybe you'll even grow sick of it."

"I would never."

I smile, "What else do you want, princess?"

She huffs out a soft breath. "Maybe I'll just keep the rest to myself."

"No," I say pulling away to look her in the eye. "Tell me."

"Seriously, Xander. You're not a genie and you're not magic. You can't just flip a wand or your wrist and fulfil all my heart desires," she mutters.

I wish I could. If I could make her happier by doing, so I would.

"Tell me," I repeat, my tone leaving no room for argument.

She breaks eye contact, staring off at the wall. It takes her a long time before she's able to say the words.

"I want to be able to love you without feeling so terrified."

My stomach hollows at that and a burn radiates in my chest.

"Why is that so terrifying, Katerina?" I ask softly.

Instead of replying, she starts to climb off the bed. I try to ignore the way heat rolls through me at the sight of her naked body. Her ass jiggles as she walks and my cock twitches which is crazy because after what we were up to all afternoon, it should be completely out of commission. Katerina heads for a closet and grabs a dress, pulling it on and effectively hiding her body from view.

"I'm going to tell you my last wish. But first I have to try and show you the answer to that question," she tells me. "Come on."

I get off the bed as well, and put on my clothes before following her out the door. Katerina starts to lead me towards the end of the narrow hallway. The large brown door I saw earlier, the one she deftly tried to pull me away from. My heart pounds with the possibilities of what could be behind the door.

"We're not going to enter," Katerina says once we're standing in front of it. "I don't think I physically can."

I don't need to voice the question. She sees it in the way I look at her.

"Because this was my mother's room. The room she shared with my father before she died."

The pain behind those words, the look in her eyes, undoes whatever shred of hesitation I'd been feeling ever since I kissed her. Because if there's one thing I know for sure, it's that I wanted to hunt down every single thing that causes her pain and destroy them.

When I notice a tremble go through her hand, I immediately slip mine into hers.

"You don't have to talk about it if you don't want to, Katerina," I tell her.

"No," she shakes her head. "I didn't tell you ten years ago because I was a coward. Maybe if I had let you see all of me, we wouldn't be in this position. I won't make the same mistakes again."

"I'm listening," I say quietly.

She takes a deep breath. "I was eight years old when my mother died. She passed away from cancer. Losing a family member is always a terrible thing. But losing someone to cancer, eats away at you in an inexplicable way. Because it's watching that person die and being unable to do anything about it. Watching them suffer in pain and being helpless. I hated feeling like that. I was only a child but I remember praying so hard, trying so hard. I would always hound the doctors for more information, beg them every day to do their best to save her. But in the end there was nothing they could do. The day she died, I was the only one in her hospital room. I watched her die."

I suck in a sharp breath at that revelation.

Katerina continues, "I've killed a lot of people over the years. I've watched as life was sucked from them. As they stopped breathing. But no matter how many people I watch die, none of it ever compares to the feeling of seeing my mother take her last breath. Watching her fight one last time as I screamed for help. I wasn't supposed to be in the hospital that day. But instead of going home I managed to convince one of my father's capos to take me there. If I had gone home, I wouldn't have had to witness something so traumatizing. I lost someone I loved more than life itself and it scared me, Xander. Because I've never felt pain like that before. And I never want to again."

She's trembling by the time she's done speaking. I pull her into my arms and hold her. The hallway is silent in a way that feels haunted. No one deserves to go through what she and her family went through. And now I understand why she tried so hard to build a wall around her heart. I might not know the full depth of her pain, but I feel it regardless.

Eventually I'm able to lead her back into her bedroom. She seems tired, so I tuck her into bed, aware that I won't be getting anything else from her today. She needs a break from all the high emotions, we both do. I tuck her into the covers, ensuring that she's comfortable before placing a kiss on her forehead. I should probably get back home anyway.

"Xander," she says softly just before I turn to leave.

"Yeah?"

"I don't want to be scared anymore."

My heart warms as I stare down at her.

"You don't have to be scared, princess."

"I wish my mom was still alive," she says quietly, so quietly that I almost don't hear it.

But I do and the words cause a searing pain through my chest. Because that's the one thing I can't do for her. No matter how much I want to.

She's fast asleep by the time I walk out of the room. I run into Rico on the way out of the house and while he does arch an eyebrow in question, he doesn't ask me anything.

"She's not feeling too well," I inform him. "Maybe just let her sleep."

He nods before telling me goodbye. Things can change in the blink of an eye. When I came to her house earlier today, I didn't expect all of this to happen. But I'm happy it did. Glad that we've at least made some progress. That we're both finding it within ourselves to heal.

TWO DAYS LATER, I'm alone in the penthouse. Katerina came over for dinner last night but aside from a few lingering looks and a secret kiss goodbye, we weren't able to talk. She has a lot of work to do and only came because Nate asked her. I'm currently biding my time until she's free so we can continue our conversation.

Because while a part of me doesn't want to be too hopeful, I'm almost sure she wanted to tell me she loved me. And hearing those words would be a defining, irrevocable change. One that would completely uproot my life. And if she can't say it yet, then I'm prepared to wait until she does. I'd wait forever to hear those words from her.

I'm working on a plan for a new job when I hear the elevator open. My brows furrow, because I wasn't expecting anyone and I should have been informed by the receptionist downstairs if I had a guest. I get to my feet and the sight that greets me is a platinum blonde woman in her early fifties, dressed head to toe in designer clothing, a fur coat thrown over her outfit. There's a large red suitcase behind her and a look of irritation on her face that clears only a bit when her eyes meet mine.

"Oh, hello darling," she greets.

My jaw grinds. "Mother."

CHAPTER 25
Katerina

> I can't do this anymore, Sophia. I gave you enough space but I'm done. You need to talk to me and let me explain. Even if you end up hating me, at least here what I have to say. Please, sorella.

I send the text with my heart in my throat. I'm worried that she won't reply. I'm also worried that she will and her answer would be for me to fuck off. After sending it, I place my phone down, sure it'll take a couple of minutes at least before she eventually replies.

"We were able to dig up some information on the man running for mayor."

My eyebrows rise as I stare at Rico.

"I thought he had a squeaky clean record," I question. "Even Roman and Christian couldn't get anything on him."

The mayoral election has been causing some problems for the outfit because the man most likely to win seems to be a hard ass and we're finding it hard to get him under our control. If the city has a mayor like that, it would make it exponentially hard for us to do our business here.

"Well yeah but then I decided to ask your boyfriend for help and he did his thing with hacking. Went as far back as Sanderson's college years and got some information a DUI and an arrest for possession."

It takes a couple seconds for me to digest all that.

"You asked Xander for help?! Rico, he's not my boyfriend and I don't want him being a part of any of this."

This is my life, it doesn't have to be his.

"He's going to be a part of your life is he not? This is the Cosa Nostra, Katerina. You're either in or you're out, there's no in between. Xander's going to have to decide if he wants to be in. But for what it's worth, he seemed happy to help when I contacted him. He didn't even blink, he just got down to the request immediately."

I chew my bottom lip as I consider it all. Xander and I are in a semi good place right now. We haven't had much time to ourselves after we had sex two days ago, thanks to me being busy managing the issues with the election but I'm hopeful that things will eventually work out. We're so close to being okay and while there haven't been any heartfelt declarations of love, I can still feel it.

And if I think back on it, he's never given me any inclination that my career bothers him. It should. Most normal people would never want to be involved with a woman that leads a criminal outfit. It's the reason I've stayed away from any serious relationships this past few years. I sigh softly, it's just one of the many issues we're going to have to work on.

"None of that matters. Don't contact him again unless I expressly ask you to, understand?"

"Yeah, I got it," he says. "But like I said, he was useful. He got me the dirt we need."

I fix him with a stare. "But will it be enough?"

"The race is pretty close. And while it won't make waves,

releasing the news could potentially damage Sanderson's campaign especially this close to the election. We just have to consider what we do with the information. Blackmail him or ruin his chances."

I lean back in my chair. "I actually like Sanderson if I'm being honest. It would be better to have as the mayor under our control, than anyone else. I don't trust his opponents."

Rico nods. "I don't either. So we're blackmailing him?"

"Yeah but we still need to think about how we'll keep him under our thumb once he's in the position. I'll have to discuss with the other Dons."

"Okay. Then I guess we're done with the meeting," he announces. "You heading to Steele's place?"

I shake my head. "Actually I'm waiting for Sophia to reply my text. I asked to see her."

He offers me a sympathetic look. "Alright, Kat. Let me know when you're ready so I can take you where you need to go."

He leaves and I'm left alone for a couple of minutes. Just as I'm considering calling Anthony and forcing him to trick his wife into a meeting, Sophia texts me back.

> Fine. I'll meet you in thirty minutes at the park near my house. Don't bring Rico.

Relief sweeps through me. Followed by dread. My gut is bunched up with nerves the entire car ride to the park. When I get there, she's already waiting for me seated on the park. My sister and I somehow manage to look so similar and then not at all. My father likes to tell me that while I favor some of his features, Sophia looks a lot like our mother. I see our mother in her sometimes. Her smile, the color of our eyes, her grace. She's the confident one, the smart one and I'm unbelievably lucky that she's my sister.

"Hey stranger," I greet, standing in front of the bench.

She looks up, blue eyes landing on my face.

"Hey, Kat."

Her expression is devoid of any warmth. I rub my hands together, thinking about how to navigate this conversation. I decide to ask about the well-being of my niece first.

"How's Nova?"

Sophia shrugs. "She's okay. She keeps asking to see you. I'm not sure how to tell her that she also has a cousin she needs to meet for the first time."

Okay... we're heading right into it.

I inhale softly. "Can I sit down?"

"You can do whatever you want. You always have," she mutters.

"Okay, enough with the passive aggressiveness," I state, taking a seat at her side. She turns to look at me. "You're angry."

Her expression darkens. "Of course I'm angry. Do you want to know what's been replaying in my mind ever since I found out the news. The moment you found out I was pregnant. I still remember how betrayed you were. You berated me for finding myself in that position. Meanwhile you had been in the exact same position yourself. You're a hypocrite, Katerina," she spits.

My guts twists with guilt.

"I was just-"

She cuts me off before I can speak. It's clear she needs to get it all off her chest.

"Your hypocrisy pisses me off but more than anger I'm hurt, Katerina. Because you could have kept the truth from Papa, to some level, I understand that. You could have kept it from Rico, from our uncle, literally everyone else but I can't believe you kept it from me. You aren't just my big sister, you're my best friend. I tell you everything but you couldn't even extend the same courtesy to me. Nine years, *sorella*. Nine years hiding such a huge secret. Do you have any idea how that feels?"

"I'm not perfect, Sophia," I begin quietly once she's done.

"I never said you were," she bursts out.

My voice is firm as I say, "No, I need you to listen to me. When mama passed away, it fell on my shoulders to take care of you, to shield you from any danger and I tried my best to do that. I loved doing that because you were mine to protect, my little sister. How was I supposed to tell my little sister that not only had I fallen pregnant but was also trapped in Moscow with a psychopath intent on finding me?"

Her eyes widen at that and she sucks in a breath.

"I still don't know the full story," Sophia mumbles.

I manage a smile. "I'll tell it to you. And I know that it's no excuse for my actions. I fucked up and I'm owning that completely. Apart from Xander and Nate, you're the person I hurt the most and I'll do my best to apologize to you for as long as you want, Soph. Because I love you so much and I need you to forgive me."

My sister doesn't say anything else. Her gaze is steady as I launch into the story. By the time I'm done, we're both crying.

"You're the most annoyingly, selfless, egotistical, stubborn person I've ever met," Sophia says wiping at the side of her face.

"I know," I say in agreement.

"Would it have been so hard to tell me? I could have shared in your pain. Nine years and you couldn't see your son. It must have been killing you."

"I was able to bare it, because I knew he was safe. He had his father and I knew his father would do right by him."

"He should have had his mother too," Sophia whispers.

"Yes, he should have. But he has me now and I'm never going to leave him again."

Sophia looks away from me and runs a hand across her face. "I still hate what you did."

"I know."

"You don't really deserve forgiveness."

"Of course," I say nodding.

"But the truth is, I could never hate you despite how much I want to. You are so incredibly lucky that you're my sister, Katerina. If anyone else had hidden such a huge secret I would have never been able to get past it."

It's not forgiveness. But it's close.

"So what do I do now?" I ask her.

"Just tell me one thing first, do you love him?"

I stare at her for a second. "He's my son, Soph. Of course I love him."

She shakes her head. "Not Nate. Alexander. Are you in love with him?"

"Oh," I say in surprise before quickly recovering "I loved him nine years ago, Soph but I was too afraid to say it. Now it feels like the universe is giving me a second chance and I'm so scared of ruining it."

Sophia nods like my answer pleases her. She stands up and I follow suit.

"Do right by him first, *sorella*. If you manage to find happiness and hold on to it, then maybe I'll forgive you."

My jaw drops, "Wait, what?"

"You heard me. You're great at working hard to get what you want. Just fight for love. For once, fight for something worthwhile. I promise I'll be there on the other side if you do."

We stare at each other for a couple of seconds. Before she

goes, I realize there's something I need to tell her. Something I should have been telling her all this while.

"Mom would have been proud of you, Sophia," I say softly.

Because despite it all, I know our mother would have preferred that we lived our lives away from the outfit. She would have wanted us to be happy with a family of our own and Sophia succeeded in that. She managed to forge her own path.

My sister's eyes soften. "She would have been proud of you too."

I know that to be true as well. I kept my promise to our mother. I took care of Sophia, I kept our family together. So even if I know in my heart she would have not been comfortable with my position as Don, I know she would understand that I am what I was made.

I am my father's daughter.

After leaving Sophia, I drive to Xander's penthouse. Right now, all I want if for him to hold me and tell me everything will be okay. For some reason, hearing him say the words always manages to put me at ease. I think about the condition Sophia gave me for forgiveness. It all seems so simple, but if there's one thing I know about love and matters of the heart, they never are.

I take the elevator up to the house and as soon as it opens, I hear shouting.

"For fucks sake. I said you can't stay here. I'll find you a hotel somewhere but I don't want you anywhere near me or Nate."

Xander rarely ever raises his voice.

"How dare you speak to me this way? Is this how I raised you?!" a woman shouts back.

My footsteps fall to a stop at that.

"Please, don't make me laugh. You didn't raise me, mother. All you did was give birth to me."

I stay quietly at the entrance to the living room, barely breathing. Xander doesn't talk much about his mother. I know their relationship is strained, I also know she was absent for most of his life. But hearing the pain in his voice as he addresses her causes a painful crack in my chest.

"Enough with this victim complex you have. I am here for you, Alexander. To help you," his mother says, her voice manipulative.

Each word feels like dripping honey mixed with poison.

"No, you're here to help yourself. You're here out of spite because you can't bear the thought of me losing the company to Graham or hell even Mikayla. You have never cared about me."

"Your judgment is warped, Alexander. I am not going to abandon you because you're my son."

"You've overstayed your welcome. Good bye, mother."

I realize a second too late that I'm standing right by the entrance. My breath stops as Jessica Steele appears in view, pulling a red suitcase behind her.

Fuck.

She recognizes me. It's clear in the way her lips curl in disgust at the sight of me. I make sure to meet her glare with one of my own. She laughs coldly.

"Of course you would be here," she states. "Katerina, is it? It's good that you're here. I've wanting to meet you all this while."

CHAPTER 26
Xander

I move across the room lightning fast until I'm standing in front of Katerina.

My mother has been here for over an hour. At first I was content to let her drone on and on about how tiring her trip was. I even provided her with some refreshments. I was perfectly polite, until she mentioned staying in my home. Which is where I had to draw the line. I lost my cool when she started acting like she had a right to demand to stay here. Nate barely even knows her. He's aware he has another grandmother, has seen pictures of her and might remember meeting her once or twice, but in his mind, the only grandmother he's ever known is Isabella. And I intend on keeping it that way.

I feel Katerina's arm on my shirt, her touch searing.

"Xander, it's okay," she tells me before moving to stand at my side. "It's nice to meet you, Miss Steele."

My mother rolls her eyes. "Don't say things you don't mean, child. I definitely don't think it is nice to meet you. In fact all I can think right now as I look at you is how much I dislike you for ruining my son's life."

Katerina flinches at that and my jaw clenches.

"That's enough. Get out."

Her gaze lands on me, brown eyes roaming my face, taking in the situation.

"You're protecting her?" my mother asks on a laugh. "Are you really this dense, Alexander? You're going to just forget all she did to you? I thought you were smart enough not to throw your life away all for a pretty face."

"I don't have to explain myself to you."

She doesn't reply instead turning to face Katerina again.

"I understand people in your line of work tend to be cruel, but if you feel even a modicum of anything for your son and my son, you'll get out of their lives for good."

Katerina opens her mouth to speak, but I cut in.

"She'll do no such thing. You're the one that needs to get out of our lives for good, mother."

After a couple more tense seconds of her glaring at us both, she walks out of the penthouse, entering the elevator. I let out a breath of relief once she's gone. When I look to my side, Katerina's wearing a disapproving frown.

"I don't need you to fight my battles for me, Xander," she states.

"Actually, princess. My mother is my battle and mine only."

"And what did you mean when you said you would lose the company to Graham or Mikayla? What happened?"

She wasn't supposed to hear that.

"Oh. Well my father and I had a bit of a falling out. I walked out on him after telling him I had no interest in the company ever again."

Katerina gasps. "You did what?"

"No need to get your panties in a twist, princess," I say lightly.

"Are you kidding me? That company's your entire life. It's all you've ever known. I know without a doubt that you worked hard to get to your position and now that you're so close you're going to let it go? Because of me?" she asks, her voice cracking slightly.

"Hey, hey, no," I say, placing my hand on her chin. I incline her head up so she's looking right into my eyes. "It's not because of you. It's because of me. I think I need to do this, princess. Maybe it's time for me to find something else to do, venture out on my own."

"So you're just going to let Graham take over?" she asks still frowning. "Don't think I don't know he was responsible for leaking our picture to the press in the first place. I'm just letting him go because he's your brother."

I chuckle. "Graham has always wanted to be CEO. He's always had more of a passion for it than I did. That being said, he won't be able to get the position if he doesn't grow up. Recent problems aside, I know without a doubt that he can rise to the occasion. He may be an asshole, but he would actually do well in the position."

"That… incredibly mature of you," Katerina murmurs.

"Whoever takes over my father's company is his problem from now," I tell her. "All I want to do is take care of my family. Of Nate, you," I add gently.

Her eyes grow soft and glassy. She looks away from me, clearing her throat.

"Okay, issues with your company aside, what did you mother want? Why is she back?"

"She's here to find me a wife."

Katerina's eyes widen. "She's what?"

"Here to find me a wife, Katerina," I repeat. "She seems to have gotten it into her head that if I get married to a respectable woman that my father finds acceptable, then all my problems will disappear."

"She might be right."

"She's wrong," I counter firmly. "I'm not getting married, Katerina. I already have so much shit going on and my mother's meddling is an unwelcome addition to all that."

"Well, she certainly seems like an interesting woman," Katerina mutters.

"Jessica Steele is an incredibly selfish woman who only cares about two things. Money and herself. She abandoned her son for years without a care in the world."

Katerina's face falls at that and I realize too late how that sounds.

"Princess..."

"I guess I'm a little similar to your mother," she says sadly, a far off expression in her face.

"No," I retort vehemently. "There's one glaring difference. You know what you did was wrong. You were in pain every year that you were away from Nate. I know that with certainty. My mother on the other has yet to realize her mistakes and still believes she did nothing wrong by abandoning me. You're not like her, princess. I promise."

She still looks a little uncertain but manages a small nod. When I pull her into my arms, she sighs before wrapping her arms around my waist.

"Where's Nate?" she mumbles against my chest.

"I asked Mikayla to go pick him up and distract him for a couple of hours," I inform her. "I didn't want him seeing my mother."

"Okay."

She falls quiet but doesn't let go of me. I don't mind, holding her in my arms feels like a blessing I have no plans of being ungrateful for. Eventually, I have to break the silence.

"What's going on, Katerina?"

"I just back from seeing Sophia," she says softly. "It went well. Or at least as well as it could have gone. She hasn't forgiven me completely but at least I know my sister doesn't hate me."

"That's good. But why do you still seem so sad?" I ask.

"I guess I'm just thinking about how none of this would have ever happened if I hadn't made so many mistakes." She finally looks up at me. "I wanted to tell Sophia the truth. But by the time I worked up the nerve to, a month had passed, then two, before I knew it, years had flown by and I had no idea how to bring it up. I'm a horrible person."

"No, you're not," I insist. "You're human. You're allowed to fuck up every once in a while."

She sucks in a deep breath, eyes fixed on my face. "I'm starting to believe you're a saint, Xan. How can you even bear to look at me after everything I've done?"

"Are you kidding? You're so beautiful, I never want to look away," I say, my voice light and teasing.

"Xander," she says, slapping my chest gently.

I chuckle gently. "But seriously, I'm not a saint. I was angry too. But I got over it because I care about you, more than anything. And I could see you were willing to make things work."

"I am," she promises.

"Now can we end the hug session here and head up to the bedroom? Make the most of our time before Nate comes home?" I ask suggestively.

Her eyes simmer with heat. "We could but first I need to talk about something else."

A groan escapes my lips, causing her to frown.

"Rico told me he had you hack into some confidential records."

"Oh yeah. How'd that go? Did it help?"

"Yes, but that's not the point. You don't have to do illegal things for me."

"Please, what use are my skills if I can't use them for illegal things?"

"Xander," she warns.

"Princess, I'm a great hacker. And also currently in a relationship with you," I say carefully, her expression doesn't change at the inclination so I forge on. "If I can provide you with any help, I will."

"You don't care that you would be helping the bad guys in the process?"

"There are no bad guys or good guys. Life isn't black or white. And even if it was, the shades don't matter. I'm on your side."

Her face softens. She runs her hand across her face. "You know you tend to say the sweetest things that almost make me cry, don't you?"

"I do and I honestly revel in it," I grin. "Its fun watching the big bad Don get all soft."

"Only for you," she mutters and my heart swells at that. Then her expression turns serious. "So what's your plan? If you're not going back to your father's company, then what do you want to do? Because being my family's hacker is not a viable career choice."

"Obviously not," I tell her, moving towards the couch. I sit down in front of the open laptop on the table and gesture for her to come sit beside me.

Once she does, I switch on the laptop. "I've actually been working on something the past couple days. A business plan. I think I want to establish my own company. A tech start up to be exact."

Katerina's eyes widen. She's the first person I'm telling

this to. I've been toying with the idea, wondering if it would be the right move.

"To be honest, princess, I've always had this burning desire to create something of my own, bring my own ideas to life. Working at my family's company felt like I was following someone else's vision. But if I started my own company, I'd get the freedom and creative control I've always wanted."

"That sounds amazing, Xander," Katerina says, eyes gleaming. "But it's also a bold move. Where would you get funding? Investment? Your father will probably never agree to this."

"I have some money saved up and my father's agreement doesn't matter to me. Plus I happen to be dating a woman I'm sure would happily invest in my company," I say, shooing her a sly wink.

She rolls her eyes. "We'll see. Keep going though, I want to hear all your ideas."

She listens attentively as I drone on and all about all my plans, interjecting at all the right moments and even providing some ideas of her own. By the time we're done talking about it thirty minutes later, my plan is practically air tight and I'm more confident.

Katerina places a kiss on my cheek. "I am so proud of you."

"Thanks I'm proud of me, too," I state and she laughs. "Would be nice if I got that kiss somewhere else though."

She smiles before wrapping her arms around my neck and kissing me, soft and slow. Her lips gliding over mine. Too slow for me however and she lets out a breathless laugh as I push her onto her back on the couch, before straddling her. She lands with a soft thud and then I'm pressing my lips to hers, tasting her the way I wished I could all those years we were apart. She has no idea. How I searched for her in every woman that I was with. How I would lie awake at night, wishing she was right beside me. Maybe one day I'll tell her.

My heart thunders in my chest as I deepen the kiss, sensations coursing through my body. All I can taste is her, all I feel is her. Her hips cant into mine, her hands pulling me closer as I feast on her mouth. My hands reach up into her hair, fisting blonde locks.

"We should probably head up to my room, baby," I tell her, lifting my head so my lips graze hers with each word.

She nods and then I'm climbing off her, intertwining our fingers as I lead her up the stairs. She's never been inside my room before. But I doubt I let her catch even a glimpse because once we're inside, I'm on her again, pulling her closer by the waist. I place a soft kiss on her mouth as I walk us backwards towards the bed, Katerina climbs onto it without complaint. I can see in her expression that she wants this, she's ready.

Once I climb on top of her, a voice whispers in my ear to go slow. To enjoy this, enjoy her. The last time we had sex, I was impatient, a starving man, denied of what he wanted for so long. But now, I get to savor this. Savor her. I slowly unzip her dress. The silk material slackens and I gently lift her so I could ease off the rest of her clothes. I let my touch linger on every curve and dip, mapping her body with my mouth and caressing her breasts through her bra. It's slow and tortuous and soon Katerina is whimpering in frustration.

"Xander, please,' she breathes, her skin flushed with pleasure.

My groan vibrates against her skin but with one word from her, my wishes come undone. I manage to lose her underwear to the side leaving her completely naked. Then I'm fumbling to take my clothes off as well. Once I'm done, I stare down at her, marveling at how perfect she is. She might not see herself as perfect, but she is, to me.

"You're a blessing I promise never to take for granted, Katerina."

She moans loudly as I slowly slide into her. Another groan climbs up my throat at how tight and wet she is. Her body fits mine effortlessly, naturally. I hold still, kissing my way up her neck and capturing her mouth in a kiss before I start moving. This isn't just sex, it's what I imagine people to mean when they talk about making love.

Her sighs of pleasure vibrate through my body as I glide in and out of her in a slow, sensual rhythm. It takes all my willpower to maintain the pace but I want to savor every single second I get to spend inside of her. When her nails scrape against my back, I feel my control start to slip. She lets out a soft cry.

"Xander, I need you to go faster," she pleads, voice breathy with desire.

I grit my teeth as my muscles strain before gripping her hips and giving her exactly what she asked for. If fuck her harder and faster, sure that her nails are making indents on my back. Her eyes are half closed, her lips parted as she continues to moan.

My gaze lingers on her face, trying to imprint every detail of it to memory before I kiss her again. She breaks the kiss after a second to cry out as she comes, her pussy gripping onto my cock, tight as a vise. I hold on for only a moment or so before my control finally snaps as well and my orgasm washes through me, blinding me for a second.

My heart pounds, my head swims as I wonder at the incredible feeling. I roll onto my side next to her and Katerina turns to look at me.

"I really don't deserve you," she says sweetly.

"That was just one orgasm, princess. No need to get all sappy."

She slaps my shoulder. "You're an idiot."

The both of us fall silent, breathing heavily as we try to recover. When a few minutes place, Katerina taps my shoulder.

"We need to get dressed before Nate comes back," she tells me, placing a kiss on my cheek.

I groan softly before sitting up on the bed. Katerina sits up as well and my gaze slides down to her perky breasts. My cock twitches and she notices. Her eyes narrow.

"No. We're going downstairs and being responsible parents," she warns.

I chuckle. "You want know something I absolutely love?" I ask, leaning over to steal one last kiss.

"Sure," she tells me, smiling up at me happily.

"That I'm the only one that gets to hear you beg like that.

"Shut up, Xan," she mumbles, rolling her eyes.

We both get dressed and make it downstairs in the nick of time. Because almost as soon as we get there, Nate arrives with Mikayla in tow. And I really, really hate my sister's perceptiveness because she only has to take one look at us before her eyebrows climb.

I shake my head, fighting back a groan. While Katerina goes to greet them both, I'm stopped by the sound of a text entering my phone. I pick it up and open it, finding one from my father.

> You and I need to have a talk, son.
> Tomorrow, 5pm. Bring her along as well.

There's no mistaking the "her" he's talking about. I run my hand through my hair, letting out a soft breath.

Fucking great.

CHAPTER 27
Katerina

"Katerina," Nate says enthusiastically when he sees me.

I crouch down as soon as I'm in front of him and he doesn't hesitate to hug me back.

"Hey, sweetie. How was school today?" I question.

"It was great. We got to blow up an apple," he informs me.

My eyebrow arches and I look up at his aunt.

"Science project," Mikayla explains with a grin. "He also got in trouble for blowing up the apple. Why don't you tell your mom about that?"

"Oh yeah," my son mutters. "Daniel and I got yelled at by our teacher because we shouldn't have been playing around with chemicals in the first place."

"How did you even know what to do to get it to blow up?"

"Daniel's really smart. He's going to be an astronaut one day," he says grinning.

"And what do you want to be, sweetie?"

He shrugs. "I don't know. I guess I'll think about it when I'm older."

It suddenly hits me that owing to the fact that he's my son, Nate's next in line to become Don. It's a troubling thought, because I fought hard to ensure he wasn't brought up in the outfit and I'm not able to re-introduce him to it. His father might not have a problem with my being in the mafia but I have a problem with it. It's dangerous and I want more than anything to protect them.

"You can be anything you want, Nate," I tell him. "But you shouldn't be breaking the rules at school."

"It was worth it though."

I smile, running a hand through his dark hair. "Sweetie, it doesn't matter if something's worth it or not if it's a bad thing."

He nods, expression thoughtful. "Next time we'll ask for permission before doing a science project."

"How about you not do any at all until you're older? I don't want you getting hurt."

He wrinkles his nose. "I'm not a baby, I'll be fine."

Something pangs in my chest. He really isn't a baby anymore. He's a young boy, a willful stubborn one like his dad and I guess me as well.

"Okay, sweetie. Why don't you go tell your dad about your day?"

He immediately heads for his father who is still standing at the foot of the stairs. Xander grins before picking him up and I watch them for a couple of seconds feeling my heart grow.

"You're pretty good at being a mom," Mikayla says and I turn to her in surprise.

I completely forgot she was still here.

"Hi, Mikayla. Thanks for picking him up," I tell her.

"It's fine. I love hanging out with him. But I don't want to talk about Nate right now. I see my brother's finally taken my advice," the dark haired woman says with a mischievous smile.

I blink. "I have no idea what you're talking about."

"You're together, right? Please tell me you're together," she implores.

"Oh. Yes, we're together," I say carefully.

The words feel a little fragile. Maybe because I'm afraid to break this newfound bubble of happiness and contentment.

Mikalya lets out a breath of relief. "Oh thank God. I was worried for a while there that you wouldn't find your way back to one another. Honestly, the two of you should be thanking me."

I smirk, "Oh really?"

"Yes. If I hadn't meddled then that big doofus would have never realized his undying love for you. You're welcome."

I laugh. She reminds me of her brother with the sass and the unwavering confidence.

"For what it's worth, thank you, Mikayla. For being accepting and supportive," I state. As far as I know she's the only person in Xander's face on my side.

"I'm just trying to make sure my elder brother is happy. And my mom also asked me to tell you that she supports you as well. She always used to tell me how much she regrets not standing up for you at that dinner many years ago. Maybe if she had none of this would have happened."

"She sounds like a wonderful woman," I say.

"She's the best. My rock. Anyway, enough of all the sappiness," she states and I have to roll my eyes at how similar that is to what Xander said earlier.

Siblings, I think, shaking my head.

"You and I need to plan a girl's day," Mikayla says. "We can go to the spa and then shopping. It'll be great."

I smile. "I would love to."

"Think about all the embarrassing stories I have of Xander. I'll tell you everything."

I feel his presence at my back before he places a hand on my hip. "You'll do no such thing," Xander states.

Mikayla sticks her tongue out at him, "Try and stop me, Xan."

I laugh at the way Xander's expression darkens. "Let's just get started on dinner," he says resigned. "You're helping, Kay."

His sister shakes her head. "No, I'm going upstairs to play with the kid. Call me when it's ready."

She blows us a kiss before heading up the stairs. I laugh softly under my breath.

"I swear she's an absolute menace," he mutters.

"She's amazing," I counter. "Come on, I'll help you with dinner. I should actually get cooking lessons one of these days. You can't be the only one cooking all the time."

He smiles. "Actually, I don't mind. I know you find it hot, seeing me in the kitchen, apron tied to my waist. That kind of thing gets me going," he teases.

"It does not," I retort, feeling my cheeks heat.

After dinner, Xander manages to convince me to sleep over. We inform Nate that I'll be staying but as soon as we tuck him into bed and confirm he's asleep, I head up to Xander's room. We're lying in his bed, arms wrapped around me when he informs me about the meeting his father requested.

"We don't have to go if you don't want to," he's telling me. "Honestly not sure what he could possibly have to say."

"We're going," I tell him. "I'm not going to let you be

estranged from half your family because of me. We'll go and we'll listen to whatever it is he has to say."

"You don't have to force yourself, princess. I know you don't like him."

He's right. I don't like how big of an impact Richard Steele had in the reasons I made the decisions I made nine years ago. I don't like how he prevented me from seeing Nate again five years ago. But everyone deserves a chance, even him.

"You never know. He might surprise me. Maybe he's changed since the last time I saw him."

Xander snorts. "Don't hold your breath."

"Even if he hasn't we're still going. Who knows, maybe after I meet your father, you can finally meet mine."

He groans at that making me laugh.

"My dad's not that bad. He's actually much nicer now that he's not Don anymore. The position has relaxed him," I lie.

"Bullshit," Xander mutters. "We sure do make a pair, you and me. Fathers that drive us crazy."

"Mothers that couldn't be there for us growing up," I add softly.

Xander places a kiss on the top of my head at that. "Tell me about her. Your mom."

So I do. Everything is easier when I do it with him. Even talking. The words that I would have found impossibly to voice are said gently. He listens to it all attentively. My mother's grace, her strength. She left a country and the only home she had ever known to marry my father, relocating to the U.S from Moscow.

The rest of the night flies by with us talking. Xander asks me to say something sexy in Russian, I refrain from punching him in the jaw. He tells me about his childhood. His favorite memories, one of which involved beating Graham at a race. We trade stories like that in the dark.

And I can almost feel our yearning hearts becoming one. Xander was right when he spoke about the invisible string between us, the one that always leads us back to each other. I just hope it never cuts.

I DRINK a cup of coffee as I try to ignore my nerves arising from the meeting later today. Xander and Nate already left, him going to drop him off. I managed to wake up with just enough time to head into the guest bedroom downstairs in order to act like I slept there all night. When he saw me earlier, Nate had no idea anything was amiss.

But we're going to have to tell him eventually. I know Xander's not hiding it because he's worried about his reaction. I'm sure Nate wouldn't care if we told him we were together. But in the past couple of months, with moving from D.C and finding out I'm actually alive, meeting me, it's been a lot of change. Kids thrive more in a permanent environment and neither Xander nor I want to destabilize him even further. At least for now.

After finishing my coffee, I decide to take a shower in order to get ready for the day. By the time Xander comes back, I'm dressed and waiting for Rico to come pick me up. He is not happy about that.

"Would have been nice if I left and came back to find you in my bed, princess," he points out.

I smile, reaching up to cup my cheek. "I know and I'm sorry, Xan. But I have a ton of work to get to at the office. I'll be back later this evening so we can head to the meeting together," I assure him.

He blows out a breathe before inclining his head to brush his lips against mine.

"Think about all the things I could have done to you if you had stayed," he murmurs, voice like sin. "Too bad."

My insides heat and I start considering the repercussions of delaying Rico for a couple of minutes. Then Xander pulls away, leaving me hanging. I blink at the sudden empty space in front of me.

"Have a nice day at work, princess," he tells me, laughing as he walks into the kitchen.

I briefly consider throwing an apple at the back of his head. But I decide to be the mature one, heading into the elevator and then into the car Rico arrives to pick me up in.

It's a progressive day at work and I find myself wishing the day wasn't so good because now it'll inevitably get ruined by whatever it is Richard Steele has to say. Xander and I walk into the restaurant together that evening, arm in arm, dressed semi-formally. Me in a long floral maxi dress and him in a black suit without a tie. I try to imagine the picture we must make to the outside world. I hope people look at us and think we're right for each other.

It doesn't matter what anyone else thinks though. I know we're right for each other.

Richard Steele is already seated, waiting for us to arrive. The restaurant is pretty, with a nice ambience but it all goes over my head as I set my eyes on Xander's father for the first time in five years. He hasn't changed much. Still the same uninviting aura. The same lingering frown of disapproval. Facial expression etched in ice, intimidating green eyes.

I continue walking towards him. We both stop once we arrive at the table.

"Father," Xander says, clearing his throat. "You summoned us."

My grip on his arm grows tighter. A silent warning for him to act more serious. Richard's expression doesn't so much as waiver. He looks from his son, to me and then to our conjoined arms. Then he's waving a hand towards the two chairs on the other side of the table.

"Have a seat."

We do and almost immediately the first course of food is brought towards the table. I watch as it's all set down. Xander and I exchange a look. I decide to speak up.

"Actually, Mr. Steele. We were hoping to talk first," I state.

"Eat," he says. There's no disguising the word as a command. My jaw clenches. Beneath the table, Xander gets a hold of my thigh, rubbing small calming circles through my dress. "It's good manners, Miss Mincetti. I invited you as a show of hospitality. Let us have a nice dinner."

I nod slowly before sitting up straighter and digging into the meal. It's great but I can barely concentrate because I'm too worried about what he could possibly have to say to us.

"How about dessert?" he suggests once we're done with the meal.

I glare at him and he manages a small chuckle before looking at his son.

"Would I be right in assuming that the both of you are in a relationship now?"

Xander nods, without hesitation. "We're trying to make this work, dad. I know you don't approve."

"Actually. You've made it clear that you don't give a fuck whether I approve of anything you do anymore. So I'll be keeping my opinions to myself. This meeting was called, to warn the two of you of what would be expected in your future. Because I'm not sure either of you understand what is at stake."

I blink at that, looking towards Xander who is equally as confused.

His father continues. "First off, Alexander. I want to believe you have a plan for your future. It's been weeks, since you walked away from your family's legacy, I'm sure you've thought long and hard on what you plan to do."

Xander informs him about the tech start-up and if I didn't know better I'd almost say that Richard Steele is impressed. When he finishes speaking, his father clears his throat.

"All I can say is that the company has lost a formidable asset in you, Alexander. But I have no doubt you'll pave your own way. You are my son and a Steele, we don't fail."

Xander cocks his head to the side, "Alright, what's going on?" he finally asks. "Are you dying? Is that it? They say people sometimes do out of character things when they're close to death. Is that what's going on here?"

Richard's lips thin. "What's going on here is that I'm trying to have dinner with my son and his girlfriend. This is my way of making an effort."

"Sure, but why?" Xander presses.

"Well, if I'm being honest, I received a call from your mother. A particularly distressing one where she wouldn't stop complaining about Katerina's presence in your life. I suddenly realized that if your mother was so against it, then it was probably not the worst thing."

My jaw practically drops. Beside me Xander stares at his father incredulously.

"You're agreeing to our relationship just to spite my mother?"

He shrugs. "I never said that, Xander. And all that matters is that I'm agreeing to the relationship. But like I said, there are a few things I need to make sure of. The first of which being Nathaniel's safety. If I'm not wrong, you will all continue to remain in New York?" he questions.

"Yes, we will," I reply.

New York is my home. I couldn't imagine living anywhere else. Nate loves the city and he's finally managed to make friends and grow comfortable. And Xander already told me that he plans on establishing the start up here.

"Good, given your position, Katerina. I'm going to need you to ensure that he has adequate security wherever he goes. Being the son of a Don is a dangerous prospect and who knows, he could be targeted by anyone looking to provoke or threaten you."

My skin prickles. "No one would dare."

"Just make sure he's well protected," Richard states. "He's my grandchild. I do not want anything happening to him."

"I won't let anything happen to him," I say fiercely.

The table relapses into silence and the more I sit here in front of him, the more I start to grow impatient.

"Is that all you have to say, Richard? How about an apology for kicking me out of your home, not once but twice?"

He waves a nonchalant hand in the air. "I'm not going to apologize for that, Katerina. I was protecting my family the way I knew best. You should understand considering you're the head of yours. Sometimes all we can do is what we think is best. If anything the both of you should be grateful to me for fostering your reunion. If I hadn't sent Xander to New York then all of this would have never happened."

I'm silent, stewing on his words.

"We're very grateful," Xander says dryly. "Now if that's all, I think Katerina and I are going to head home."

He doesn't object. "Think about what I said. Nate's safety comes first."

We walk out of the restaurant. When we arrive in front of our car, Xander looks at me, and I can still see the confusion in his expression.

"I still think he's terminally ill," he mutters.

That makes me laugh. "Or maybe your father actually is capable of change."

"Maybe," he agrees.

CHAPTER 28

Xander

Katerina smiles at me devilishly before getting on her knees and stepping between my legs. I'm already hard, I have been since we woke up but instead of fucking her like I wanted to but I chose to get in some work before Nate woke up. It's been two weeks since the start of our relationship and we've found a rhythm that works for us.

Right now it's 6am and she's tracked me down to the kitchen. I'm standing in place while she stares at my cock which she managed to work out of my pants. When she licks her lips, it sends a bolt of lust through me.

My cock thickens, already dripping with pre-cum.

"Baby, I'd honestly rather be inside of you," I say, fighting back a groan as she places her hand on me.

Katerina looks up at me, brown eyes sensual and open. "Just shut up and let me do what I want to, okay?"

I smile, placing my hand on her cheek for a second. I have to let go quickly though. My eyes grow wide as she slowly take me down her throat. She takes me all the way to the hilt and stays there for a minute with her lips stretched wide against the base of my shaft. Her pace is slow at first, unhurried as she sucks me hard. My breathing turns erratic and I fight the battle to fuck her mouth hard.

I lets out a soft curse, before my hands tangle in her hair. She flattens her tongue and runs it along the underside of my cock before gently sucking the head and sliding me all the way down to her throat once again. My grip tightens in her hair.

"Fuck, you're so good at this, Katerina," I groan softly. "There you go. That's it. You have no idea how perfect you look right now, baby."

She moans at the praise and it spurs her on to go faster. When she gags around the base of my cock, my breath hitches and my muscles go taut. I tap her face gently trying to warn her that I'm about to come. She increases the suction, her hands continue to work me up and down my shaft.

My cock throbs in her mouth and I grip the granite countertop with one hand as I come with a loud groan. Katerina takes every last drop of my come down her throat. Swallows it all like a good girl. My legs turn to jelly for a second and I find it hard to hold myself up. Once she's done, she gets to her feet, her lips stretched into a grin. I pull her closer, holding her tight around her waist.

"Fuck, princess," I breathe. "That might be my new favorite morning routine. What did I do to deserve that?"

She places her head on my chest. "So much, Xan. You did so much," she whispers softly.

Our relationship still has some hijinks it needs to work through. For example, she still hasn't moved in here, despite spending all our nights at the penthouse. And it mostly has to do with the fact that we've yet to tell Nate about our relationship. I think Katerina's nervous that if we cross that line then there's no going back. It'll be permanent because neither of us wants to hurt him. And considering she still hasn't been able to tell me she loves me, it's good we're taking things slow on that front.

We're also not sure where we want to live. It's a topic we've both skirted around the past couple of weeks. I know she loves the penthouse but security wise, it would be better to move into her family's home. I'm just not sure whether Nate would be comfortable there.

He went there for a visit last week. To officially meet Katerina's family. Everyone was there. Her father, her sister, her uncle, his cousin. He met them all and I could tell he was a little overwhelmed. Everyone was on their best behavior though. Even her father, although he did pull me aside to threaten murder if I ever hurt his daughter. It was nothing more than I expected. Nate seems happy with such a big family. But I have no idea how he would react to moving into the mansion. I don't think I have problems with it. But I am hesitant that it's not the right time.

Katerina climbs onto the counter, watching me as I move to pull out the ingredients for breakfast.

"I'm going out later today on a date," she announces and my movements fall to a stop.

I slowly place the cucumber down before turning to face my girlfriend, sure that I didn't just hear her tell me that she was going on a date. The smile on her face is cheeky and gloating.

"Repeat that, Katerina," I state, my voice low.

"I said I was going out on a date with a man," she says confidently.

My eyes narrow. "You're doing no such thing."

She makes a face. "You know you can't make me do something I don't want to, right?"

"I can damn well try. Maybe I'll tie you to the bed. And then spend a couple of hours reminding your body why I'm the only one it belongs to. You're mine," I say fiercely, stepping between her legs and looking up at her. She swallows softly. "Now, care to tell me who this man is so I can plan his murder?"

She rolls her eyes. "You're such a caveman. The man is Roman De Luca. As in the Don of the De Lucas. We're friends, remember?"

"Sure," I mutter, still unhappy with what she said.

"He's happily married, Xander. It's not a date. I was just trying to mess with you."

"Consider me messed with."

She sighs, placing a hand on my chest. "We try to go out to a shooting range once in a while to talk. Roman's one of the only friends I have. He's a good man too and I like hanging out with him."

"I'm sure the both of you will be able to hang out fine with me present," I state.

Her lips part. "You're kidding?"

"No, princess. I'll be joining you on this 'date'. It actually works out well. I've been meaning to continue to learn to shoot. You and Roman can give me some pointers."

She frowns. "No one invited you, Xander."

"Sure, but I'm going regardless."

"No, you're not," she shakes her head.

One good perk to having the Don wrapped around your finger, is that I get to do whatever the hell I want all in exchange for a few orgasms. By the time afternoon rolls around, we're stepping out of the door to meet Roman De Luca. Nate's nanny has arrived to keep watch on him while we're gone.

I sneak a glance at Katerina on the ride to the shooting range. She looks content, happy and I'm so glad every day that I get to see her like that. That I contributed to it. Every single day, I try my best to ensure that I'm able to fulfil at least one of her heart desires.

When we arrive at the rink, I'm surprised to find a couple of men already situated on the outside of it. Most of the time when Katerina has security following her or Nate, they're inconspicuous, she gives them strict orders to blend in. I'm sure the men standing outside are Roman De Luca's protection.

I arch an eyebrow as we pass them, heading inside the building.

"It's a meeting between two Dons and while it's completely friendly, there's always an underlying threat that shouldn't be ignored," Katerina explains.

"A threat from the outside, or a threat of a fight that could occur between the both of you?"

"Both."

Roman De Luca's expression grows intrigued as we approach. He's a tall man at nearly six foot three, with eyes so blue they're practically black. His intrigue is bordering on amusement by the time we're standing in front of him.

"So you can bring your boyfriend along but when your brother in law asks to tag along, it's a no?" Roman asks the woman beside me.

Katerina shrugs. "My brother in law doesn't give me orgasms now does he?"

That makes me grin, meanwhile Roman lets out a chuckle.

"True," he says before looking towards me. He stretches his hand for a shake. "I'm Roman De Luca."

"Alexander Steele," I reply shaking his hand. His grip is firm. "Nice to meet you."

The both of them give off the same aura. I'm guessing from having a shared reality.

"You too. But take it from you, Anthony's going to be really pissed when he finds out you're here."

"He'll get over it," I say shrugging.

Katerina laughs. "He's a child. He doesn't get over anything."

"Don't be mean to my best friend," Roman warns.

I like seeing her like this. Being somewhat free around people that aren't her family, me or Nate. She glows even brighter when she's not feeling weighed down by all her emotions and feelings of expectation.

"So, Alexander," Roman drawls. "Do you shoot?"

"He doesn't," Katerina answers for me.

I give her a sideways glance. "Really, princess?"

"You tried it once and had beginners luck," she states.

"You said I was a natural," I shoot back. "And I know you're only doing this because you're jealous that I'm better than you."

At that, Roman's eyes shoot upward. "Better than Katerina? Now that I would love to see."

"He's not better than me," Katerina insists. "Xander likes to think of himself as God's gift to man."

"It's not like that's completely untrue," I state.

She looks at Roman in exasperation. "You see what I have to deal with every day. He's insufferable."

Roman chuckles. "But seriously, Xander, why don't the two of us make a wager. We play and whoever makes the most shot on target, wins."

I grin, liking the sound of that. "Sure let's do it."

Roman moves to get into position. I stand behind Katerina for a moment, leaning down to whisper in her ear.

"And when I win, I want something from you too, princess," I murmur, kissing the shell of her ear softly.

I feel a shiver roll through her.

"When you lose, I'm going to gloat for days."

"Trust me, baby. I'm not going to lose."

I never say things I don't mean and by the time I'm done shooting every bullet in the canister of the gun handed to me, it's pretty clear that I really am God's gift to man. Or at least to shooting. When I turn to my girlfriend, her eyes are wide with shock.

She really has no trust in me.

Beside me, Roman De Luca's also similarly surprised. Although his is more muted.

"Mincetti, I think I'm just going to stop playing with anyone belonging to your family," he calls out to Katerina.

"That would be advisable," she retorts.

I smile. It's the little things that matter and Roman referring to me as her family has a sort of easy feeling settling over my chest.

"You could be an ace shooter if you wanted, man," Roman says to me visibly impressed. "You and Sophia are pretty gifted, huh?"

"Yeah, we get that a lot," I quip.

I've only met Katerina's little sister once, but she seemed cool. My type of person.

"So, what do you want?"

I don't even have to think about my request. I tell him about my tech start up that's launching in less than two months.

"I'm looking for investors," I inform the Don.

Katerina has sidled up beside me, "Opportunistic," she says under her breath.

I don't miss it. I wrap my arm around her waist, pulling her closer.

"It's called being a business man, baby. I have to milk every chance I get."

Roman nods in understanding. "I'll get in touch with you. We can work out the terms for my investment."

"Thanks man. You want to go another round with Kat?" I question.

"Actually, I think I'm just going to leave. My ego's taken enough of a hit. It's pretty humbling, the fact that I can't seem to beat any of you."

"How about Tony? I bet you could beat him."

Katerina's brother in law, while a great person, tends to take everything and anything as a joke. He's never serious. It's pretty endearing. I've only met him once, but I like him, despite the shadows of darkness I know lie beneath his character.

Beside me, Katerina snorts at my suggestion. Roman grins.

"What?" I ask.

"I once watched Tony throw a knife at someone and hit him right in the chest. That someone is Rico and Tony was somehow able to throw the knife with enough precision and calculation that it wouldn't be a fatal wound," Katerina informs me

"That's insane," I say, trying to imagine the incident.

Throwing a knife on target is a scary skill. One I'm sure not a lot of people possess.

"It's Tony. Insane is practically his middle name," Roman chuckles.

Katerina looks up at m, "Rico still has the scar to prove it."

"I'll ask him to show it to me some time," I joke.

We talk for a few more minutes before Roman suddenly falls quiet.

"I almost forgot to tell you, Katerina. I received a report yesterday."

"About?" Katerina prompts.

"Apparently a man claims to have sighted Sokolov in one of the underground boxing rings."

As soon as he says the name, the smiles on our faces melt. Katerina stiffens and I notice her growing paler.

"He's in New York?"

"That's what this man claims but I'm not so sure. He's still a Boss in the bratva, Katerina. What would he be doing in an underground boxing ring? And I looked into him a little, the man's a little unhinged and he thrives on attention. If he was in the city, he would want us all to know. I'm not completely sure what the history is between the both of you but I don't think we have anything to be worried about."

"Of course," Katerina nods. "Thank you for telling me, Roman."

He inclines his head respectfully before saying good bye and leaving. Once he's gone, I stand in front of Katerina, placing my hand under her chin to tilt her head up.

"Hey, you still with me?" I ask softly.

She inhales a shaky breath. "Yes. Yes I am. Roman's right. If he was in New York, we would know. I have several programs up and running, alerting me about everyone of importance that arrives in the city from Moscow. He's not here. If he was here, I would have known."

She sounds like she's trying to convince herself more than me. I lead her towards the car, because it's clear she won't be able to get anything else done today. When we arrive back at the penthouse, I go straight to the kitchen to make her a glass of hot chocolate.

I hate that she can be formidable in literally every other area, but when it comes to that bastard, she seems to crumble. Even the mere mention of his name has her shaken up. It's clear she went through so much more during her time with him that she's unwilling to talk about.

I marvel at the strength she possesses all the time.

"Where's Nate?" she questions, looking around the house.

"His nanny sent me a text. They went to get some ice-cream and then he asked to go to the cinema to watch a movie."

She blinks, her expression growing troubled. "I want him back here."

I shift forward to press a kiss on her forehead. "He'll be back soon, princess. Just relax."

I wait quietly as she finishes her cup of hot chocolate.

"Do you want me to put you in bed?" I ask her, already knowing the answer.

She nods, stretching her arms out for me to carry her.

"Big baby," I say affectionately as I move to lift her head, carrying her up the stairs.

Sleeping is Katerina's coping mechanism. As soon as I tuck her in, she's out like a light. I head back downstairs to try and get some work done but I'm on edge as well, discomfited at the news.

Still my worries are nothing in the face of Katerina's when she wakes up less than two hours later.

"I think we should move into the mansion now," she tells me, padding across the kitchen floors to the dining table where I'm seated.

I look up from my laptop to her face.

"Why?"

"Because it's safer," she says simply.

"Baby, we're not going to upend our entire lives because there's a slim possibility that man will be in the city."

"It wouldn't be upending it," she says on a frown. "I just want us to be safe. Anything could happen in this house."

"Katerina, I don't think you're looking at this clearly."

"I also don't think Nate should be going to school. At least for the time being."

There's science in the face of that proclamation. I stare at her, my jaw clenching.

"I'm sorry, what?"

"It's not safe," she repeats.

"Princess, you're starting to sound like a broken record here," I tell her getting to my feet.

"I'm just trying to protect you both."

"So what? You're going to move him out of his house into another one? And then keep him away from school? Why don't you wrap him in some bubble wrap while you're at it?" I question.

She places a hand on her forehead in frustration. "Xander, you're not listening to me."

"No, I need you to listen to me. You don't get to tell me what I can or can't do with my son."

"Our son!' she yells. "He's our son and I have as much say in how we protect him."

"He already has two men shadowing him everywhere he goes. Why can't that be enough?"

"Because this is the Cosa Nostra," she says in exasperation. "I've heard of too many child abductions to delude myself into thinking anything we do will be enough. I need to do this, Xander. Because I can't. I can't lose him. Please," she says desperately.

I notice her breathing speed up and I'm immediately there, holding her in my arms. I rub comforting circles on her back in an effort to calm her down.

"Breathe, Katerina. You need to calm down."

"Why isn't he back yet?" she says, her breathing still

erratic. "Something's wrong. Xander I swear something's wrong."

My heart threatens to cave in on itself. I've never seen her like this. I'm about to grab my phone to ask the nanny to bring Nate back when it starts to ring. Katerina and I look at each other and I don't know if it's her hysteria rubbing off on me, but my heart skips several beats as I grab the phone to answer the call.

Katerina's eyes are shut and I'm pretty sure she's praying.

"Addison," I say sharply, speaking to Nate's nanny. "Where is he?"

As soon as she starts to cry, I feel my heart leap into my throat.

"I'm so sorry, Mr. Steele. We were in the park. One minute I was holding his hand and the next a car was driving past us. They rushed towards me and snatched Nate from me. The men wore masks. There was nothing I could do to stop it. I am so sorry sir," the woman explains in a rush.

Each words feels with even more dread than the last. Katerina's back is against the wall. I can see the stark terror on her face as she sidles down to the floor, crouching as her shoulder shake with sobs. Numbly, I drop the phone to the ground.

"I told you, Xander. I told you something was wrong," she says quietly.

My chest aches with the realization. "That bastard has our son."

CHAPTER 29
Katerina

"How much more fucking incompetent can you all possibly get? The city's not that big. I dispersed every man to look for him and you bring me nothing?" I scream.

It's been five hours and seventeen minutes since my baby was kidnapped. Five hours and seventeen minutes since I haven't been able to take an easy breath. After Xander and I got over our shock at the news, we immediately leapt into action. He went to the police for help and I came here to the mansion. In the past three hours I've asked from help from all the Dons. Roman, Christian, Enzo, every single one of them has dispatched men to search through every corner of the city. And so far, there's been no news.

"We'll find him, Don," one of the capos standing in front says to me.

"You'd better. Because if my son doesn't turn up alive and well, I swear I'll turn this house into a blood bath. Maybe I'll start with your head," I threaten.

He swallows nervously and the men hurriedly disperse. I feel a soft hand on my shoulder and turn to look at my sister.

Sophia came here as soon as she heard the news. Right now, Rico, Tony and Xander are out there, driving around the city, trying to find him as well.

"Kat, you need to sit down," my sister says gently. "You look pale."

"I'm fine," I mutter, turning to walk towards my office.

I've been looking through every CCTV camera in the area of Nate's abduction, trying to figure out what route the kidnappers took. Not only were their faces covered, but they managed to avoid streets with cameras that could help to pinpoint their location. I'm not daunted. If I have to hack into a satellite to find my son, I will.

When I reach the door to my office, I sway on my feet. My father's there immediately, his face etched in concern.

"You're of no help to anyone if you collapse, *mia cara*," he says to me.

Like Sophia, I brush off his concern, heading for my laptop. A few minutes later, Sophia enters the room with a plate of food. I shake my head at the sight.

"I'm not hungry."

"You need to eat to at least have some strength, Katerina. You can't save Nate if you have no energy."

I grit my teeth, looking up at her. "I said I was fine, Soph, I just need to keep working on this. I'll eat when I find him. I just need to find him first."

Behind her, Xander suddenly appears, walking up to my table. I see the same bone deep expression in his eyes, I'm sure can be found in mine. His jaw is clenched as his eyes roam my face. Then he's accepting the plate of food from Sophia.

"Thanks. I got this," he says to her, offering a small smile.

My sister nods, walking out of the room and shutting the door behind her. Xander doesn't say a word for several seconds. He places the food on the table in front of me, before sitting on the other side.

"What's it going to take to get you to eat something and rest, princess?" he finally asks.

"Finding my son. And bringing him back to me," I mutter.

He sighs softly. "We'll find, Nate, Katerina. It's only a matter of when we do. It's killing me every single moment he's away from us. But I'm not going to sit here and watch you destroy yourself in the process. I can't."

I fix him with a hard stare. "Then don't watch," I snap.

"No. You don't get to shut me out, baby. I know you're in pain. I get that you think all your worst fears are being confirmed. But whatever it is you're going through, we do so together."

My face crumbles at that. My chest fucking aches. "Xander, he could be dead," I whisper.

"He's not dead," he retorts, assuredly. "He's alive. I can feel that our son is alive, I know you feel it too. Sokolov wouldn't have gone through the trouble of kidnapping him just to kill him. He wants something. We just have to wait until he asks for it."

"And what am I supposed to do until then?" I question.

"There's a whole army out there looking for our son. I'm sure they'll find him soon. What I need you to do right now is have a few bites of that salad at least, and then take a nap. You don't have to sleep for too long. Just an hour or two to clear your head. If there's any news, you know we'll be told immediately."

I hesitate, feeling my chest tighten.

"Okay fine. I'll do it, but only if you lie down with me."

He agrees and after eating, he leads me towards my bedroom. The two of us climb into it. Xander holds me from behind and I shut my eyes trying not to imagine what my baby must be going through at the moment. Like I expected, it's impossible for me to fall asleep.

But I stay still because I can hear Xander's soft breaths. He hasn't had a wink of sleep since earlier this morning. It's almost 11pm and he must have been exhausted. I don't move a muscle for an hour. Until my phone suddenly lights up on the bedside table.

My heart starts to pound at the sight. I manage to wiggle out of Xadner's grasp without waking him to read the text.

Come here alone if you want to save your son. Katerina, you know who this is. And you know what happens if you disobey me. I want you here, alone.

I hold my breath as I read the text over and over again. There's a location attached to it. Directions to the place he's keeping Nate. My gut reaction is to wake Xander and show him the text. But I can't help but think about the fact that he'll be in danger as well if he goes.

I couldn't live with myself if anything happened to him. He and Nate are my whole entire heart. I have to do everything in my power to keep them safe. So I manage to sneak out of the room and then the house, although it's no easy task. When one of the capos catches sight of me in the garage, I ask him to keep quiet. Not to raise any alarms until I'm gone. He does, handing me a key to one of the cars. I drive out of the compound as fast as I can, imputing the location in the DPS.

I arrive there nearly an hour later. I'm not surprised to find an abandoned warehouse. It's usually a criminal's first choice when it comes to conducting unsavory activities. The large doors that lead into the warehouse are unguarded.

I walk in with my heart in my throat, wondering if I've made a mistake. Finally when I've stepped up to the middle of the cold and dusty room, there's the sound of laughter at my side. My head snaps up and my gaze connects with Maxim Sokolov's for the first time in ten years.

"Katerina, how nice to see you again," he says grinning. "I'm not surprised you came. You always did have bigger balls than half the men I've met in my entire life. Welcome, *moya lyubov*," he says calling me his love in Russian. "It's been too long."

The first thing I feel at the sight of his face is disgust. And not just because a side of it has been burnt badly beyond recognition. My stomach roils because I can't believe I ever for one second ever thought he was charming enough to sleep with him. The Maxim I knew back then was good looking enough. With blonde hair and blue eyes. The man that stands in front of me is nothing like him. He's older, probably in his early forties and he's holding a cane, limping as he starts to walk towards me.

"What the hell happened to you?" I can't help but ask.

He stops short. "Oh, you mean all this?" he questions, waving at his face. "Occupational hazard, my sweet kitty cat. I was in the hospital for several months after you left Moscow. I feared that I would never recover and I would never see you again but eventually I began to heal."

"That's too bad," I mutter, reaching behind me and pulling out the gun tucked into my chest. "Where is my son?"

"You mean our son," he intones, looking at me with a serious expression.

My heart thuds in my chest. "Are you kidding me? You can't possibly still be delusional enough to think he's yours."

Sokolov cocks his head to the side, before chuckling.

"No, of course not. All I had to do was look at him to realize he's not mine. Such a shame he'll have to die for it."

The carefree way he delivers that statement has my eyes widening.

"Maxim," I swallow softly. "He's only a child. He doesn't deserve all this."

"Relax, Katerina. I'm not going to kill him immediately. He's fine actually, asleep somewhere in this building. Maybe I'll even let you see him before I kill you. After I kill you, then I'll kill him and destroy your family."

"Big words for a handicap that's a thousand miles from his home," I spit.

He smirks. "That may be true but I'm quite tenacious, Katerina. I never stop going after the things that I want. Now be a good girl and come over here. Maybe if you give me a sweet enough kiss, I'll reconsider your death sentence."

My lips part. He walks towards me and I move away until we're circling each other, a good deal of space between us.

"You're insane," I tell him. "Have you ever considered checking into a mental hospital? Or at least seeing a shrink."

"Your wit is as sharp as ever, kitty cat. But your time is up. Drop the gun. Or the kid dies."

I let out a soft breath before slowly lowering my gun to the ground.

"Okay. I'll do as you say. Just please don't hurt him."

I never should have come here on my own. I think about Xander back at home. He's going to be so angry. But I also didn't leave him without a plan. I brought my phone along, left it in the car. My best guess is that Sokolov has put in place something to jam the signal around the building. Which is why I parked my car as far away from it as I could without it being suspicious.

Xander's coming for me. I know it in my heart. I just have to stall for time. I have to wait for him. Sokolov watches me hungrily as I place the gun down, raising my hands in surrender.

"Before you kill me, at least tell me where he is," I plead.

"He's up there," he tells me, pointing at a gallery on the second floor of the warehouse. "One of my men gave him some pills to make him sleep. He will not wake until the morning. Maybe I'll kill him in his sleep. Give the little boy a peaceful death. That would be a mercy, no?"

"You'll do no such thing," I say through gritted teeth.

My muscles are bunched up tight. Everything in me screams to go up there and see my son. But I can't make any sudden movements. That much is made clear when Sokolov steps forward and picks my gun from the ground.

"Again with the fucking orders. You may be a Don, Katerina. But you are nowhere near my level. You're a female. You're weak, pathetic."

Each of those words being thrown at me, feels like a gun shot. I clench my fists as he draws even nearer. His hand wraps around my wrist and my heart skips a beat as I come face to face with him. He's always been a monster. But now he really looks like one.

He's about to say something when we hear the sound of successive gunshots and a struggle outside the warehouse. My entire body nearly sags with relief. I know it can only mean that help has arrived. I say a quick prayer for the people I love. For every member of my family. Sokolov's face twists into rage.

"What have you done?" he asks, hands gripping mine tightly.

"My family's come to rescue me," I whisper, reveling in his fear. "And not just them. The Dons of New York City stand with me, Sokolov. You're going to die today."

He makes a low harsh sound at the back of his throat.

Before I can blink he's lifting his gun and jabbing it into the side of my forehead. I cry out, stumbling back as my vision blurs.

"I'm not fucking going down unless I take you with me, Katerina," he says, lifting the gun in his hand and pointing it at my chest.

My breathing slows. Time seems to fall still around me as I stare down at the barrel of the gun. I'm terrified that that will be the last thing I see. Not my son's smiling face, not Xander but this. A monster that's intent on killing me.

And then I think to myself that I'm still such a fucking idiot. I should have told Xander I loved him. I never said it. Not once. And now it might be too late.

"Good bye, Katerina," Sokolov says, eyes filled with triumph.

He starts to squeeze the trigger and my eyes fall shut. A shot goes off in the next second. I gasp at the sound. Then slowly my eyes open when I realize the shot wasn't for me. I place my hand over my stomach, my chest, realizing that I'm fine, unhurt.

I look up at Sokolov and he's on the ground, a bullet wound in his head. I whirl around with my heart in my throat. Standing there is Xander, holding a gun in one hand while he also tries to clutch his bleeding arm. My eyes widen and I'm rushing towards him before I can blink.

"Xander," I cry, reaching him the moment he falls to his knees.

"You good, princess?" he asks, looking pale.

I nod as tears start to fall down my eyes. I press my hand on his wound, praying that it's not serious.

"I'll be fine," he assures me, eyes roaming my face. "Where's our boy?"

"He-he's up there," I say shakily.

"Could you please go get him? Now, Katerina."

I don't want to leave him. But the urge to see our son is stronger.

"Just stay here, I'll be right back," I tell him, getting to my feet.

"Not going anywhere, princess," he mutters, still clutching his bleeding arm.

I manage to find the stairs leading up to the gallery and then I'm running as fast as my legs can carry me. Relief nearly knocks me to my feet when I arrive and find Nate sleeping soundly in a cot, completely oblivious. I move closer to the bed and lift him, searching his body for any bruises, making sure he's not in pain.

After confirming he's okay, I manage to lift him up. He stirs once I do so, his green eyes landing on my face.

"Mom?" he asks and my heart nearly drops at that.

"Hi, sweetie. I'm here, you're okay."

His eyes fall closed again and I can't help but be scared that whatever they gave him to sleep was too strong. I'm also terrified that his dad won't okay. I'm not sure where I get the burst of strength from, but I carry him down the stairs, back to his father who is still in the same position I left him.

He exhales in relief at the sight of us, reaching for his son. I place Nate on the floor and Xander runs a hand across his face reverently.

"Is he okay? He's okay, right, Princess?"

I nod, "He's fine. I'm fine. You saved us, Xander. You saved us."

I'm still crying. Out of fear, gratitude, and relief. My emotions are a roller coaster. I reach for Xander and he cries out in pain.

"Oh God, I'm so sorry, Xander," I mutter.

"It's alright, baby. Just get me to a hospital," he says

softly still staring at our son. And then his eyes meet mine. I can see the strain in them. He's barely fighting to stay conscious. He must have lost a lot of blood. I have no idea how he got shot in the first place.

"Katerina, remind me to kill you for going off on your own when I get better."

Despite the situation I laugh. "I will," I say through tears.

He touches my face with his injured arm for a second, frowning at the bruise that's forming at the side of his head. His eyes start to fall close and I manage to catch him just before his head thuds against the floor as he falls unconscious.

I stay right next to the two most important people in my world. I wait until help arrives. It only takes a minute or two until my cousins' face shows up in my peripheral. And once I finally see Rico, everything in me sighs with relief. And then my vision goes black.

CHAPTER 30
Katerina

When I wake up I'm in a hospital bed. My sister's asleep with her head on the bed but she wakes up as soon I move.

"Kat," she says and I watch her eyes well up with tears.

"I'm okay, *sorella*," I assure her.

"How could you have been so stupid? You should have never gone there alone."

"I know," I mutter. "As if it wasn't already obvious, I seem to have a talent for making stupid decisions." Where are they?"

She's quick to reassure me. I've been unconscious for half a day. They kept me for observation because they wanted to ensure that I didn't have a concussion. In that time Xander's had surgery and is currently out of danger. He's still unconscious and will continue to be so for the rest of the day. Nate's at home resting. Richard and Isabella came to take him away after the hospital confirmed that he was okay. He doesn't remember much of what happened because he was unconscious the entire time.

I listen quietly as she tells me everything.

"And everyone is okay?" I confirm. "No one was hurt."

"There were some casualties. Sokolov hired about fifty armed men to guard the warehouse. We lost about five capos, the De Luca's lost some too. But all in all, the casualty rate was low. I was so scared, Katerina. When we found out you were gone, Xander got to work on tracking you immediately. It was difficult because your location kept changing. And then it started to look like something was jamming the signal. But he managed to work around it all. He was so focused on finding you. That man loves you so much, sorella."

"I know," I whisper.

"After we got your location, everyone practically raced out of the mansion. Even Papa. I stayed behind but Tony already told me everything that happened. As soon as they arrived, the fighting started and it was a mess. He thinks Xander got hit when he was trying to get in. According to Tony, he's never seen anyone fight that hard before. Are you sure he's never had any combat training?"

I smile. "Positive."

"Well, he's great at it. And a good shot. He took down three of the men outside before rushing inside the warehouse. He must have gotten shot in the middle of it all. Thank God, the bullet wasn't too deep."

"Yeah," I breathe. "Soph, I need to see him. I need to see him and confirm he's okay."

My sister nods in understanding. She helps me out of the bed, leading me to Xander's room. At the door, I run into the last person I was expecting to see leaving his hospital room, Jessica Steele. She stills when she notices my approach.

I brace myself for whatever she has to say. I'm sure she blames me for what happened. And rightly so. It's all my fault. Instead of yelling at me though, Jessica sighs.

"I know you think of me as a horrible mother," she begins. "And maybe I am. But you need to understand, child. That I did what I thought was best for him."

"We all think we're doing what's best. Most of the time we're wrong," I tell her.

"I love my son," Jessica says. "And I know you don't believe me. He probably doesn't believe it either. But I'm going to do my best to work towards getting him to do so. After what happened, almost losing him," her voice cracks on the last word.

"I understand, Jessica," I say gently. "And I'm sure Xander will forgive you eventually."

She offers me a small smile. "His brother and sister are in there with him," she informs me before walking away.

I ask Sophia to leave while I enter the hospital room. I find Mikayla and Graham on opposite sides of Xander's bed, seated with worry on their faces. They get to their feet as soon as they notice me.

"Katerina," Mikayla says softly, moving to hug me. "I'm so glad you're okay."

"Thanks, Kay."

My gaze moves to the silent man in the room. He clears his throat, rubbing the back of his neck.

"Hey, Katerina," he greets.

Despite everything I'm glad he's here. At his brother's side when he needs him the most. Xander was right. There might be hope for him yet.

"Kay and I are going to leave now," he says, nodding at his sister.

"Wait. Can you ask your parents to bring Nate here?" I question.

They assure me that they will and then they leave. I take a seat beside Xander's bed to wait for him to wake up.

When his eyes finally open, the first thing I do is call his doctor and nurses into the room. After they confirm that he'll be okay, we're left alone once again. I stare at him for a couple of seconds, trying to memorize every inch of his face.

"I love you, Xander," I say softly, the words leaving my lips as easy as breathing.

His green eyes land on me and the sight of it is like a punch to the stomach. "I love you and I'm so sorry that it took me so long to be able to say it. But I'm saying it now and I'll say it every single day for as long as you continue to find me worthy of your love. Thank you so much for taking care of me. For saving me, for always being there, even when we were apart."

I'm crying by the time I'm done. Xander doesn't say anything for a few seconds. Then he's trying to sit up.

"You probably shouldn't," I start, trying to stop him.

He raises an eyebrow. "Just help me, woman."

So I do, placing his back against the wall. "You know the first thing I want to do?" he asks and I shake my head.

"I want to hug you and Nate for as long as it takes to convince me we're all safe. Then I want to kiss you for as long as I want."

My breath leaves me in a rush. "You'll get to do both those things soon, I promise."

"Good. Because I also need you to understand that you don't need to thank me. Being with you is as easy as breathing, Katerina. You've owned my heart for so long I'm not even sure it belongs to me anymore. It belongs to you. Every inch of it."

I smile, feeling my chest threatening to cave in on itself as my heart swells.

"I love you, princess," he tells me, eyes never leaving mine.

I shift forward and throw my arms around his neck, carefully not to hurt him.

"I love you too."

All the years we've been apart add up to about twenty eight years. Counting the 9 years after Nate and the 18 years before I met him for the first time. Twenty seven years wasted. It only seems fair to me that we should get two or three times as long to make up for it.

Nate arrives at the hospital about two hours later. His expression is worried as he enters his father's hospital room, but we're quick to assure him that nothing is amiss. After a hug session in Xander's bed, we both share a look, coming to a wordless agreement.

"Sweetie your father and I have something to tell you," I start.

"Your mother's going to move in with us. Actually we'll be moving into her house. The mansion. You like the mansion, right?" Xander asks our son.

He nods. "It's big. Lots of space to play in. I like it."

I smile, glad that he's at an age where things like this are still easy for him to accept.

"That's good, buddy. And there's one more thing. Your mother and I are in a relationship."

He blinks, letting that sink in. "Like Daniel's parents are in a relationship?" he finally asks.

I nod once. "Exactly like that."

When he beams, it feels like a boulder is lifted off my chest. He tugs my hand and I crouch down so I'm eye level with him.

"So does this mean I get to call you mom?" Nate asks softly.

My eyes well up with tears, I hug him to my chest as tight as I can, "Yes, sweetie. You can call me mom. In fact, it would make me very happy if you did."

He smiles and nods once before looking up at his dad. "Get well soon, dad. You said we were going to Paris."

I arch an eyebrow at that. "Paris?"

"Dad said he was going to ask you an important question there. He said you love Paris."

When I look back at Xander, he's rolling his eyes. "I asked you to keep it a secret from her, sport."

Our son giggles. "I'm sorry."

My heart races as I consider exactly what important question he could possibly want to ask.

"Don't think too much about it, princess," Xander says. "At least not until I get down on one knee."

I gasp softly, "Xander."

"You're going to say yes when I ask, right?" he prompts, uncertainty in his green eyes.

"Of course," I say softly, feeling a shiver roll through me. "I would say yes a thousand times to a future with you, Xander."

THE END.

Did you like this book? Then you'll love...

Marrying the Mafia Boss
An Enemies to Lovers Romance

A forced marriage, a surprise pregnancy, and the mafia boss I suddenly belong to.

What began as a chance encounter on a hotel rooftop with the hot millionaire,

soon became an arranged marriage to my sworn enemy.

Tony is as captivating as he is dangerous.

Unhinged, unpredictable, and... unforgettable.

But he has a vendetta against my family and wants my father unalive.

Despite our fiery clashes, there was an undeniable pull between us.

One reckless night led to an unexpected pregnancy.

And now, to avoid a mob war, for better or worse, I'm stuck...

Marrying the mafia boss.

Read Marrying the Mafia Boss NOW!
https://www.amazon.com/dp/B0CWP41MM8

Made in the USA
Monee, IL
10 October 2024